BIRTH OF AN AGE

BOOK TWO OF
THE CHRIST CLONE
TRILOGY

Praise for The Christ Clone Trilogy

"...a lively three-part novel dramatizing the end times events described in Revelation...BeauSeigneur's *Christ Clone Trilogy* livens things up with a sci-fi premise" — Alex Heard & Peter Klebnikov, *The New York Times*

"...an engrossing and ingenious story around the biggest possible subject. James BeauSeigneur brings to bear a fine mix of scientific, political, and religious knowledge to illuminate this powerful tale."
— Charles Sheffield, *Hugo and Nebula Award*-winning sci-fi author

"Finally, out of the ghetto of the evangelical subculture comes a refreshing, well thought out, and methodically researched look at the end of the age. And not since C.S. Lewis have we seen such creativity and imagination in its presentation. Bravo! More!"
— Jeremy Nordmoe, **Vanderbilt University Librarian**

"Breathtaking...It's as fine a piece of work as I have read, on several different levels. Thanks for writing a plausible, well researched and well written series."
— Kerry Livgren, primary songwriter of 8 gold and platinum albums for "**Kansas**." Songs include "**Carry On Wayward Son**" and "**Dust in the Wind**"

"...a brilliant and fascinating narrative that kept me on the edge of my seat."
— Ian Wilson, noted historian and best selling author

"Pulling together apocalyptic prophecies, science, military detail, current events and Jewish and Christian Scripture and traditions, BeauSeigneur weaves together a believable, ingeniously constructed tale."
— *NAPRA ReVIEW* (New Age Publishing and Retailing Association)

"By far the most exciting, true-to-life portrayal of end-time events I've ever read. It is on my "MUST READ" list for any serious student of prophecy."
— John Terry, **Editor**, *PropheZine*

"...grabbed me by the throat and never let go...C.S. Lewis couldn't have done it better!" — Larry Lindner, **Editor**, *Tickled by Thunder*

"I'm so impressed with this intriguing and captivating series. I'm also encouraged to note the careful research Jim has done. The validity of the message is enhanced greatly by it."
— E. Brandt Gustavson, **President, National Religious Broadcasters**

"His accuracy in presenting historical events makes *The Christ Clone Trilogy* incredibly believable."
— Barbara Meister Vitale, author of *Unicorns Are Real* and *Free Flight*

BIRTH OF AN AGE

BOOK TWO OF
THE CHRIST CLONE TRILOGY

by
James BeauSeigneur

SelectiveHouse Publishers, Inc.   Rockville, Maryland

Requests for information should be addressed to:
SelectiveHouse Publishers, Inc.
P.O. Box 10095
Gaithersburg, Maryland 20898

Credit card orders, phone toll free: 1-888-CLONE-99
Web site: selectivehouse.com

Publisher's Cataloging-in-Publication
BeauSeigneur, James
    Birth of an age: book two of the Christ clone trilogy / James BeauSeigneur. – 2nd ed.
    p. cm.
    Includes bibliographical references.
    ISBN: 0-9656948-3-6

    1. Jesus Christ--Fiction. 2. Cloning--Fiction. 3. Fantastic fiction. I. Title.

PS3552.E387I6458 2001   813'.54
                                                         QBI97-40319
    Library of Congress Catalog Card Number: 97-92166

Cover design by James BeauSeigneur & Chris Chon. Edited by Gerilynne Seigneur.

First Edition:
    First Printing 1997; Second Printing Revised 2001
Second Edition:
    First printing 2001
Unabridged audio version available December 2001 from Recorded Books, L.L.C.
    Web site: recordedbooks.com

---

10   9   8   7   6   5   4   3   2   1

Second Edition – November 2001

Printed on acid-free paper – Manufactured in the United States of America

For Gerilynne, Faith, and Abigail who sacrificed so much to allow this trilogy to become a reality;

But most of all for Shiloh, who sacrificed far more. May it serve you well.

Acknowledgments

I wish to acknowledge and express my appreciation for the contributions of so many. Over the ten years I spent writing **The Christ Clone Trilogy**, I called upon the support of specialists in many fields of endeavor to ensure the accuracy and plausibility of my work. Others have provided editorial support and direction, professional guidance, moral sustenance, or have helped in some other way.

Professor John Jefferson, Ph.D.
Michael Haire, Ph.D.
Peter Ramsey Helt, J.D.
Christy Beadle, M.D.
Eugene Walter, Ph.D.
Clement Walchshauser, D.Min.
Col. Arthur & Elizabeth Winn, Ph.D.
Bernadine Asher
Roy & Jeannie Blocher (and Martha)
Scott Brown
Curt & Phyllis Brudos
Estelle Ducharme
Georgia O'Dell
Paul & Debbie Quinn
Bryan Seigneur
Fred Seigneur
Gordy & Sue Stauffer

James Russell, M.D.
Robert Seevers, Ph.D.
James Beadle, Ph.D.
Ken Newberger, Th.M.
Ian Wilson, Historian
Jeanne Gehret, M.A.
Linda Alexander
Wally & Betty Bishop
Matthew Belsky
Dale Brubaker
Dave & Deb Dibert
Tony Fantham
Mike Pinkston
Doug & Beth Ross
Doris Seigneur
Mike Skinner
Doug & Susy Stites

Sincere appreciation to poet and political martyr Nguyen Chi Thien for his unfaltering spirit, and to

The staffs of the libraries of Montgomery County, Maryland
The staff of the Library of Congress
The Jewish Publication Society of America
The Zondervan Corporation
Yale Southeast Asia Studies
The hundreds of others whose work provided background for this book

This novel is a work of historic and prophetic fiction. While well-known public personalities and widely-reported historic events are referenced, only those events which have been widely-reported by reliable nonfiction sources should be assumed to be true; all others should be assumed to be the product of the author's imagination. Additionally, the names of several "public persons," institutions and organizations such as the Catholic Church, the United Nations and numerous world governments are incorporated into this work. References to events involving any such persons, institutions, organizations, or governments following the publication date of the first printing of the first edition of this book are entirely the product of the author's imagination.

With the exceptions noted above, all other names, characters, and incidents are either the product of the author's imagination or are used fictitiously, and any resemblance to actual events, organizations, or persons, living or dead, is entirely coincidental and beyond the intent of either the author or the publisher.

□   □   □

James BeauSeigneur has been writing professionally for eighteen years. His published works include technical manuals on strategic defense and military avionics, newspaper and magazine articles, speeches for U.S. Congressional and Senatorial candidates, and lyrics for several published songs. Formerly involved full-time in politics, Mr. BeauSeigneur has managed several U.S. Congressional and Senatorial campaigns and in 1980 ran for U.S. Congress against Al Gore. He has four years of experience in military intelligence, including two and a half years with the National Security Agency. Mr. BeauSeigneur and his wife, Gerilynne, have two daughters, Faith and Abigail.

Table of Contents

The Power Within Him — The Power Within Us All 1

Birth Pains 13

Closed Circles 29

When Worlds Collide 41

Eve of Destruction 55

Alien Stone 69

Cat Strike 87

Wormwood 95

God Amok 105

Swarm 113

Naorimashita 121

The Source of These Powers 135

What He Must Do 145

The Avenger of Blood 157

Dark Legion 179

Avatar Dawn 193

The Origin of God — The Destiny of Man 203

Clearing the Temple 235

Behold the Hosts of Heaven 247

"Are these the shadows of things that will be, or are they the shadows of things that may be?"

Charles Dickens
A Christmas Carol

"For false Christs and false prophets will appear and perform great signs and miracles to deceive even the elect – if that were possible."

Matthew 24:24

Prologue[1]

████████████

The Power Within Him —
The Power Within Us All

January 20, 2021 — Israel

It was just after dawn. Robert Milner acted as navigator while Decker Hawthorne drove the rented jeep through the mountain pass on their way to meet Christopher. In the jeep Decker had brought food, bottled water, and a first aid kit. His thoughts alternated between worry about the condition in which they would find Christopher and anticipation of what Robert Milner had told him in the lobby of the Ramada Renaissance forty days earlier. The barren countryside brought back memories of Decker's own wilderness experience eighteen years earlier, when he and Tom Donafin had made their way through Lebanon toward Israel before being rescued by Jon Hansen. He recalled the powerful shift of his emotions in that moment as he lay on the

---

[1] Chapter 28 from *In His Image, Book One of The Christ Clone Trilogy* is included here as a prologue.

1

ground, tangled in barbed wire, with three rifles pointed at his head, expecting to be shot; and then suddenly recognizing the U.N. emblems on the soldiers' helmets, and realizing that he and Tom were safe.

In the past, when Decker recalled that moment, he thought of it as just another case of being in the right place at the right time. Now he could not help but believe it was much more. Had it not happened, he would not have met Jon Hansen and he surely would never have become his press secretary. And had Decker not worked for Hansen, who later became Secretary-General, then Christopher would not have had the opportunities he did to work in the U.N. and later to head a major U.N. agency, and then to become a U.N. ambassador serving on the Security Council. Surely this was more than chance.

It occurred to him that this chain of events had not just started on that road in Lebanon. There was the destruction of the Wailing Wall, and then he and Tom were taken hostage; and before that, there were the events which had allowed him to go to Turin, Italy, in the first place. If he had not gone to Turin, he certainly never would have been called by Professor Harry Goodman on that cold November night back in 1988, to come and see what Goodman had discovered on the Shroud.

As he continued to think through the chain of circumstances that had brought him to this point, he tried to find the single weakest link in the chain, the seemingly least important event which, had it not occurred, would have averted any of the later events.

"Some things we must assign to fate," Robert Milner said, breaking the silence. It was as though he had been listening to Decker's thoughts.

"Uh . . . yeah, I guess so," Decker answered.

The days leading up to his return to Israel to find Christopher had been the most anxious of Decker's life. At times he could barely concentrate on his work as he counted the days until Christopher's return and anticipated what would follow. Milner had talked about a time so dark and bleak that the destruction of the Russian Federation and the Disaster would seem mild by comparison. Somehow the horror which might otherwise have consumed Decker at such a thought was mitigated by the hope which Milner also foresaw. Certainly, to this point, nothing cataclysmic had occurred — though the unrest in India and Pakistan might well foreshadow such events. Decker realized he would have to accept the bad along with the good. He just didn't want to dwell on it, especially if, as Milner indicated, such events were inevitable.

Ahead on the trail, a shapeless form began to take on definition. Had Decker noticed it before, he would have thought it was a bush or a tree stump or perhaps an animal, but until this moment it had blended so well into the background that it seemed an inseparable part of its surroundings. "There he is," said Milner.

Decker pressed a little harder on the gas pedal. As they got closer, he began to wonder again in what condition they would find Christopher. The last time they were together, Christopher had told Decker that he was beginning to wonder whether in the final analysis, his life had been a mistake. Now, forty days later, he was — according to Milner — the man who would lead mankind into 'the final and most glorious step in its evolution.'

In another moment they could see him clearly. His coat and clothes were dirty and tattered. He looked thin but strong. Over the forty days his hair had grown over his ears and he now had a full beard. When Decker saw his face, he was startled for a moment by the astounding resemblance to the face on the Shroud. One thing, however, was very obviously different. The face on the Shroud was peaceful and accepting in death: on Christopher's face was the look of a man driven to achieve his mission.

Milner was the first one out of the jeep. He ran to Christopher and embraced him. Patting Christopher on the back caused a small cloud of dust to rise from his clothes. Christopher then went to Decker, who reached out his hand but Christopher refused it, then instead hugged him as well. He smelled awful, but

Decker held him for a long time anyway.

"Are you all right?" Decker asked. "I've been worried about you."

"Yes, yes. I'm fine." Then turning slightly to address both Decker and Milner, he continued. "It's all clear now. It was all part of the plan."

"What plan?" asked Decker.

"I've spoken with my father. He wants me to finish the task."

"You mean . . . God? You talked with God?!"

Christopher nodded. "Yes," he said quietly. "He wants me to complete the mission I began 2000 years ago. And I need your help; both of you."

Decker felt as though he was standing on the crest of a tidal wave. Suddenly his life had more meaning than he ever imagined possible. He believed what Milner had told him about Christopher's destiny; if he hadn't he never would have left Christopher alone in the desert. But then it had all been cerebral. Now he was hearing it from Christopher's own lips. This was a turning point, not only in the lives of these three men, but of time itself. Just as the coming of Christ had divided time between B.C. and A.D., this too, would be a line of demarcation from which all else would be measured. This undoubtedly *was* the birth of a New Age. Decker wished that Elizabeth were alive to share it with him.

"What can we do?" Decker managed.

"We must return to New York immediately," Christopher answered. "Millions of lives are at stake."

□   □   □

Before leaving New York, Decker had arranged for the loan of a private jet from David Bragford, telling him that it was for Milner. As planned, the jet and crew were waiting at Ben Gurion airport when Decker, Christopher and Milner arrived. Decker had brought clothes and a shaving kit from home for

Christopher, but though he eagerly took advantage of the shower on Bragford's plane and welcomed the clean clothes, Christopher decided to forego the razor and keep the beard.

As Christopher ate his first meal in forty days, Decker briefed him on events at the U.N. Afterward Christopher began to pore over the reams of documents Decker had brought for him to review.

Three hours into the flight, one of the crew members came into the cabin, obviously very concerned about something. "What is it?" Decker asked.

"Sir," he said, "the captain has just picked up a report on the radio. Apparently all hell has broken loose in India."

"We're too late," Christopher whispered to himself as he let his head fall into his open hands.

The crewman continued, "The Pakistani Guard have detonated two nuclear bombs in New Delhi. Millions are dead."

For a long moment they sat in stunned silence, then Decker turned to Milner. "This is what you were talking about in Jerusalem, isn't it?"

"Only the beginning," he said as he reached over and hit the remote control to turn on the satellite television.

Immediately the screen showed the mushroom cloud of the first atomic bomb set off in New Delhi. The billowing cloud of debris seemed to roll back the sky like an immense scroll of ancient tattered parchment. Two days after the Pakistani Guard first made threats of hidden nuclear weapons, the television network had set up remote cameras to run twenty-four hours a day outside the threatened cities just in case the Guard carried out its threats. Even from ten miles away, the camera began to shake violently as the earth trembled from the blast's awesome shock wave. Several hundred yards in front of the camera a small two-story building vibrated with the quake and then collapsed. An instant later a bright flash on the screen marked the second explosion.

"That was the scene approximately one hour ago," the

network commentator said, his voice registering his horror, "as two atomic blasts, set off by the Pakistani Guard, rocked the Indian subcontinent. It is believed that the action came in response to the successful interdiction of weapons into Pakistan from China and a new ultimatum issued by General Brooks, commander of U.N. forces in the region. According to sources close to the Pakistani Guard, leaders of the Guard were convinced that U.N. special forces were close to locating the bombs, which would have left little to prevent India from invading Pakistan.

"Within minutes of the explosions the Pakistani government strongly condemned the action by the Guard who, they repeated, are rogue forces *not* associated with the Pakistani government. But by then India had already retaliated, launching two nuclear-tipped missiles on Pakistan. Apparently prepared for such a response from India, China immediately launched interceptors which successfully brought down the Indian missiles before they could reach their targets.

"Prior to that launch, China had attempted to maintain a neutral position in the long-running conflict between its neighbors. That neutrality was frequently called into question, however, because of the Chinese arms merchants who served as the main source of arms for Pakistan."

As Christopher, Decker, and Milner watched, new information poured in at an incredible rate. In a matter of only a few hours, the entire war was unfolding. In response to China's action, India launched a conventional attack on the Chinese interceptor bases, while simultaneously launching five additional missiles on Pakistan. Three were intercepted; two reached their targets.

Pakistan then responded to India's attack by launching a volley of its own nuclear weapons and within minutes the Pakistani Guard set off the remaining seven bombs they had planted in Indian cities.

In a temporary lull in the action, the scene on television switched to a satellite feed from a camera mounted on the top of a remotely-controlled all-terrain rover, which showed the first horrifying scenes from the suburban areas of New Delhi. Fire was everywhere. Rubble filled the streets. The sky was filled with thick black smoke from the fires and radioactive fallout, which blocked out the setting sun as though it were covered by a loosely-woven black cloth. Scattered around the landscape were hundreds of people, dead and dying. Immediately in front of the vehicle, the mostly nude body of a young Indian woman lay sprawled in the street. All but a few scraps of her clothing had been burned away. On the less charred parts of her body, where some skin remained, the flowered pattern of the sari she had been wearing was seared into her flesh like a tattoo.

Sitting on the street beside the woman's body, a startled young girl, three or four years old, looked up at the rover and began screaming. The bombs had not been so merciful to her as to her mother; she might languish two or three days before life fully released its grip on her. For a moment the camera dwelled on her, her skin covered with numerous open blisters.

Christopher turned away from the screen. "I could have prevented this," he said. It took a moment for the statement to sink through the horror and register with Decker.

"Christopher, there's nothing you could have done," Decker answered. "It's useless to blame yourself."

"But there *is* something I could have done. I told you before we left New York that I felt Moore was going to do something which would lead to catastrophe, and that there was nothing I could do to stop it. But it wasn't true. There was *one* thing I could have done. And now, because I hesitated, millions have been killed and millions more will die. Even after the war is over there will be untold deaths from fallout and radiation poisoning. And unless the U.N. acts to provide immediate relief, millions more will die of starvation and disease."

"But it's crazy to blame yourself for this. If this is the result of something Moore did, then the responsibility rests with him alone."

"Oh, the responsibility does indeed rest with Moore. It

was he who put General Brooks back in control, and it was he who directed Brooks to issue the two ultimatums. With the first, Moore was hoping to bring the war to a quick close in India's favor. In return, he expected to gain Nikhil Gandhi's support for his bid to become Secretary-General. With the second ultimatum, Moore believed he could force the hand of the Pakistani Guard. General Brooks assured him that the Guard didn't really have nuclear devices planted in India, but Moore knew the risk he was taking. If there were no bombs, then the ultimatum would call the Pakistani Guard's bluff. On the other hand, if the threat was real, he knew that a war would destabilize India to the point that Gandhi would likely return to rebuild India and Rajiv Advani would replace him as Primary on the Security Council. Either way, he calculated that he would benefit."

"Are you sure about all this?" Decker asked, unable to believe that Moore would sacrifice so many people to become Secretary-General.

"I am," Christopher answered.

"Christopher is correct," Milner said with certainty.

"Moore is also responsible for the murder of Ambassador Lee," Christopher added. "And he is planning the assassination of Yuri Kruszkegin. There is nothing he will not do to achieve his goals. I must stop him now, before he can do any more."

"Why didn't Moore just kill Gandhi, instead of risking the lives of so many?" Decker asked, still struggling to believe the magnitude of Moore's malevolence.

"The death of Ambassador Lee was believed to be an accident," Milner answered. "If Kruszkegin died, most would assume it was coincidence. But no one would believe that the death of three Primary members was just a fluke, especially if soon after that Moore became Secretary-General precisely because of the replacement of those three members. Besides, killing Gandhi would still leave him the problems in India and Pakistan to deal with as Secretary-General — better to try to end the war quickly in India's favor and ingratiate himself to Gandhi, rather than bring suspicion on himself with three untimely deaths."

"What are you going to do?" Decker asked Christopher.

"In the third chapter of Ecclesiastes," Christopher answered, "King Solomon wrote, 'There is a time for everything: a time to be born and a time to die; a time to plant and a time to reap; a time to heal and a time to kill.'"

Decker looked back and forth from Christopher to Milner and then back to the television screen. As the camera panned the devastation, in the distance, where the smoke and radioactive cloud had not yet entirely shrouded the earth, the moon rose above the horizon, glowing blood red through the desecrated sky.

□   □   □

It was another two hours before their plane landed in New York. From there they went directly to the United Nations, where the Security Council was meeting in closed session. As night had fallen in the east, the war continued to spread. Nuclear warheads dropped like overripe fruit, appearing as falling stars in the night sky. The destruction spread six hundred miles into China and to the south nearly as far as *Hyderābād*, India. West and north of Pakistan, the people of Afghanistan, southeastern Iran, and southern *Tajikstan* gathered their families and all they could carry on their backs, and beat a hurried path away from the war. In just days the local weather patterns would fill their fields, rivers, and streams with toxic fallout.

Pakistan was little more than an open grave. India's arsenal was completely spent. What was left of its army survived in small clusters that were cut off from all command and control. Most would die soon from radiation. China was the only participant still in control of its military and it had no interest in going any further with the war.

In the few hours it had taken them to fly from Israel and arrive at the U.N., the war had begun and ended. The final estimate of the number killed would exceed four hundred and twenty million. There were no winners.

□   □   □

In quick strides Christopher reached the door of the Security Council Chamber and burst through, followed closely by Decker and Milner. For a moment the members stared at the intruders. Everyone knew Decker but they had not seen Milner in a year and a half, and the change in Christopher was more than the hair and the beard; his whole demeanor had changed. When he recognized Christopher, Gerard Poupardin, who sat some distance from Moore, looked over at another staffer and laughed, "Who the hell does he think he is: Jesus Christ?"

Christopher seized the opportunity provided by the startled silence. "Mr. President," Christopher said, addressing the Canadian ambassador who sat in the position designated for the President of the Security Council. "Though I have no desire to disrupt the urgent business of this body in its goal of providing relief to the peoples of India, Pakistan, China, and the surrounding countries, there is one among us who is not fit even to cast his vote among an assembly of thieves, much less this August body!"

"You're out of order!" Moore shouted as he jumped to his feet. "Mr. President, the Alternate from Europe is out of order." The Canadian ambassador reached for his gavel but froze at the sheer power of Christopher's glance.

"Gentlemen of the Security Council," Christopher continued.

"You're out of order!" Moore shouted again. Christopher looked at Moore and suddenly and inexplicably Moore fell back into his chair, silent.

Christopher continued. "Gentlemen of the Security Council, seldom in history can the cause of a war be traced to one man. On this occasion, it can be. One man sitting among you bears nearly the total burden of guilt for this senseless war. That man is the ambassador from France, Albert Moore."

Moore struggled to his feet. "That's a lie!" he shouted.

Christopher stated the charges against Moore.

"Lies! All lies!" Moore shouted. "Mr. President, this outrage has gone on long enough. Ambassador Goodman has obviously gone completely mad." Moore could feel his strength returning. "I insist that he be restrained and removed from this chamber and that . . ." Moore once again fell silent as Christopher turned and pointed, his arm fully extended toward him.

"Confess," Christopher said in a quiet but powerful voice.

Moore stared at Christopher in disbelief and began to laugh out loud.

"Confess!" Christopher said again, this time a little louder.

Abruptly, Moore's laughter ceased. The panic in his eyes could not begin to reveal the magnitude of his torment. Without warning he felt as though his blood were turning to acid as it coursed through his veins. His whole body felt as if he were on fire from the inside.

"Confess!" Christopher said a third time, now shouting his demand.

Moore looked in Christopher's eyes and what he saw there left no doubt as to the source of his sudden anguish. He stumbled in pain and caught himself on the table in front of him. Blood began to trickle from his mouth and down his chin as he bit through the tender flesh of his lower lip; his jaw clenched uncontrollably like a vice under the unbearable agony. Gerard Poupardin ran toward Moore as those near him helped him to his seat.

The pain grew steadily worse. There was no way out. "Yes! Yes!" he cried suddenly in excruciating anguish, as he pulled free of the grip of those helping him. "It's all true! Everything he has said is true! The war; Ambassador Lee's death; the plan to kill Kruszkegin; all of it!" Everyone in the room stared wide-eyed in disbelief. No one understood what was happening, least of all Gerard Poupardin. But everyone heard him — Moore had clearly confessed.

Moore hoped only that his confession would bring relief from his torment, and in that he was not disappointed. No sooner had he finished his confession than he fell to the floor, dead.

Someone ran for a doctor and for about fifteen minutes the chamber was filled with confusion, until finally Moore's lifeless body was taken from the room.

"Gentlemen," came a somber voice from near the spot where Moore had fallen. It was Christopher. "A quarter of the world's population is dead or threatened by death in China, India, and the eastern portions of the Middle East. There is so much that must be done, and it must be done quickly. As indelicate as it may seem: with the death of Ambassador Moore, until France can send a new ambassador and the nations of Europe can elect a new Primary, as Alternate from Europe, I am now that region's acting Primary representative. Gentlemen, let us get to the business at hand."

□   □   □

The coroner's report would find that Albert Moore died of a massive heart attack, brought on, it seemed, by the tremendous burden of guilt for what he had done. For Decker, no explanation was necessary: Christopher had begun to exercise the unexplored powers within him. He could only hope and pray that these powers would be equal to the challenges the world would soon face as Christopher led mankind into the final stage of its evolution and into the dawn of the New Age of humankind.

Chapter 1

Birth Pains

January 24, 2021 — The United Nations, New York

The China-India-Pakistan War lasted only a day but the dead numbered in the hundreds of millions. Millions more would die from radiation poisoning, disease, and starvation. Nature, too, demanded her toll as wild animals, driven from their natural habitats, attacked weakened human survivors fleeing the holocaust. At the U.N. the ensuing days were filled with endless meetings of the Security Council working to provide relief to the war's survivors. Because providing food was a major priority, Christopher's experience with the Food and Agriculture Organization made him the center of much discussion and he showed himself to possess both skill and untiring drive. There was no mourning for Albert Moore as there had been for Secretary-General Hansen and Ambassador Lee. Even if there had been time, there would be no tears for one who had caused so much misery. France quickly named a new ambassador and an election for a successor to Moore on the Security Council was scheduled for Monday, the first day of February.

The return of former Assistant Secretary-General Robert Milner was celebrated with great excitement at a reception held by the Lucius Trust, which was attended by several hundred members and supporters, including many U.N. delegates. Milner took advantage of the opportunity to express his sincere approval of Ms. Gaia Love as Alice Bernley's successor as director, and he encouraged the members to be diligent in advancing the work of the Trust. He concluded his address to thunderous applause by confirming the rumor circulating among the Trust's supporters that his return from Israel was evidence that the 'time' was very near.

Decker Hawthorne spent the next three days responding to a deluge of requests for information on the war and its consequences; the meetings of the Security Council; the investigation of Albert Moore's records; and, as Decker was pleased to see, a growing number of requests for information about Christopher.

It was not until the morning of Sunday, the 24th of January, that Decker, Christopher, and Milner were once again able to meet together in Christopher's office. The three men sat in comfortable high-backed English chairs around a low table as coffee was served. "Do you have the article you told me about?" Christopher asked. Decker nodded and reached into his briefcase to retrieve a copy of *The New York Times*. "I think you should hear this, Mr. Secretary," Christopher told Milner.

"This is from yesterday's paper," Decker began, "page sixteen, dateline Jerusalem."

While the attention of most of the world focuses on the still unfolding tragedy in the East, two men in Israel, one claiming to be the 2,000-year-old Apostle John, the other to be 'one who comes in the spirit and power of the prophet Elijah,' are predicting far worse tragedy to come. The men, leaders of a large and very active cult in Israel called the Koum Damah Patar (KDP), say that the earth is about to undergo such cataclysmic events as fire falling from the sky, the collision of a large meteor or asteroid with the earth, poisoning of one-third of the earth's fresh water, and the blacking out of one-third of the sun and stars.

While most Israelis consider the two men simply an annoyance, there are some who take them very seriously and claim that they are responsible for causing the drought that has stricken Israel and the rest of the Middle East for the past sixteen months. Their followers believe that one of the men, whom they call Rabbi Yochanan — the Hebrew equivalent of John — is actually the Apostle John of the Christian New Testament, and that even though he appears to be in his late fifties, he is actually over 2,000 years old. The other man, who says he comes like John the Baptist before him, 'in the spirit and power of Elijah,' is a former Hasidic rabbi named Saul Cohen. Like Israel's High Priest Chaim Levin, Cohen was originally a follower of New York Rabbi Menachem Schneerson. Cohen was disowned by the rest of Judaism nearly twenty years ago when he began to teach that Jesus was the Jewish Messiah.

Dressed in robes made of burlap or 'sackcloth,' John and Cohen walk through the streets of Jewish towns and cities proclaiming their messages of God's wrath on the earth. Adding to the general unkempt appearance of the men, reportedly they seldom bathe and cover the tops of their heads with ashes and soot in accordance with ancient religious traditions for those in mourning. They refuse to be interviewed by members of the press, preferring the endless recitation of their warnings.

Members of the KDP cult, which reportedly has

nearly 150,000 followers, have been a constant irritant to their fellow Israelis and tourists alike, and have been blamed for a major drop in the already flagging tourist business in Israel. Cult members approach their unsuspecting targets and accuse them of acts or thoughts which the cult considers immoral, and then threaten eternal damnation to any who do not repent. Even High Priest Levin has been assaulted by their verbal harangue.

Membership in the KDP is apparently limited to single Jewish males, though the group also has a large number of additional followers. Actual KDP members are easily identified by the blood-red Hebrew writing which each bears on his forehead. Many in Israel believe KDP members possess psychic abilities and most say that the KDP members who have approached them have very detailed personal information about their lives.

According to the proclamations of the two KDP leaders, the events they prophesy will befall the people of the earth because mankind has 'refused to follow God's laws and to accept God's mercy.' They say the reason that the prophesied punishment will come from the heavens is because instead of worshiping the 'true God, men have instead worshiped the sun, moon and stars' — an apparent reference to astrology — and other 'false gods.'

Should their prophecies about the collision between the earth and an asteroid prove true, it would not be the first time such an event has occurred. Many scientists believe that it was just such a collision with an asteroid that may have caused the extinction of the dinosaurs about 65 million years ago at the end of the Cretaceous Period. According to Dr. Jean Spring of the Palomar Planet-Crossing Asteroid Survey at Mt.

Palomar Observatory in the U.S., there are several thousand asteroids whose orbits intersect the earth's orbit, approximately 950 of which are one kilometer (.6 mile) or more in diameter. She is quick to add, however, that the chances are extremely small of a large asteroid colliding with the earth anytime in the next 20 billion years.

When KDP members first began appearing in Israel, police arrested hundreds of them on charges of disturbing the peace. Very soon, however, it became impossible to find sufficient jail space for them. According to sources inside the Israeli government, police have attempted to arrest the cult's two leaders, but despite help from Israel's intelligence service, they have found it impossible to infiltrate KDP ranks. Even though the two men have now come out into the open, police have been unable to arrest them because of their uncanny ability to quickly slip away whenever police, even undercover police, come near."

As Decker read the last paragraph of the article, Christopher rose from his chair and went to one of his bookshelves. "Listen to this," Christopher said, as he walked back from the bookshelf with a leather-bound book open in his hands. It was a Bible.

The first angel sounded his trumpet, and there came hail and fire mixed with blood, and it was hurled down upon the earth. A third of the earth was burned up, a third of the trees were burned up, and all the green grass was burned up. The second angel sounded his trumpet, and something like a huge mountain, all ablaze, was thrown into the sea. A third part of the sea turned into blood, a third of the living creatures in the sea died, and a third of the ships were destroyed. The third angel sounded his trumpet, and a great star, blazing like a torch, fell from the sky on a third of the rivers and on the springs of water — the name of the star is Wormwood. A third of the waters turned bitter and many people died from the waters that had become bitter. The fourth angel sounded his trumpet, and a third of the sun was struck, a third of the moon, and a third of the stars, so that a third of them turned dark. A third of the day was without light, and also a third of the night.[2]

"That sounds frighteningly similar to what John and Cohen are predicting," Christopher concluded, as he flipped to another page.

"You mean that stuff is in the Bible?!" Decker asked.

"Yes, in the book of Revelation," Christopher said. "But there's more."

And I will give power to my two witnesses, and they will prophesy for 1,260 days, clothed in sackcloth. These are the two olive trees, and the two lampstands that stand before the Lord of the earth. If anyone tries to harm them, fire comes from their mouths, and devours their enemies. This is how anyone who wants to harm them must die. These men have power to shut up the sky so that it will not rain during the time they are prophesying; and they have power to turn the waters into blood and to strike the earth with every kind of plague as often as they want.[3]

"So everything they're predicting will happen?" Decker asked, his voice filled with concern.

"I believe they may have the power to *make* it happen,"

---

[2] Revelation 8:7-12.
[3] Revelation 11:3-6.

Milner answered. "This is what I told you about that morning in the hotel lobby in Jerusalem."

Decker looked at Christopher and suddenly a sick look came over Christopher's face. "What's the matter?" Decker asked.

"According to what I just read," Christopher said, "John and Cohen — if they are the 'two witnesses' referred to — they're prophets. They're servants of God."

"Yeah, but wasn't it John who wrote Revelation?" Decker responded.

"That's right!" Christopher agreed, the realization apparently occurring to him only an instant after it had to Decker.

"Is it possible," Christopher asked, turning to Milner, "that what John wrote in Revelation, he's now attempting to carry out?"

"It would certainly appear so," answered Milner. "And as I said, I think that he and Cohen may have the power to make these things happen. Whether this is what John had in mind all those years ago when he wrote the book of Revelation is highly unlikely. His psychic and telekinetic abilities have only recently grown to the magnitude that they are now. And I doubt that 2,000 years ago he had any idea they'd ever grow to this point. It's more likely that now, finding himself possessed of such powers, he's chosen to use what he wrote then as a blueprint. It wouldn't be the first time Bible prophecy was used in a similar manner. Cult leader Charles Manson did much the same thing back in the 1970s, combining the words of Revelation and lyrics by the Beatles. But Manson's crimes will pale by comparison to what John and Cohen have planned."

"Okay, hold it a minute," Decker said. "Perhaps I'm a little slow," he began self-effacingly, "but obviously there are a few things here that I'm not catching. Would somebody please explain to me why these guys have all this power and why they want to cause all this destruction?"

"I'm sorry, Decker," Milner responded. "All of this has been happening pretty fast. I'll try to explain. As I told you at the hotel in Israel, humankind is about to enter the final phase in its evolutionary process.   At the completion of this final phase — which we call the New Age — humans will have evolved as far beyond what we are now, as we now are above the insects. The KDP are the first to enter that phase.

"Decker, haven't you ever wondered what it is about the Jewish people that allowed them to survive for nearly 1,900 years without a country? They survived dispersion and literally dozens of attempts by kings, government, and bigots to wipe them from the face of the earth. They have flourished despite the cruelest discrimination, and most amazing of all, they have avoided assimilation into the civilizations around them.   No other nationality in history has ever done that. Decker, they really are different from non-Jews. Now, I know that may sound like a racist statement, but what I'm saying is that they are actually slightly farther along on the evolutionary scale. The difference is so small that it's not measurable by any known standard, but it has allowed them to survive as a people, and that is why the first concrete manifestations of the New Age are being seen among the Jews. The KDP are the spearhead of the evolutionary changes to come.   Soon the changes will spread throughout the world, to people of every nation and race."

"So how do John and Cohen fit in?" asked Decker.

"Like the biblical Jewish prophets before them," Milner answered, "both John and Cohen were born with certain psychic abilities. I suspect that Jesus recognized that ability in John and that is why he chose John to be among his disciples, even though John was much younger than the other apostles." Decker looked over at Christopher, thinking that perhaps Milner's supposition would spur a memory from his former life. Christopher shrugged to indicate he had no recollection of the matter.

"Thousands of years ago, men like John and Cohen would have been acclaimed as major prophets. A few years ago, they would have been just two among hundreds of moderately successful psychics. Now, as the New Age approaches, they have been catapulted beyond anything the world has previously known. And yet the power they have now will soon seem like nothing at all. I cannot begin to tell you the magnitude of what lies ahead for humankind. As the potential of the human mind is revealed, we will begin to see our fellow humans not only through our physical eyes but also through the mind's eye. We will begin, as the members of the KDP already have, to see the innermost part of those around us: their needs and desires; their hopes and their fears; their pain and their joy; their true selves! We will all be stripped bare of the facade which makes some of us seem beautiful and some of us ugly, some of us seem charming and others dull, some of us attractive and others repulsive.

"When we can truly see those around us, when we are forced to see not just their outward appearance but into their very souls, then we will begin to truly understand each other. Certainly, all that we see will not be pleasant; indeed, much will be dark and corrupted. But we will also be able to see beyond the corruption to its root cause. And as we learn to understand what has made each of us what we are, we will quickly lose our desire to hate."

The excitement in Milner's voice grew with every sentence and it was contagious. Milner picked up the Bible that Christopher had closed and put on the coffee table. "The Apostle Paul put it beautifully in First Corinthians.

> *For we know in part, and we prophesy in part, but when perfection comes, the imperfect disappears. When I was a child, I talked as a child, I thought like a child, I reasoned like a child. When I became a man, I put childish ways behind me. Now we see but a poor reflection as in a mirror; then we shall see face to face. Now I know in part; then I shall know fully, even as I am fully known.*[4]

---

[4] I Corinthians 13: 9-12.

Milner put the Bible down and continued. "For a while, a short while, the embarrassment of having others see our innermost thoughts will be more than some of us can bear. But soon, as we and all around us are stripped bare of pretense and deceit, we will begin to understand that those around us are really no different than we are, that they share the *same* hopes and fears, the same needs and desires. And when we see that, we will come to realize that understanding others is just as great a blessing as being understood.

"As we learn to speak and listen with our hearts, true cooperation among people will begin. There is no end to what we will be able to do when we really work together! But even this is only the beginning! All of this will happen in just the next few decades. It is merely the foredawn of the glorious New Age!" Milner was nearly out of his seat with his enthusiasm.

"As the transcendent dawn becomes full, we will grow beyond the realm of our own bodies. Now we know only matter and energy, and we operate within their constraints. Then we shall know a whole new form. To call that form 'spirit' would not be inappropriate, but that term would limit it to what we can now imagine it to mean; and it is so much more. The solar system, the galaxy, indeed the very universe, will be ours! We will travel to places, times, and dimensions unimaginable! There will be no end!"

Decker's eyes had grown wide and his eyebrows arched halfway up his forehead. Never had he imagined the awesome magnitude of the promise this New Age held. In that brief moment, Decker swore himself to its fulfillment.

"And yet," Milner continued, "it is possible that all of this could be torn from us. The next five to six years will determine whether we boldly enter the glorious light of the New Age or retreat into the darkness of our hatred and fear. If the latter course is chosen, on that day we will surely begin to die as a species. It may take a hundred years, perhaps even two, but man will certainly destroy himself and the earth with him."

"'Man must evolve or perish,'" Christopher said, introspectively. "That's what my father told me in the desert: 'Man must evolve or perish.'"

"Even as we see the emergence of so great a promise as the New Age," Milner said, "we also see the specter of a hideous and macabre threat. History, it has been said, is the record of man's inhumanity to man. Our history since the Disaster certainly bears grim witness to that: the destruction of Russia, the China-India-Pakistan war. And even where there is no war there is individual brutality. Violent crime has risen dramatically each year since the Disaster," he said, referring to the day seventeen years earlier which saw the mysterious sudden deaths of nearly one fifth of the world's population.

"Does the Disaster have something to do with all of this?" Decker asked.

"No, not at all. I use it only as a point of reference. What I'm saying is that as the New Age approaches, the old age struggles to hold on. It is not that the age in itself has any power, but rather that humankind, sensing the coming of anything new and unknown, foolishly grasps onto what it knows, no matter how self-destructive it may be. We cling to our past like a man clinging to the mast of sinking ship rather than swimming to a lifeboat a few feet away. By appealing to man's fear of the unknown, John and Cohen have perverted the role of those in the KDP."

"If the KDP is just misled," Decker asked, "then the real threat to mankind's future is from John and Cohen. Could you," he said, looking at Christopher, "just do something like you did with Albert Moore? If they're really going to cause the destruction they're claiming in that newspaper article, then surely they deserve it. And even if they don't deserve it *yet,* can't we take some kind of preemptive action?"

Milner answered for Christopher. "Unfortunately, it is not that simple."

"No, I didn't think it would be," Decker said with a sigh of resignation. "Still, humor me: why not?"

"Entry into the New Age must be a conscious choice. No one can be forced or dragged into it. In that way, this step in the evolutionary process is entirely unlike all that preceded it. Evolution, as the world has experienced it to this point, is 'material evolution.' That is, the force of evolution has caused physical changes, with creatures progressing along divergent paths of advancement. There was never any choice involved: those species that adapted and evolved survived; those that did not, perished. The path of material evolution followed by the human species has achieved its full realization; the next and final step is not *material* evolution but *spiritual* evolution. That is why there must be a choice. Choice is the impetus and catalyst to allow the change to begin. We must each choose for ourselves either to enter the New Age or to remain in the past.

"Eliminating John and Cohen would not facilitate a correct decision; it would simply remove the possibility of choice. It may seem ironic, but without the option of choosing to remain in the present age, it is impossible to enter the New Age."

"So, in effect, John and Cohen are a 'necessary evil'?"

Milner nodded. "I admire your succinctness," he said. "Had it not been John and Cohen, it would have been someone or something else. The 'evil' is necessary for the 'good' to emerge."

"But if choice is required, what about the KDP? By following John and Cohen they've obviously made the wrong choice, yet they've already entered the New Age."

"No, Decker. No one enters the New Age apart from everyone else; the threshold must be crossed as a species, not as individuals. Certain manifestations will appear before that time. Just as the dawn is preceded by the brightening of the night sky, so we see the signs of the coming of the New Age manifested in the KDP. But the day begins not with predawn brightening of the sky, but rather with the first appearance of the sun."

Milner continued. "Just because the manifestations are most evident in the KDP does not mean they have entered the New

Age. The choice of entering the new day or of turning back into the darkness still remains for them. The choice is theirs to continue to follow John and Cohen, or to follow Christopher. The same choice will be offered to everyone else in the world."

"But how will they make that choice? When will they know?" Decker asked.

"I don't know the exact timing. The opportunity to choose will come only when the world is ready to decide. I *do* know that until that time, John and Cohen must be given full reign to do as they will."

"You mean we just have to sit by and let them do their worst?"

"I'm afraid so," Milner answered. "Only in that way will humankind be prepared to take the step of volition that is required."

"So, basically what you're saying is that Christopher can't give the world the choice to stop beating their heads against the wall until they've so bloodied themselves that they're willing to stop?"

"Uh . . . yes," Milner said, with a hint of a smile. "Once again I compliment your ability to cut to the heart of the matter."

"Okay," Decker said, "just one more question . . . for now anyway."

"Yes?"

"How do you know all this?"

"Well, that's a very long story. Suffice it to say that we can be sure that despite John and Cohen's prophetic abilities, and their ability to cause the things they prophesy, there is at least one thing they have claimed in that article which is patently false: Saul Cohen does not come in the power and spirit of the prophet Elijah . . . I do."

"What do you mean?"

"You may remember that Alice Bernley had a 'spirit guide' whom she called Master Djwlij Kajm or sometimes 'the Tibetan.'" Decker nodded. "Well, when Alice died, Master Djwlij Kajm came to me. During the sixteen months I was in Israel, before you and Christopher arrived, I went through a period of preparation under Djwlij Kajm's guidance. At the conclusion of that period, in a process that's a bit difficult to explain, I received into myself the spirit of Elijah. We are both here." Decker blinked back his astonishment.

"Jewish prophecy says that the prophet Elijah, who was perhaps the greatest of all of the Jewish prophets, and who, according to his successor, Elisha, did not die, but was taken up alive into heaven,[5] will return. That is why Saul Cohen claims that he comes in the spirit and power of Elijah. He intends to counterfeit the return of Elijah to the Jewish people. But, in fact, that is impossible because the spirit of Elijah dwells here within me. We are one. I am his mouth and he is my eyes."

"So, do you know everything that is going to happen?" Decker asked.

"The knowledge is within us," Milner said, referring in the plural to himself and the one who possessed him. "But there is a veil beyond which I have been forbidden to look. I suspect that beyond it is something which will prove personally very painful for me and from which Elijah seeks to protect me for as long as possible. When the time is right the veil will be lifted."

"So where do we go from here?" Decker asked. "Do we just sit and wait while John and Cohen wreak havoc with the earth?"

"Not at all," Milner answered.

"Well then, what? Do we reveal who Christopher is and put the religion of the New Age on the 'fast track,' or what?"

"No!" Christopher answered abruptly, as if scolding Decker. "I'm sorry," he said after a moment. "I didn't mean to bark at you. It's just that, despite Secretary Milner's magnificent explanation, there's still so much that remains unclear. It's one thing to talk about what may lie ahead, it's another altogether to bear the responsibility for making it happen. My time with my

---

[5] II Kings 2:11.

father was so brief. There is much I still don't know. But of one thing there can be no doubt: the New Age is not about replacing one religion with another. In fact, it's just the opposite. This is about humankind coming to rely upon itself; upon the god that is within all of us.

"Karl Marx said that religion is the opiate of the people, but he was wrong. Religion is not the opiate, it is the **incendiary** of the people! Never is evil done so well as when it is done in the name of religion! Never is cruelty so absolute as when it is empowered by self-righteous anger! Never has so convenient an excuse as religion been found for one man to rob or murder another! Religion has been the cause of more wars, more damnable crusades, more pious inquisitions, more discrimination, more inequity, more prejudice, more injury, more intolerance, more fanaticism, more narrow-mindedness, more injustice than any other cause known throughout history! Hindus murder Muslims, Muslims murder Jews, Catholics murder Protestants, Buddhists murder Hin . . . there's just no end."

For a moment there was profound silence as Decker pondered, amazed that he had never realized these things himself. Now it all seemed so obvious. It was, after all, religious differences that had served as the line of demarcation in the war between India and Pakistan, and as a key factor in China's support of Pakistan.

"In answer to your question, Decker," Milner interjected, "what must be done is not religious but political — though I hesitate to use that word because of its negative connotations. The first step is Christopher's election as the Primary from Europe. Much has been done toward that goal already. We require the votes of eight of the fifteen countries in the European Region. I believe that he has that many votes already."

"That's great!" Decker said. "But how can you be sure?"

"Over the past three days, since our return from Israel, I've met with several European members. They're quite impressed, as are most of the members, with Christopher's handling of the situation with Moore. Their logic constrains them to believe Moore's confession was simply the result of his unbearable guilt and that Christopher merely exposed that guilt. No one seriously thinks Christopher had any direct involvement in Moore's death. But even more important," Milner continued, "has been the magnificent way Christopher has stepped into the position of acting Primary. The eyes of the world have been on the televised meetings of the Security Council and — as the man of the hour — on Christopher. At a critical time such as this, following such a senseless war, the world needs a hero, and Christopher neatly fits that role." Decker was well aware of that sentiment, but he enjoyed hearing Milner say it. "In fact, I would not be surprised if he were elected unanimously.

"At the proper time," Milner continued, "the second step will be Christopher's election as Secretary General. Much of the foundation has already been laid through years of work by myself and by the Lucius Trust. I believe we can already count on the support of over a third of the general membership and at least four of the members of the Security Council."

"You mean that all those people know about Christopher?"

"No. Of course not. Only a very small group outside of this room knows about him — only those in whom I have the utmost trust. The rest have only nebulous imaginations of the New Age, and a vague knowledge that a mighty leader of that age is coming; one whose right and destiny it is to rule the earth as a benevolent and compassionate sovereign."

Chapter 2

Closed Circles

March 30, 2021 — New York City

The waiter at the Wan Fu Chinese restaurant on Second and 43rd near the U.N. brought the check and four fortune cookies. As was his long-time habit, Decker waited to take the last one, as though that might increase the odds that the fortune he got was actually his and not just the result of hastily grabbing the wrong cookie.

"Mine says, 'You will soon be embarking on a long journey,'" Jackie Hansen said.

"Mine says the same thing," said Jody MacArthur, one of the secretarial staff who worked for Decker.

"Great!" said Jackie. "Where shall we go?"

"Well, while you two are off on your journey, I'm going to be here spending my winnings from the lottery," said Debbie Marz, Decker's lead administrative assistant.

"Why? What does yours say?" Jody asked.

"It says, 'A small investment could result in major returns.'

And my horoscope said that today is a good day to take a risk. It sounds to me like it's a perfect day to buy a lottery ticket."

"I'll go with you," Decker said. "You don't mind if I play the same numbers, do you?"

"What, and have to split the winnings? Sorry, sir; you're on your own."

"What does yours say, Decker?" Jackie asked.

"It says, 'You like Chinese food.'"

"No, really," Jackie laughed. Decker handed her the fortune and she read it. "He's right," she told the others at the table.

"Well, it was *you* who picked Chinese," Debbie Marz commented.

The weather seemed particularly agreeable as they left the restaurant. The bright sun gently coaxed the March air to a delicate early spring warmth. Birds flew overhead and pecked at crumbs on the sidewalks around them. Street vendors peddled sunglasses, neckties, pepper spray, New York City souvenirs, and flowers. It was hard for Decker to imagine that the events predicted by John and Cohen would actually occur. For a while it was all he could think about. For several nights after Christopher's election as Europe's Primary member on the Security Council, Decker had hardly slept because of persistent nightmares. Now, two months later, the thought of worldwide destruction seemed unimaginable. Perhaps, he thought, the damage would just be localized. It's a big planet. Maybe it would happen somewhere else, not here. A little distance could make all the difference in the world. After all, even the India-China-Pakistan War, as bad as it was, really didn't affect life here in New York. Sure, there was a lot of work going on at the United Nations aimed at rebuilding the affected countries, caring for the sick, and assisting with quick and painless deaths for those suffering from radiation-related illness; but such discussions took place in comfortable meeting rooms where the worst that had to be endured were the stories and photographs of other people's suffering. It was not that Decker didn't care about those directly affected by the war, it was just that as he looked around on this beautiful spring day the thought of such things seemed so remote. Today, right now, there was only the spring.

As frequently happened when left to his thoughts for very long, Decker began to think of Elizabeth and his daughters. The years since their deaths only seemed to intensify his longing. Elizabeth loved spring. They met in spring in the same coffee house where Decker met Tom Donafin. She walked in while Decker was trying to play a song he had written on the guitar. It had seemed like a pretty good song when he had practiced it earlier; then strangely, when she walked in it seemed inane and his playing was even worse. That had been forty-four years ago, but thinking back, he could feel every emotion as if it were occurring only now.

Just ahead on the sidewalk, there was a noisy commotion as a small crowd gathered around a bearded man. Jackie, Jody, and Debbie all slowed to look. Decker — pulled back from his memories — did the same. Just as Decker became aware of what was happening, the bearded man turned and looked directly at him. The man's forehead seemed covered with blood. Decker recognized the marks.

"Religion is not the cause of evil, Mr. Hawthorne," the man began. "It is only a convenient excuse used by men for the evil they do! As surely as the Sovereign Lord lives, He takes no pleasure in the death of the wicked, but would rather that they turn from their ways and live."

"Keep walking!" Decker told his companions as he reached out, quickly gathering them up like chicks and herding them along.

On the sidewalk in front of the United Nations they saw two more KDP, both with small groups gathered around them. As Decker soon learned, all but a few thousand of the Koum Damah Patar had left Israel and spread out to countries all around the world. Their primary targets appeared to be cities with large Jewish populations, and New York had one of the largest.

June 2, 2021 — Harvard-Smithsonian Center for Astrophysics, Cambridge, Massachusetts (10:30 p.m.)

University of Mississippi graduate student Mary Ludford rubbed her eyes and took another swallow of lukewarm coffee from the cup she had owned since she was fourteen. It was her only souvenir of her father, who had abandoned her and her mother eight years before. She and her mother had sold everything else that belonged to him to make ends meet and what they couldn't sell they burned, smashed, or threw away. Her mother never understood why Mary kept the cup, and Mary wasn't quite sure herself. She had bought it for her father on Father's Day a year before he left. On the cup was a panel from *Calvin and Hobbes*, his favorite comic strip, and hers as well. It was an unauthorized ripoff of the comic's trademark, as counterfeit as her father's love. Of one thing she was certain: if not the caffeine in the coffee, then the bitterness of the memories the cup held would always drive away the sleep. At this moment, however, her mind was far from her hatred for her father.

For several hours she had been studying computer-enhanced images on the ultra-high resolution monitor before her, plotting the positions of some of the galaxies most distant from the earth. The images, captured by electronic detectors sensitive enough to register a single photon of light, had been taken from the 120-inch telescope at Mount Wilson Observatory in California. As part of her thesis project, Mary Ludford was analyzing the amount of redshift registered from each of the galaxies in order to calculate their rate of recession away from the earth. The redshift effect, discovered by astronomer Edwin Hubble, results from the fact that, as the universe expands and other galaxies recede relative to the position of the Milky Way, light from those galaxies is either more or less red depending on their distance from the earth. As a result, the amount of redshift is used as a kind of cosmic tape measure to determine both distance and speed away from the earth.

Mary confined her study to a small region on the edge of one of the voids of space located by the naked eye in the constellation Boötes. As she moved to the next image she found something unexpected. Three dots of light appeared not to be moving away from the earth, but toward it. Quickly she skipped ahead to two other images of the same area which had been taken two and four hours after the first. Both of them had the same three points of light. There was only one logical explanation, but when she checked a recent update of the *Astrological Survey* she found that no known major asteroids should have appeared in the area.

Looking at her watch, she decided this was as good a stopping point as any and shut off her equipment. In the morning she would report the discovery to her thesis advisor. For now she would celebrate her apparent find with a pizza. Identifying new asteroids was not a major discovery, but it was a first for Mary. No matter how insignificant to the body of science, the joy of discovery was the same.

□   □   □

The next morning, Mary Ludford showed the images to her advisor, Dr. Jung Xiou, who agreed with her conclusion that the unidentified bodies were most likely asteroids. "It's not my specialty," Dr. Xiou admitted, "but they appear to be fairly large. When were these made?"

She checked her log even though she was sure of the answer. "Two weeks ago," she answered.

"Okay, you need to make out a report of the discovery and get a copy over to CBAT," he said, referring to the Central Bureau for Astronomical Telegrams of the International Astronomical Union, which serves as a clearinghouse for astronomy reporting. "I'll call and let them know you're coming."

"Great," she said. "I'll get right to work on the report."

"I'll also call Dr. Waters at Mount Wilson to see if we can schedule some additional shots of it."

"Good luck. I understand they're pretty booked up."

"There would be something wrong if they weren't," Xiou responded. "So, how is the rest of your work progressing?" he asked, referring to her thesis project.

"Oh, plodding along. I should have another interim report ready to show you in about a week." Dr. Xiou nodded approval. "Let me know what you find out from Mount Wilson," she said, as she started to leave.

"Of course," Xiou answered, going back to his work. "Oh, Mary," he called, catching her before she got out the door, "have you come up with names for them?"

Mary Ludford knew that initially the asteroids would be assigned a code for the year and month in which they were first sighted — in this case, 2021 K for the first half of June in the year 2021 — followed by the order of the sighting during that period. Later, when the asteroids were sighted again on their next orbit, they would officially come to be known by the names she selected. She also knew that the convention for naming asteroids is pretty much left up to the imagination of the discoverer. There are some named for Greek and Roman gods, others for scientists, political figures, poets, and philosophers; a few are named for cities; there are even four discovered in the early 1990s named John, Paul, George, and Ringo. "I think I like Calvin, Hobbes, and Wormwood," she said with a smile.

The idea evoked only confusion from Dr. Xiou. "Calvin and Hobbes I think I understand. They're from that old comic strip. But Wormwood? You mean like in Hamlet?" he asked, referring to a line from the Shakespearean play.[6]

"No," Mary answered. "*Miss* Wormwood. That was the name of Calvin's first grade teacher."

"Well, that's a trivia question I would have missed," Xiou confessed.

"I guess it's kinda silly, really," Mary admitted. "I tried to

---

[6] Hamlet, Act III, Scene 2, William Shakespeare.

think of the name of the little girl in the comic strip but all I could think of was his teacher." Mary was becoming a little embarrassed. "If you don't like it, maybe I could . . ."

"No, it's fine," he said reassuringly. "I was just sort of hoping you'd name one after me."

"Who could pronounce it?" she said with a laugh.

June 21, 2021

Two and a half weeks passed before Mount Wilson Observatory in California could schedule another set of images of the three asteroids Mary Ludford had discovered. What the images revealed was significant enough to merit a face-to-face call. By a fortunate coincidence, Mary Ludford was with Xiou when the call arrived. At the request of Dr. James Waters at Mount Wilson Observatory on the other side of the country, the call was switched to Xiou's wall display monitor. In a moment the large flat board blinked on and Dr. Waters appeared life-sized before them. The clarity of the picture gave the distractingly persistent impression that he was in the next office and that someone had simply cut a window between the two rooms. The impression was dramatically reinforced by the screen's most remarkable feature: each hexagonal centimeter of the screen also functioned as a camera, sending its individual signal to the corresponding hexagon on the receiving screen. With some help from the system's computer, which compensated for the edges between camera tiles, the multiple angles of view made the image appear virtually three-dimensional. This impression was reinforced by the fact that as the viewer moved about the room he gained a different perspective of the people and objects in the other room.

Dr. Xiou introduced Mary to Dr. Waters; everything was there but the handshake.

"Hi, Mary. I'm glad you're here to see this," Dr. Waters said, blurring even further the distinction between 'here' and 'there.'

"Hello, Dr. Waters," Mary responded. "It's nice to finally meet you."

"You, too, Mary; and please, call me Jim." Mary nodded agreement.

"Frankly, Mary," Waters began, "what you've found has got all of us stumped out here." Waters pressed one of the function keys on his computer keyboard and the picture on Xiou's wall display was instantly replaced by a composite image with a close-up of Waters in the upper right corner and the rest of the screen filled with what Mary quickly recognized as one of the images on which she had made her discovery. "This first shot," Waters began, "is one of those taken last month, on May 20th, with the three objects appearing here, here and here." As he spoke, he used his mouse to point to each of the objects in turn. "The second picture," he continued, as the image changed, "was taken last night. You'll note that the albedo of each of the objects — again, here, here, and here — has increased noticeably as they've moved closer to earth."

"Excuse me, Jim," Dr. Xiou said. "You keep referring to them as objects; are they asteroids or not?"

"The best answer I can give you at this point," Waters answered, "is, I guess so. Their orbits are much more like what we'd expect from comets than from asteroids, with an aphelion well beyond the orbit of Neptune and a perihelion halfway between the orbits of Mercury and Venus. What has us stumped is where they came from and why we haven't seen them before. Based on their course and speed, we've plotted their orbits and have determined that they are definitely earth-crossing, which would make them Apollo-class asteroids, and yet none of our previous surveys has identified them."

"Any theories at all?" Xiou asked.

"Well, according to our projections, their orbits bring them inside the orbit of Jupiter for a period of only about two and a half years of their fifteen-year orbit. It's possible that we've simply not been looking in the right place when they've been near enough to be of interest, but, frankly, I doubt that with the amount of attention that's been focused on the Apollo-class asteroids, that *everyone* could have missed three asteroids of this size. We're going through the archives researching that right now. Another possibility is that they are wandering planetoids from outside our solar systems which have only recently been captured by the sun's gravitation.

"The two asteroids closest to the earth, 2021 KD and 2021 KE — I understand you're calling them Calvin and Hobbes," Mary smiled and nodded, "are only about 350,000 kilometers apart, which is relatively close. The largest one, 2021 KF — the one you've named Wormwood — is lagging approximately 67 million kilometers behind. As I mentioned, all three of them are fairly large as the Apollo asteroids go. The first one, 2021 KD, is irregular, being roughly kidney-shaped, and has an average diameter of about twenty kilometers. The second one, 2021 KE, is spherical and has a diameter of about three kilometers. 2021 KF, though, is a monster with a diameter of nearly fifty kilometers, which would make it the largest of the earth-crossing asteroids, dwarfing even Eros, which is oblong with a width of about twenty kilometers," he said, referring to the largest of the previously-discovered asteroids whose orbits intersect the orbit of the earth.

"How close will their orbits bring them to the earth?" Dr. Xiou asked.

"That's why I'm calling." Dr. Waters reached for his keyboard and pressed another function key. As quickly as he had completed the task, the image on the screen rotated to give a computer-generated overhead view of the portion of the solar system between the sun and a point beyond the orbit of Mars where the asteroids were located in the most recent photographs. At the upper center of the screen were the three asteroids, which appeared as no more than specks of light against the vastness of even this tiny fraction of the solar system. "We ran the data we have on the asteroids' paths through the computer and came up with a simulation. This is what we got." Waters started the simulation and each of the bodies began to move, tracing out their orbits across the screen. Quickly the asteroids moved through a steep arch, dropping counterclockwise toward the lower left. In the upper left hand corner of the screen a counter showed the dates as the simulation progressed. Lower down on the screen, the earth traveled along its nearly circular path around the sun.

As the simulation progressed, a sick feeling came over Dr. Jung Xiou. Mary Ludford's mouth dropped open and then quickly shut as she bit her lip. As the counter clicked off each additional day, the orbits of the two leading asteroids brought them closer and closer to the earth, and a conclusion began to appear frighteningly inescapable. Just as a collision seemed imminent, the picture on the screen zoomed in for a much closer view, from which it was evident that the first two asteroids would actually just miss the earth.

"As you can see, we're talking about two very close passes," Dr. Waters said as the two asteroids on the simulation passed by the earth, barely avoiding a collision. Waters stopped the simulation for a moment in order to elaborate on what they had just seen. The simulation's calendar stopped on July third. "We're running these estimates through again," he said, "and watching the asteroids very closely, but it appears that 2021 KD could come as close as 800 kilometers. 2021 KE may come even closer, within about 500 kilometers. It could even come in brief contact with the outermost atmosphere. If so, then based on the trajectory, it will simply skip off the atmosphere the way a stone skips across water when it's thrown at a shallow angle. Both 2021 KD and 2021 KE should provide an exciting opportunity for some once-in-a-lifetime viewing. At the expected distances, 2021 KD will appear in the sky more than twice as large as the moon, and if 2021 KE does indeed skip off the atmosphere, there will be some fantastic fireworks."

"That's great, Jim," Xiou said. "But I have to admit, you had me worried."

"Well, that was the *good* news."

"What do you mean?" Xiou asked.

"The problem is with 2021 KF. The orbits of all three asteroids have a similar inclination, ranging from 41 degrees to the ecliptic for 2021 KD and 2021 KE to just less than 38 degrees for 2021 KF. But, whereas 2021 KD and 2021 KE are in nearly identical orbits around the sun, 2021 KF's orbit is much larger. Right now the three are fairly close in cosmic terms, but that's merely a coincidence. Their paths will continue to grow farther apart as they come closer to the sun. What that means, as you'll see when we run the rest of the simulation, is that 2021 KD will intersect the earth's orbit at point A on July third followed by 2021 KE less than three hours later." As he spoke, a white capital 'A' appeared on the screen at the appropriate location where the orbits of the first two asteroids had passed the earth. "2021 KF's orbit, however, will intersect approximately forty-three days later at point B." A capital 'B' now appeared below and to the left of the capital 'A.' "Were their orbits more alike, so that 2021 KF would also intersect somewhere near point A, then by the time it got there, the earth would be 64 million miles farther through its orbit, and well out of danger. Instead, if our preliminary calculations are correct, it will intersect the earth's orbit at point B on August fifteenth."

Waters pressed a key to restart the simulation. The third and largest of the asteroids had been just beyond the scope of the close-up and so had momentarily disappeared from the screen, but now reemerged just to the upper left of the screen. The vision was quite arresting and Dr. Waters could clearly hear the collective gasp as the simulation played through. "A collision?" Xiou asked, struggling to maintain his professionalism despite the scene unfolding before him. It was not necessary for Dr. Waters to respond; in another moment, an instant after the counter changed to August fifteenth, the asteroid struck the earth. In the simulation the earth, with a diameter of about 8,000 miles, merely absorbed the much smaller body and continued about its orbit. Although that might accurately represent the view from space, the view from the earth would be much more dramatic.

"At this point the simulation is based on a limited amount of data," Waters said. "It's still possible that my calculations could be wrong. We're going to get some additional shots of the asteroids tonight and try to tie this thing down, but it appears we're looking at the possibility of a direct hit on the earth."

There was a long, uncomfortable silence, and then Dr. Xiou asked, "How much damage are we talking about?"

"From a combination of primary and secondary effects," Dr. Waters answered, "the destruction of all, or nearly all, life on the planet."

Chapter 3

When Worlds Collide

June 23, 2021 — United Nations Security Council

Ambassador Jeremiah Ngordon of Chad, who represented Western Africa and whose turn in the rotation it was to serve as President of the Security Council, called the special meeting to order. The meeting had been requested by Dr. Samuel Johnson of the United Nations Space Science Foundation and Ambassador Hella Winkler of Germany, who had replaced Christopher as the Alternate from Europe when he was elected as Europe's Primary. Winkler had also replaced Christopher as Chairman of the World Peace Organization (WPO), and it was in that capacity that she now joined Dr. Johnson in requesting the meeting.

By now everyone allowed into this closed meeting was aware of its purpose. Nevertheless, following the requisite introductions of guests and obligatory statements of mutual admiration which always precede meetings where politicians are involved, the meeting began with a summary of the events which had precipitated it. Among the contingent of eight scientists and three

WPO generals on hand to brief and answer questions from the Security Council were Dr. James Waters of Mount Wilson Observatory and Dr. Jung Xiou of the Harvard-Smithsonian Center for Astrophysics. Mary Ludford, who had discovered the asteroids, was also present, but it was not anticipated that she would address the council.

The meeting was closed to the press and public but there was no intent to keep the information secret for long. The only thing worse than letting the truth out would be having it leak out. But it was important that the information be presented to the public in the calmest possible terms and tones. Certainly the peril was real, but the crisis was not without a remedy: the sole purpose of this meeting was to assure that the cure would have a chance to work. Science believed it had found the solution and now government would provide the needed finances and logistical support.

Decker Hawthorne, whose office was the gatekeeper for information from the meeting, had hand-picked the staff, including those who would handle the audio and video recording of the proceedings. Selected portions of the tapes would be released to the press, but only after judicious editing. Now that the meeting was underway, Decker sat, pen poised over a legal pad, ready to note any statements that might need to be edited out to avoid unjustified anxiety among the public. There was no evidence of distress in his manner, but Decker was keenly aware that there was far more to this matter than anyone in this room, other than he and Christopher, could begin to understand. No one had yet made any connection between the asteroids and what the men, John and Cohen, had prophesied five months earlier. But, then why should they? Most of the people in this room didn't even know who John and Cohen were; those who *did* assumed they were just garden-variety kooks. Still, by this time no one could have avoided at least hearing stories of their peculiar followers, the Koum Damah Patar. Every country in the world had a few; most had hundreds.

Dr. Alsie Johnson of the U.N. Space Science Foundation

made a few opening statements, introduced the guests, and then passed the microphone over to Dr. Waters, who provided a basic explanation of the threat and then narrated a slightly updated version of the simulation he had shown to Dr. Xiou and Mary Ludford two days earlier. Since then, refinements of the calculations of the asteroids' paths found that the first and second asteroids, 2021 KD and 2021 KE, would pass on opposite sides of the earth. The first and larger of the two asteroids would pass approximately 4,000 miles from the earth, traveling from northwest to southeast over much of North and South America on the night of July third. The second asteroid would pass three hours later, at approximately 1,000 miles, on the daylight side of the planet, also traveling from northwest to southeast, crossing much of northwest and southeast Asia, the Philippines and New Guinea.

By far the best view would be available from the Americas. There the first asteroid would be visible for several hours as it passed rapidly across the night sky. On the other side of the world, the asteroid would be somewhat harder to spot as it passed through the sunlit sky, not as a sparkling light but as a gray spot — much like the moon in daylight — easily escaping the attention of anyone not looking for it. The hope of witnessing a skip off the earth's atmosphere had been unhappily abandoned.

The real threat was the third asteroid, 2021 KF, which was by far the largest with a diameter of 50 kilometers, or about 30 miles. As indicated by Dr. Waters' initial calculations, 2021 KF was headed directly for the earth and would arrive, if nothing was done to stop it, on August fifteenth, forty-three days after the first two asteroids had safely passed. The human race, however, would not go without a fight. Modern science stood ready to prevent the cataclysm using, ironically, the same tools which before now had themselves threatened to destroy life on the planet.

Dr. Terri Hall, a former student of famed astronomer Eleanor Helin, and now one of the foremost experts on asteroids, took over when Dr. Waters completed his portion of the briefing. "There are literally millions of asteroids in our solar system," she began, "approximately one million of which are one kilometer or more in diameter. The largest asteroid, Ceres, is 1,033 kilometers (about 620 miles) in diameter. Most asteroids are in orbits between Mars and Jupiter. In addition, there are several tens of thousands of asteroids which fall into three other groups: the *Atens*, whose orbits range from just beyond the Earth to just beyond Mars; the *Apollos*, whose orbits actually cross the orbit of Earth; and the *Amors*, whose orbits range between the orbits of Earth and Venus.

"From time to time, either in the course of their normal orbits or as the result of interference from the gravity of another body or a collision between asteroids, an asteroid will come into an intersecting orbit with the Earth. However, this is a very infrequent occurrence. Over the past billion years, perhaps 400 or so asteroids larger than a quarter of a mile in diameter are believed to have collided with the earth. That equates to an average of one every two and a half million years. Because about three quarters of the earth's surface is covered with water, this number can only be estimated, based on the number of known asteroid craters on land and on the limited evidence we have of asteroids that have fallen into the oceans. The earth has approximately forty-five craters known to have been created by asteroid impact. They range in size from about 7½ kilometers to 140 kilometers, that is, about 85 miles. The largest and oldest craters are Vredefort in South Africa and the Sudbury crater in Ontario. Both are approximately 85 miles in diameter and were formed by asteroids measuring about 10 kilometers, or 6 miles, in diameter. The crater in Vredefort is 1.97 billion years old; the crater in Ontario was formed approximately 1.84 billion years ago. Other smaller craters, more than one billion years old, are believed to have disappeared with erosion.

"Probably the best known asteroid collision took place 65 million years ago when an asteroid of about 10 kilometers in diameter impacted off the coast of the Yucatan Peninsula near *Chicxulub*, Mexico. That collision is credited with the extinction of the dinosaurs. More recently — about two and a half million years ago — an asteroid of approximately 600 meters, or a third of a mile in diameter, struck in the South Pacific Ocean west of the southernmost tip of South America. The force of that impact is conservatively estimated to have been 25,000 megatons, that is, about two and a half times the destructive force of the world's combined nuclear forces — without the radiation, of course.

"Not all asteroids that enter the atmosphere impact the surface. In the early part of the last century, at 7:00 p.m. local time on June 30, 1908, an asteroid, or perhaps a comet (no one can be certain) entered the atmosphere above the *Stony Tunguska* river basin in Siberia. That body exploded in midair about seven miles above the earth. Although much about that encounter remains a mystery, it appears that the asteroid or comet was traveling nearly 19 miles per second. Because of its angle of approach, at that velocity, the air would exert a tremendous aerodynamic pressure; apparently when the pressure exceeded the body's compressive strength, it shattered.

"Even though that body never reached the earth's surface, the force of the pressure when it exploded was equal to a twelve megaton bomb. It leveled 800 square miles of mature forest; people 45 miles away were knocked down and seared by the heat; the glare was seen for hundreds of miles; and the sound was reported as far away as 600 miles.

"Another even rarer occurrence was actually captured on home movies over Wyoming in the western United States in August of 1972." Dr. Hall directed attention to the display screens which were filled with blue sky and clouds. A low rumble like a distant jet poured from the system's speakers, and then apparently from the cloud in the center of the screen — though it was actually high above it — emerged a smoky-white luminescent ball followed by what looked like a long trail of vapor. Hall continued, "In this case a large meteoroid, estimated at 200 feet in diameter and weighing about a thousand tons, actually entered the atmosphere and came to within 35.9 miles of the earth's surface. The meteoroid traveled roughly parallel to the earth's surface for just under two minutes, covering nearly a thousand miles, traveling north from Utah to Alberta, Canada, at approximately 31,000 miles per hour, before exiting the atmosphere again. Because its speed never dropped below escape velocity — 25,000 miles per hour — it was able to pierce the atmosphere and then escape the earth's gravity and continue on its course.

"Now, as to the asteroids presently headed toward earth: based on the albedo, or reflectivity, of each of the asteroids, all three appear to be class-M. Typically, that would make them about 90 percent metal and as much as 10 percent rocky materials. Of the metal content, we expect that about 95 percent is iron and 4 percent is nickel with the remaining 1 percent being other metals. As to their origins, based on their inclination, we believe they are Hungaria-type asteroids — noted for their highly inclined orbit — from the asteroid belts between Jupiter and Mars, and that they have somehow been diverted from their original orbits. The most detailed images of the asteroids are from the 1,000-foot radio telescope at Arecibo Observatory in Puerto Rico. Recent upgrades to that system provide imaging with resolution of 30 feet or better." Dr. Hall nodded to a staff member who was operating the three large display screens arranged to allow the Primary and Alternate members of the Security Council to see from their places around the table. The staff member pressed the function key to bring up the next set of images and the three asteroids appeared in a split screen format to provide the best view of all three asteroids simultaneously.

At this point Dr. Xiou continued the briefing. "We have found no conclusive evidence," he began, drawing attention to the images on the screens, "that the asteroids have suffered a recent collision sufficient to cause a major shift in their orbits. We must conclude, therefore, that some unusual gravitational effect has caused the divergence. The planet Jupiter can play havoc with the orbits of main belt asteroids, but in this case Jupiter must be ruled out as the cause because at the time we calculate that the asteroids left their normal orbits, Jupiter was hundreds of millions of miles away on the other side of the sun. There are, however, a few other theories.

"Based on all our observations and calculations," Xiou continued, "the theory most compatible with the available evidence is that the asteroids have been pulled from their normal orbits by a body small enough to have otherwise escaped our attention as it passed through our solar system. To pull asteroids of this size from their orbits, such a body would have to possess an extremely strong gravity for its size. There are two types of bodies that fit this description: either a small chunk of a white dwarf star, thrown off millions of years ago from a collision of two white dwarfs; or a very small black hole. A white dwarf is a star which, over time, has been stripped of its electrons. Such a star still has most of its mass but it is extremely dense: in its white dwarf stage a star the size of our sun could be compacted to a sphere with a diameter of only 20 kilometers, that is, about 12 miles. If two such stars collided, pieces of the stars would be thrown off at tremendous speeds. Because of its size, a piece of white dwarf could easily pass through our solar system and go completely unnoticed; and if it passed close enough to an asteroid it could certainly disrupt its orbit. The high iron content of all three asteroids tends to lend credence to this hypothesis since some white dwarf stars — for example the star 1031+234 — are known to possess magnetic fields as high as 700 million gauss, a level which approaches the maximum theoretical strength possible.

"Black holes bear a certain similarity to white dwarfs in that they, too, are produced from objects that have been crushed to incredible densities. The gravitational field of the superdense matter that makes up a black hole is strong enough to trap light itself. Most frequently, references to black holes are in terms of those that are as large as our sun or larger because it is known that certain stars collapse in upon themselves to become black holes at the end of their lifetimes. But less massive, smaller holes are also possible. Theoretically, black holes with a mass of a small moon compressed to the size of a few atoms could exist. In appearance a black hole is simply a region of darkness, so a small black hole could easily pass through the solar system without notice. And even the most infinitesimal black hole could have a gravitational field strong enough to pull asteroids from their normal orbits."

The panel continued the briefing as if teaching a class for another twenty minutes, discussing theories, showing charts and simulations, giving historical examples to demonstrate their points. Finally, Ambassador Yuri Kruszkegin of Khakassia, taking advantage of a brief pause, interrupted and asked the question that was on everyone's mind. "Can we conclude from what you've said and the documents you've provided to us, that it is your recommendation that we use nuclear weapons to destroy the third asteroid?" Kruszkegin asked.

"Yes, Mr. Ambassador," Dr. Johnson answered. Alsie Johnson dealt with politicians almost every day; he well knew that while they were among the most long-winded of the human species, they often were among the first to insist that others come to the point. It was time to get to the heart of the matter and Kruszkegin's question provided the opportunity to move the proceedings along.

"What will this involve?" Kruszkegin followed up.

"Because of the risk involved, we feel that redundancy, even overkill, is not only justified, but crucial," Johnson answered.

"I don't think anyone on the planet would disagree with you on that," one of the other members of the Security Council interjected.

"There's certainly no shortage of nuclear devices available for the task," Johnson continued. "Unfortunately, the inventories of launch vehicles capable of reaching the target and delivering a warhead are not nearly so abundant. In order to break free of the earth's gravity and deliver the warheads while the third asteroid is still at a safe distance from the earth, the launch vehicles must be capable of reaching escape velocity, that is, approximately 25,000 miles per hour.

"Ideally, with enough warning, we would detonate a series of explosions just ahead of the asteroid in order to slow its speed or slightly alter its course. With sufficient time, altering its course even one degree, or its speed by an inch per second, would be sufficient to avert a collision. Unfortunately, at this point we have neither the time nor resources to attempt this. The only option certain to ensure the safety of the earth is to completely destroy the asteroid at the earliest possible moment." Dr. Johnson nodded to Dr. James Stewart of the Ames Research Center at Moffett Field, California, to continue the briefing. Dr. Stewart nodded in turn to the staffer who was operating the display screens.

As the simulation began, Dr. Stewart narrated and explained the action. "When the asteroid is hit by our missiles, the object's mass will be sent flying out in all directions, including some pieces which will continue toward the earth. The farther from the earth the asteroid is when it is destroyed, the greater the mass that will be deflected from entering the earth's atmosphere.

"If any of the remaining parts of the asteroid are very large," Dr. Stewart continued, "they could still pose a threat. Our goal must be to not just break up the asteroid into smaller chunks, but to pulverize it. Our estimates, which are still being refined, are that this will require placement of forty warheads with an average yield of twenty megatons each over the entire earthward face of the asteroid. All of the warheads must reach their target and be detonated simultaneously, an instant before impact with the asteroid. It is a mission uniquely suited to the capabilities of Multiple Independently Targetable Reentry Vehicles, or MIRVs. This, however, further reduces our inventory of acceptable launch vehicles. Specifically, those launch vehicles capable of reaching the target and delivering MIRVs are limited to the U.S. Minuteman III and the Russian-built SS-11 Sego. Further complicating the problem is that these are both relatively old systems and most have been converted to heavy lift vehicles for orbital launches, or have been destroyed to comply with treaties. Additionally, both the Minuteman III and the Sego will require considerable modification for this mission.

"Our plan at this point is to send three waves of missiles so that, should the first volley fail to completely destroy the asteroid, a second and third line of defense will stand ready to finish the job." As the simulation showed second and third waves of missiles destroying the few remaining large pieces of asteroid, Dr. Stewart concluded by noting that all of the technology employed was proven and that all those involved were certain of the plan's feasibility.

As Dr. Stewart finished, Dr. John Jefferson of Oak Ridge National Laboratory began. "As Dr. Stewart stated, it is important that we destroy the asteroid at the earliest possible opportunity in order to limit the amount of debris that might fall to earth. There is a second reason that makes early destruction imperative: the dust which results from the explosion will initially be highly radioactive." At this revelation a sudden look of disquiet swept over the faces of those in the room as they realized the obvious — of course, after a nuclear explosion, the dust would be radioactive. "Like fallout from any nuclear explosion," Jefferson continued, "the level of radiation will drop with time. The more time between the destruction of the asteroid and the arrival of the asteroid's dust, the less radioactive the dust will be."

"How soon must we launch the missiles to keep the radiation at safe levels?" Ambassador Ngordon interrupted.

"Without knowing the exact makeup of the asteroid or of the particles that will reach the earth, it is impossible to provide a definitive answer to that question. However, based on Dr. Hall's estimates of the asteroid content, we believe it must be destroyed at least twelve days before the remaining particles reach earth. Much less than that and the effects of the radiation could be serious and in some cases, possibly even fatal. This estimate assumes that it will take an additional two days before substantial amounts of the dust begin to sift through the atmosphere."

"How soon must we launch?" asked Ngordon.

"We hope to launch in five days, on the twenty-eighth, Mr. Ambassador," Dr. Johnson answered. "If we can launch by that date, the missiles will reach the asteroid thirty-four days later on August second, at a point 20 million miles from the earth. This will allow thirteen days before the dust reaches earth, one day more than the minimum required."

"Can it be done?"

"Yes, sir. But we must have the full support of the U.N. and especially of those nations who possess the required launch vehicles."

"Mr. President," said Ambassador Jackson Clark of the United States, directing his comment to Security Council President, Ambassador Ngordon. "I think you know you can count on the full support of the American people in this effort. I know I speak for my President in saying we will provide as many of the Minutemen missiles as are available. And I'm certain that America's scientists and engineers will work around the clock to provide whatever technical support, equipment, and manpower that are required." Kruszkegin made a similar offer for the nations which once made up the republics of the Soviet Union. One of the ironies of the nuclear devastation which befell Russia as a result of its attack on Israel was that many hundreds of missiles which had not been launched came through the devastation unscarred, protected as they were by the nuclear-hardened silos.

When that was settled, Ambassador Clark turned his attention to Dr. Johnson. "What about our strategic defenses? Can they be used against this thing?"

"Unfortunately no," Dr. Johnson replied. "The directed energy weapons, which include the various types of lasers and particle beams, have sufficient range to reach the target, but even the combined energy of all such weapons in the inventory would have no significant effect on a body of this mass. Their energy sources were engineered to provide short directed bursts, not for a sustained assault on a large target. As for the kinetic energy weapons, primarily the ground-based and certain of the space-based interceptors, while they have significant destructive force, they don't have sufficient range to reach the target."

Ambassador Clark nodded in understanding.

The meeting continued for a while longer and when it seemed that all matters had been resolved as best they could be, Christopher, who had been silent to this point, raised another question to Dr. Johnson. "I'm concerned about the other two asteroids," Christopher said. "Are you certain that they pose no threat?"

"Yes, sir," Johnson answered. "As indicated in the simulation, the first two asteroids will come close — closer than any large asteroid in recorded history — but they pose no threat."

"Is there any possibility that your calculations on the paths of the first two asteroids could be in error? It seems to me we're cutting this very close."

"Sir, I appreciate your concern, but the calculations have been run independently by fourteen different observatories and universities. They've been checked, double checked and triple checked. In no case was the variance of the findings greater than plus or minus 100 kilometers, about 60 miles."

Christopher sighed and lightly tapped his pen on the table in front of him, apparently looking for another approach that might yield the answer he wanted. "But what about further down the road? From what you've said the asteroids' new orbit will make them cross the earth's path on a regular basis. Isn't there a possibility that they will pose a threat later on? Wouldn't it be better to destroy them now?"

"What we need to remember, Mr. Ambassador," Dr. Johnson answered, "is that the earth's orbit includes a tremendous amount of space. Just because an asteroid crosses the earth's orbit doesn't necessarily mean that there is a threat. As was indicated earlier, there are thousands of asteroids which cross the earth's orbit; by plotting their orbits it is possible to predict if any of the asteroids will threaten the earth any time in the next several million years. Based on these projections, we've concluded that after this pass, neither 2021 KD nor 2021 KE will come within a million miles of earth for another 3½ million years. But, of course, we will keep an eye on them just in case, just as we periodically monitor the orbits of the other Apollo and Amor asteroids."

Christopher seemed desperate to get a different answer. Decker wasn't sure whether it was a hopeless cause or not. Milner and Christopher had both insisted that, at least for the present, the destruction foretold by John and Cohen could not be stopped. It had not set well with Decker, but he was ill-equipped to argue points of prophesy and the destiny of mankind with the likes of Milner and Christopher. And yet, as Decker watched and listened, it seemed clear that what Christopher had in mind at this moment was to find some reason, any reason, to destroy the first two asteroids before they could reach the earth. Science said that asteroids 2021 KD and 2021 KE posed no threat to the earth and it would have been ridiculous for Christopher to argue that the United Nations destroy the asteroids based simply on what two religious madmen said. But John and Cohen had prophesied tremendous destruction and if the powers they possessed were great enough to hurl asteroids at the earth from deep in space, it was unlikely that they would now miss their target, no matter what the simulations indicated. Christopher himself had said that John and Cohen could not, indeed, should not be stopped until much of the destruction they prophesied had run its course. Surely Christopher, more than anyone, realized that his attempts were in vain. That Christopher would try so hard even though he was sure the effort was futile only made Decker admire him more.

"What about using the first two asteroids to test the methodology that you plan for the third asteroid?" Christopher persisted. "Doesn't it make sense to . . . well . . . to do a practice run by attempting to destroy the first two asteroids to prove the theory and technology you plan to use on the third asteroid?" The idea made a lot of sense to the other members and Alternates of the Security Council and many nodded in agreement with the logic of Christopher's suggestion. Decker held his breath. Was it possible that sheer reason could overcome John and Cohen's dark intent?

"Mr. Ambassador," Dr. Johnson answered, "while the logic behind your suggestion is sound, there are three reasons why that cannot be done. First, if we were to fire on one of the first two asteroids, and our calculations were even slightly in error, then instead of destroying the target asteroid, we might alter its course and risk hurling it directly toward earth. Second, if we successfully destroy 2021 KD or 2021 KE then, as indicated in the simulation of the destruction of the third asteroid, pieces of the asteroids would be sent out in all directions. Even if we launch five days from now, the missiles would not reach the asteroids until they were only two and a half days from the earth. The debris reaching earth from the explosion would still be highly radioactive; the number of deaths could be in the thousands. And, finally there is the problem of resources. Every resource available, including time, must be brought to bear on the third asteroid; that is where the threat lies."

The logic was indisputable; it would do no good to argue further. Science said that the first two asteroids posed no threat and there would be no convincing anyone to the contrary.

Chapter 4

Eve of Destruction

July 2, 2021 — Sacramento Peak Observatory in southern New Mexico (11:36 p.m. local time, 6:36 a.m. GMT)

Mary Ludford wiped the tears from her eyes and looked in the bathroom mirror to check her appearance. Her eyes were red, but that could easily be attributed to lost sleep; the past ten days had been punctuated by early mornings and late nights. Though she questioned her qualifications to be the recipient of so much attention, since the release of the news of the approaching asteroids, the media had made her an international heroine, and her lack of adequate rest was simply the price the world demanded of its luminaries. Now it would serve as a convenient excuse. Exhaustion was certainly an easier explanation than admitting that she had been crying.

Despite the distinctly non-heroic nature of her discovery, it was, after all, Mary who had first spotted the oncoming asteroids and had thereby given the world the time needed to prepare a defense. Besides, it was in the very nature of the media to want to put a human face on such a complex issue. So there was Mary Ludford on the covers of *NewsWeek*, *Time*, and *NewsWorld;* on the morning news/talk shows; on numerous television and radio specials about the asteroids; and at center stage, offering her commentary as the missiles were successfully launched to destroy the third giant asteroid, 2021 KF. The launches had gone flawlessly. Each missile was fired in a precisely timed sequence and then, after orbiting the earth, sent on its way toward the threatening mass 74 million miles from earth. Success seemed certain, and so, after the experts were questioned and the explanations given, after the "man in the street" was interviewed and the concerns and confusion of the world aired, again the media returned its attention to Mary Ludford.

With the destruction of the third asteroid all but a *fait accompli*, all of the attention should have provided Mary Ludford with a time of excitement and diversion, an enchanted time of posh hotels and expensive restaurants, of meeting the famous and powerful. But one thought had haunted her from the first time the spotlight was cast her way. What would happen if her father saw her on television? Would he try to call her? At first she was afraid that he *would* call. If he did, what would she say? Could she even talk to him with all the anger she harbored toward him for abandoning her and her mother? Later she determined that if he did call, she would tell him off and then hang up on him. That would show him. In her mind, she rehearsed what she would say and even practiced slamming the phone receiver. And yet later she paced anxiously, fearing that he would *not* call. If he did, she thought, abandoning her previous plan, maybe they could talk. Maybe he had an explanation for why he left. It couldn't have been a good reason but it might at least have been understandable, one that she could bring herself to forgive, providing of course he was adequately repentant.

But now she knew that she had only been fooling herself. It had been nearly three weeks since she was first interviewed on international television, and her father had not tried to contact her. He could not have missed seeing her on television or in the magazines or newspapers. Now here she was making a fool of herself, wasting tears on someone who apparently didn't care whether she even existed. Once again she concluded that when and if he did ever call, she would tell him off and then hang up. It did not even occur to her that in her resolve to stop thinking of him, she was restarting the cycle where she had begun it. In truth, she could not give up hope.

Satisfied that she was as presentable as possible and with a self-deceived determination not to spend any more time agonizing about her father, Mary Ludford left the restroom to rejoin the scientists and news media in the conference room of the Main Lab building where they had met to go over last-minute details. Afterward, they would split into groups and move to the three individual facilities that would be involved in the night's activities. When she arrived she found that the meeting had already broken up and the conference room was deserted.

Mary walked slowly northwest along the road, past reporters' vans and then made her way along the wooded path toward the Hilltop Dome. Those who lived and worked at the observatory had gotten used to the thin air but for those who were unaccustomed, Sacramento Peak's altitude of 9,700 feet above sea level did not lend itself to brisk walks. Behind her stood the rather out-of-place looking Grain Bin Dome, Sacramento Peak's first observatory, so-called because it had been constructed from an agricultural storage shed. Farther back stood the John W. Evans Solar Facility, a much more traditional-looking building which ordinarily was involved in the research of the sun's photosphere, chromosphere, and corona. To her left, Sacramento Peak's most distinguishable feature, the pearl-white Tower Telescope facility, soared upward 130 feet into the night sky. Inside the facility, the telescope extended down into the mountain through an open shaft for an additional 325 feet. It was an amazing piece of equipment but was highly specialized for use in solar observations and hence would not be useful for tracking and observing asteroids. It alone among Sacramento Peak's four observatories would be unattended tonight.

Sacramento Peak Observatory, which for seventy years had functioned almost exclusively as a solar observatory, was not the only facility which would divert its attentions from its normal pursuits. Over 200 observatories around the world were participating, many of which specialized in other fields of astronomy and had never been involved in the study of asteroids.

Despite the thin air, Mary decided to walk beyond the Hilltop Dome to the scenic overlook halfway between the dome and the Tower Telescope. The night was clear and she could see for miles across the white gypsum sands of the Tularosa Basin to the San Andres and Organ mountains to the southwest. The lights of El Paso, Texas, glowed in the distance to the south. Turning her eyes toward the northern sky, she paused to look at the two objects that had pulled her out of her quiet study of receding galaxies. Both asteroids had been visible to the naked eye for the last two nights, but now they were unmistakable in the northern sky, shining brightly just above the horizon and nearly due north. In their current positions, the second and smaller asteroid (2021 KE) was actually higher in the northern sky than the first (2021 KD). As the earth continued its orbit, however, 2021 KE would appear to drop below the first, and three hours after 2021 KD streaked across the skies of the western hemisphere, 2021 KE would drop below the horizon and traverse its path through the heavens of the eastern half of the world.

Mary walked back to the Hilltop Dome and went in. As she entered the facility she looked at the large wall monitor, which showed a telescopic view of the asteroids' approach. In addition to performing numerous tests, surveys, and studies, the observatories along the paths of the asteroids acted as tracking stations, following the asteroids' approach and providing a satellite feed to the other observatories and television stations around the world. The Hubble telescope was moved to a polar orbit to provide the best view of the asteroids' northern approach to the planet. Initially, the asteroids were both within the field of view of the orbiting telescope's optics, but as they moved closer, it became necessary to focus on only one at a time. Now in the final hours, the Hubble would focus its attention on the first asteroid until it had passed beyond the earth, and then quickly it would be rotated to focus on the second asteroid.

Television and Internet coverage included two satellite feeds showing an uninterrupted picture of the asteroids' approach. Until recently, it had been a rather unimpressive scene, appearing as no more than two tiny points of light on an otherwise blank screen. What made it interesting to watch were the two digital counters in the lower right corner of the picture as they clicked off the distance between each asteroid and the earth. Sixty-five thousand miles per hour naturally seemed fast to most viewers, but even seasoned experts were heard to exclaim when they first witnessed the counters clicking off the miles at a rate of eighteen per second. Other television stations ran special programs on the asteroids and gave frequent updates on their approach.

Despite the extensive coverage, many people wanted to see the asteroids firsthand and stores quickly sold out of amateur telescopes and high-powered binoculars. Some mild hysteria resulted as a few over-excited and inexperienced stargazers spotted various objects, both real and imagined, which they mistook for additional asteroids headed for the earth. But that was not the only hysteria. Despite repeated assurances to the contrary from the United Nations and from scientists around the world, some members of the public insisted that the event marked the end of the world. Others saw the event less as something to worry about and more as an excuse to drink and revel at raucous end-of-the-world parties.

Local authorities also noted that the increased sales of telescopes and binoculars were accompanied by a sharp rise in reports of "peeping-toms" as well as exhibitionism by those hoping to be spied upon. Police had little time to spend on such offenses, however, due to a sharp rise in more serious crimes, such as murder, rape, and robbery, perpetrated primarily by those who reasoned that, considering the possibility that the world might end, they should enjoy to the fullest what was left of it.

Many of television's daytime dramas rushed to write the approach of the asteroids into their story lines, and one long-running soap opera, which began each program with a view of the world spinning in space, added to the scene a computer-generated image of the approaching asteroids.

For some, especially those prone to depression, the fear of impending doom was more than they could bear. Appointments at life completion clinics filled up so quickly that service for walk-in clientele was entirely suspended. They simply did not have adequate medical and disposal staff to meet the needs. Some of those who found the tension of waiting for completion assistance intolerable even chose unassisted self-termination rather than waiting for the proper medical authorities at the clinics.

July 3, 2021 — The Italian ambassador's residence, New York City (1:49 a.m. local time, 6:49 a.m. GMT)

In his private study at his official residence in New York City, Italian Ambassador Christopher Goodman sat with Robert Milner and Decker Hawthorne watching television coverage of the asteroids. The commentators and news directors appeared to be having a hard time filling the final hour before the first asteroid began to traverse the sky of the western hemisphere. By now every conceivable person had been interviewed time and again and every imaginable side-bar story had been aired several times.

Decker switched channels and caught the last moments of a report on how small groups of people around the world had gathered to chant and visualize in order to create a 'positive mental envelope' to protect the earth from the asteroids. Decker shook his head. "Can you believe these guys?" he asked rhetorically.

"What they're doing is not that different than what John and Cohen did to cause the calamity that is about to befall us," Christopher answered.

"Can they prevent this?" Decker asked, pointing toward the chanters, suddenly encouraged by this unexpected glimmer of hope.

Christopher shook his head. "No, John and Cohen are too strong; and our chanting friends are still far too weak. But it is important that they try. They're like children now: with the wisdom of youth they see what must be done but do not have the strength to bring it about; and yet they try. Of such will the New Age be built."

□   □   □

Another half hour passed and those watching on television and at the observatories began to see more clearly the first asteroid's shape. Now just over 43,000 miles away, it was possible to see that it was pockmarked with small craters. Its odd shape, which resembled a slightly bent and crumpled cigar, and its span of nearly 12 miles, made it quite similar in both size and shape to the asteroid Eros. It rotated on an axis approximately one-third of its length from each end, giving the impression that it was slowly tumbling, rather than rotating. The second asteroid, now about the same distance from the earth as our moon, was far more spherical and approximately one and a half miles in diameter.

From time to time the picture on the television screen changed, sometimes focusing on only one asteroid or the other, and sometimes showing a split screen with the asteroids side by side. The asteroids were now so close to the earth that every such change in orientation revealed a dramatically new portrait of the interplanetary visitors.

The astronomers of Sacramento Peak Observatory were making final preparations for their experimental work and observations. Of the thirty-five staff scientists and twenty-two assisting graduate students, only eight would be working in the Hilltop Dome where Mary Ludford was observing the events. The reporters spread out, a few going to each of the other observatories to chronicle every moment of this historic event. Mary would have preferred to be actively involved in the work, but she wasn't familiar enough with the nuances of Sacramento Peak's equipment. Besides, the press kept her far too busy to allow her time to do any actual work.

With nearly every reporter in the world covering one aspect or another of the asteroid story, there was never a time when at least one of them was not asking her questions, or noting her reactions to the unfolding drama, or just hanging around in case she might say or do something that someone might think was newsworthy. Right now there was only one reporter and a cameraman with her, and since Mary didn't seem to be saying or doing anything newsworthy at the moment, the reporter's questions focused on what was going on around them. Mary was able to answer most of his questions. Even though she had never used equipment exactly like that at Sacramento Peak, she knew enough to answer any layman's questions.

When he was finally out of questions he sat down on a stool to watch the asteroids' approach on the giant monitor. After about five minutes, he began again. "Why is the picture shifting?" he asked, referring to the side-by-side display of the two asteroids.

Mary looked at the screen. "What do you mean?" she asked, not noticing any shift.

"The picture of the first asteroid, there on the left of the screen: it's shifting slowly toward the right." Mary watched the screen closely for a moment. She thought perhaps she saw it, too, but it was so slight she couldn't be sure. "Perhaps it only appears to be shifting because of the asteroid's rotation," she suggested.

"No, really," he insisted. "A few minutes ago it was farther to the left on the screen. It's definitely moving to the right."

Mary tried to remember if it had looked any different earlier. It did seem as if it might have been a little better centered on the screen before. "It's probably that the picture we're getting now is from a different observatory than the picture we were getting a few minutes ago. The asteroid isn't as centered in this telescope's field of vision as it was in the other telescope's."

"No, that can't be it," the reporter insisted. "I've been watching. The satellite feeds are still coming from Dominion Astrophysical Observatory in Canada." He looked at his notes and tapped his pen to indicate where he had made note of it, then added, "It hasn't changed in the past twenty minutes."

Mary looked at the monitor, which indicated the point of origin of the satellite feeds on the composite picture. She wasn't sure, but she thought the reporter might be right. It really didn't matter though; it was now even more apparent that the first asteroid was moving ever so slowly to the right. "I'll go find out," she said.

Mary walked over to Dr. Alvin Taylor, the senior scientist at the John W. Evans Solar Facility of the Sacramento Observatory. The reporters had been told to stay back from the equipment and out of the way so as not to interrupt the scientists' work, but Mary felt no obligation to accede to those rules.

"Excuse me," Mary said to Dr. Taylor, who was just finishing a conversation with one of the staff scientists.

"Yes," Dr. Taylor responded, as the other scientist picked up a phone and began to dial.

"We were just noticing the picture of 2021 KD," she began, referring to the first asteroid. "The picture seems to be drifting slowly to the right on the screen."

"We noticed that, too," Taylor answered. "Dr. Lane is calling Dominion Astrophysical Observatory to find out what's going on," he added, nodding toward the woman on the phone. Mary and Dr. Taylor stood quietly for a moment, listening to their end of the conversation, trying to make out what was being said, but the call was far too brief to make any sense of it.

"Yeah. Okay. Good luck," they heard Dr. Lane say, and then the call was over.

"They're aware of the problem," Dr. Lane told Dr. Taylor as soon as she hung up the phone. "They think it's a cumulative error caused by their segmented positioning system. They're attempting to correct it now."

Dominion Astrophysical Observatory, located on a wooded hill just north of Victoria on the southern end of Vancouver Island in British Columbia, was best known for its study of variable stars, Beta Cephei stars, the orbits of double stars, and the examination of the frequency distribution of chemical elements. Asteroids were hardly its mainstay, but like many other observatories, Dominion had postponed its regular work to participate in this once-in-a-million-year opportunity. Dominion had been chosen as the primary observatory for this portion of the coverage because of its northern location and because of its recently commissioned 25-foot segmented mirror telescope (SMT). With one and a half times the equivalent diameter, and two and a quarter times the light-gathering power of the once-famous 200-inch telescope at Mount Palomar, the Dominion SMT used a mosaic of hexagonal mirror segments that functioned optically in close approximation to a monolithic mirror. For coherency each segment had to be continuously positioned with respect to the other mirror segments that made up the mosaic. This was accomplished by means of position sensors and actuators built into the mirrors' supports which maintained a common focus with all the other segments. It was these sensors and actuators that appeared to be the cause of the problem.

"If they can't get it fixed," Dr. Lane said, "they'll switch to the feed from the backup observatory. I believe . . ." Lane looked at a schedule she had on a clipboard, "yes, that would be Kitt Peak."

July 3, 2021 — Kitt Peak Observatory, Papago Indian Reservation, Arizona (12:21 a.m. local, 7:21 a.m. GMT)

High above the Papago Indian reservation, nestled among the

granite crags and cliffs of Kitt Peak, the white dome of Steward Observatory stood like a giant white mushroom. Home to the largest concentration of operating telescopes in the northern hemisphere and credited with numerous astronomical firsts, Kitt Peak served on this occasion as the backup to Canada's Dominion Astrophysical Observatory. It was not a role the scientists of Kitt Peak expected to be called upon to fulfill, but it should have been a simple matter of turning on their broadcast equipment and synchronizing the hand-off from Dominion. At the moment the call came, however, Dr. Chapman of Kitt Peak was busy with a problem of his own. He and his colleagues had not even noticed the problem with the broadcast picture from Dominion.

"Dr. Chapman, this is Dr. Watson at Dominion Observatory in Canada," the call began. "We have a problem here with our 7.7- meter telescope. So far we've been able to compensate, but I wanted to give you the 'heads up' just in case."

"Thanks," Chapman said, "but I'm afraid we have some problems of our own with our 11-meter SMT. For some reason — we can't seem to isolate the cause — but it appears we have a cumulative error in our segment positioning system, making it look as though asteroid 2021 KD has changed its course."

For a long moment there was silence.

"Hello?" Dr. Chapman said, as he began to wonder if they had been cut off.

"I'm here," responded Dr. Watson at Dominion. "How long ago did this start?"

"We first noticed it about ten minutes ago," Chapman answered.

Again there was silence. "Have you been monitoring our picture?" Watson asked after a moment.

"Well, not for the last few minutes. Like I said, we've been pretty busy with our own equipment. Why? What's the problem?"

"You'd better have a look."

Dr. Chapman leaned back in his chair and twisted his neck to look around a table at the large split screen monitor of the two asteroids. It took a moment for him to see the shift and when he did, he could not believe what he saw. Jumping up from his chair, he took the phone with him so that he could see the screen more clearly. The unobstructed view and new orientation changed nothing. It took only seconds for Dr. Chapman to realize what was happening. This wasn't coincidence. It couldn't be.

On his end of the phone, Dr. Watson heard only the sound of men talking in the background. "Tom! Frank!" Chapman called to his associates. "Look at this!" he shouted, pointing toward the monitor.

Chapman's two associates looked at the monitor, then back at the image from their own telescope, and then back at Chapman, their eyes asking the same question: Was the image on the monitor coming from their telescope? Chapman shook his head in answer. The taller of the two men looked at a small monitor which indicated the picture's source; the other stared back at the picture on the large monitor. For a long moment there was silence.

"What is it?" Dr. Watson's voice asked over the phone, but Chapman didn't respond.

"Shit!" Dr. Watson heard someone on Chapman's end of the phone yell, offering confirmation of his worst fears.

"Have you verified this with anyone else?!" Chapman asked Watson hurriedly. "What about with the Hubble?!"

"Stay on the line," Watson said. "We'll do that right now." It really wasn't necessary: Kitt Peak was well-equipped to verify what was happening, but for about forty-five seconds Chapman held the phone as he listened to the ensuing hysteria that erupted when Watson passed along the content of the call to the others at Dominion Astrophysical Observatory. Then he hung up and sat back down, not waiting for Watson to return to the phone. Behind him reporters, now ignoring the boundaries meant to keep them out of the way of the astronomers, demanded to know what was happening. The other two astronomers quickly called other observatories, hoping to find something that would tell them they were wrong, but there was no mistake. It took only a few moments to be sure. Asteroid 2021 KD had inexplicably changed course and was now headed dangerously close to a collision course with the earth. It was impossible to determine **where**, or even **if** it would hit; there was no time to run simulations now. The asteroid was now only 8,640 miles away and would reach the earth's outer atmosphere in less than eight minutes.

Chapter 5

Alien Stone

At 7:33:22 a.m. Greenwich Mean Time (GMT), July 3, 2021, 317 miles above the earth's surface and directly over the northern Siberian village of Tiksi near the Lena Delta, asteroid 2021 KD, traveling at a speed of 18 miles per second (64,440 miles per hour), entered the most extent region of the earth's ionosphere. Its angle of descent was so slight that it traveled over seven miles horizontally to the earth's surface for every one mile it dropped. At that angle, the density of the atmosphere increased relatively slowly, with the result that the asteroid's surface temperature rose only about a dozen degrees Celsius with each passing second. The slow but steady increase in resistance of the denser atmosphere against the asteroid's irregular shape, combined with its unusual axis of rotation, caused the asteroid to begin to tumble and spin.

Eighty-one seconds after entering the ionosphere, at an altitude of 108 miles, the friction of the atmosphere caused the skin of the tumbling asteroid to superheat and glow. Sixteen seconds later it penetrated the outer regions of the stratosphere, 60 miles above the earth's surface. Nearly coincident to this, the asteroid's surface temperature reached 1,527 degrees Celsius, the melting point of the nickel-iron alloy which made up the great majority of its now wildly tumbling mass. As it did, millions of tiny droplets, or ablation flakes, of molten metal began to peel away from the twelve-mile wide colossus, leaving a visible metallic trail of red-hot nickel iron and combining with the friction of the asteroid to superheat the atmosphere around it.

Had it been a more spherical object, the asteroid would have maintained the same trajectory it had when it entered the atmosphere. That course would have brought it to within 29 miles of the earth's surface over northern Canada — never actually coming in contact with the earth, but continuing on after a six and a half minute sojourn, back into space. Such had been the case in August 1972 when a large meteoroid passed through the atmosphere over the western United States and Canada. What made this incident different was the asteroid's irregular shape. As the asteroid encountered denser and denser air, two forces worked increasingly against each other: inertia and drag. Just as the design of an airplane wing gives the airplane lift, so the shape and tumbling of the asteroid combined to impel it in the opposite direction, that is, to force it down toward the earth. At this point, inertia was winning. But drag had already forced the asteroid several miles lower and with each mile the air grew thicker and the drag grew greater.

It would be erroneous to say that the asteroid was falling; the earth's gravity played almost no part in the asteroid's course. Its speed when it entered the atmosphere was more than two and a half times the velocity needed to escape the earth's gravity, and thus far, that speed had decayed by only a relatively insignificant .6 miles per second. Other factors, however, *did* come into play to affect the asteroid's course relative to the earth's surface. These included the continuing orbit of the earth around the sun; the curvature of the earth; and to a small extent, even the earth's rotation, at the comparatively slow speed of about 1,000 miles per hour. Combined, the effect was that the path of the asteroid arched like a pitcher's curve ball, carrying it slightly to the east in its predominantly southern course, as it moved ever closer to the earth's surface.

Seconds later, above the Beaufort Sea, north of Mackenzie Bay in Canada's Northwest Territory, the asteroid reached a critical point in its approach. Because of atmospheric physics, a sonic boom generated at heights above 37 miles reflects upward off of the denser atmosphere below, thereby preventing any sound from reaching ground level. Now, however, 111 seconds after entering the atmosphere, as the asteroid dropped to less than 37 miles, a sonic boom as powerful as the strongest earthquake issued forth through the heat-blistered sky.

Below the asteroid, near Key Point, south of Herschel Island, the men of a half-dozen Inuit Eskimo families waited patiently in their boats, some with hand-held harpoons, others with high-powered rifles, scanning the bay for the dingy gray-white backs of Beluga whales to break the surface. It was 11:35 p.m. local time, but that hardly mattered this far north and at this time of year in the 'land of the midnight sun.' The last sunrise had been on June twenty-first, twelve days before, and the next sunset would not come for another fifteen days, on July eighteenth. On the shore a few hundred yards away, the men's families slept in tents, waiting for the next kill when they would strip the *muktuk* and despoil the white whale of every usable part. Suddenly, all eyes turned toward the sky and stared in awe at heaven's display. In mere seconds it was gone, trailing off into the southern sky.

For a moment after the asteroid passed, the men stood frozen in silence. And then all at once they shouted to each other in their native Inuktitut with such great excitement that, for the moment, they totally ignored the pair of Beluga whales that had surfaced just 20 meters away. Then someone pointed and called out. Quickly the men in the boats nearest the whales put the asteroid out of their minds and went to work, starting their small outboard motors and maneuvering their 18-foot crafts as close to the unsuspecting Beluga as possible. Near the bow of each boat, two men stood ready, one poised with a hand-held harpoon connected by rope to a pair of empty aluminum beer kegs, the other with a rifle, hoping to finish the job quickly after the harpoon was set.

Traveling at 1,100 feet per second, it would be nearly three full minutes before the asteroid's sonic boom reached the boats below. When it did it would hit like a brick wall, shattering the fiberglass boat hulls as if they were cheap stage glass, and splintering the bones of the men and their families like balsa, reducing their lifeless bodies to formless heaps.

Behind the asteroid a tremendous vacuum formed, which the surrounding atmosphere rushed to fill, creating a tail of supersaturated air from above the Arctic Ocean and a wake of wind which curled off, forming row upon row of super cyclones like giant eddies behind the paddle of a boat.

To the residents of Kaktovik, Alaska, 125 miles to the west, the asteroid appeared in the sky as an enormous flaming star. (It would be eight and a half minutes before the first winds reached them. Less than two minutes later, no one would be left alive as the entire town was blown into the arctic sea.) To the ill-fated Inuit Eskimos near Kay Point, directly beneath the asteroid, it had seemed as though the midnight sun had exploded. Twelve seconds later, to the people of Fort McPherson, 200 miles farther south, at which point the asteroid streaked by only 26 miles overhead, it was as if the heavens themselves were on fire.

No one at Ft. McPherson understood what was happening. The news of the change in the asteroid's course was only now being broadcast on television and radio and, without time to run computer simulations, no one could even begin to project the asteroid's course or where, when, or if, it would actually collide with the earth. In Ft. McPherson, parents pointed and young children clapped in delight as if viewing fireworks. Nearly everyone, young and old alike, was up despite the late hour to watch the asteroid. They had been told to expect no more than a bright light, like a huge star, traveling swiftly across the sky. What they saw instead was a flaming tumbling mountain the size of Manhattan Island hurling past them at unbelievable speed, followed by a fiery trail as bright as morning itself. It was an awesome sight that no one really had time to take in. Four seconds later, with the asteroid already 66 miles farther south but still clearly in view because of its enormous size, the people of Fort McPherson still stared in wonder as they were engulfed from behind in a nuclear-force wall of heat.

There was no chance to escape, but at least their deaths were quick. Everyone and everything for 15 miles to the east and west of Fort McPherson were incinerated and turned to ash within seconds. What didn't burn, melted, and all was swept away in the asteroid's tremendous wake, leaving no trace on the suddenly-barren landscape of the homes, schools, or lives of the 720 stalwart souls who had lived there.

Rich with moisture from the arctic and from the Peel and Channel Rivers, the hurricane-force winds in the asteroid's wake spread in mere minutes across hundreds of miles to the east and west, uprooting and flattening thousands of square miles of virgin Canadian forest, erasing whole towns, and reducing everything in their path to rubble. Ignited by the super-heated atmosphere and molten metal of the asteroid, enormous fireballs followed close behind and were blown by the winds like the flames of hell, consuming everything that remained in an immense blast furnace, reducing hundreds of years of forest growth to smoldering cinders in minutes. Whole lakes and rivers boiled violently, killing all the life within them, and then were sucked up by the immense force of the winds. Vapor condensed on cooled droplets of melted asteroid, dirt, and other debris, forming rain. Some fell to the earth, and some was swept into the upper atmosphere by the tremendous winds, freezing into hail stones; falling and repeating the cycle until finally huge hailstones — some weighing up to twenty-five pounds — fell to the earth, sizzling like butter in a pan on the scorched landscape where they fell.

Beneath the asteroid, debris from the ground, including objects weighing up to several tons, was picked up and swept along at speeds of thousands of miles per hour. Cars, trucks, trailers, boats, mobile homes, aircraft, slabs of rock and concrete, pieces of homes and other structures and all they contained — so twisted and smashed as to bear no resemblance to their former state — were carried aloft and towed along for hundreds of miles.

A hundred miles south of Ft. McPherson, at 66 degrees north latitude, the asteroid first began to enter darkness. Sixty-three seconds later, 1,200 miles south of where Ft. McPherson had stood, the asteroid passed 18.84 miles overhead just west of Edmonton, Alberta, the first heavily populated area in its path, and delivered the same devastation to Edmonton's three quarters of a million people that it had brought on the populations of Ft. McPherson, Ft. Goodhope, Norman Wells, Ft. Norman, and Wrigley, along its path. In seconds every structure in the city and its suburbs were engulfed in flame. Most of the population died in the initial blast of heat and shower of molten iron; the rest died within moments from the fires, or were sucked up into the asteroid's wake. Explosions from natural gas, petroleum, and other chemicals added to the deadly amalgam to incinerate the remains of the towns and homes around Edmonton like the stubble of hay. In the streets, flaming asphalt ran like water, puddling in ruts wherever the ground was low. In a few places the heat was great enough to melt shards of glass from the demolished buildings.

In the next seventeen seconds the asteroid passed over Red Deer, Calgary, and Medicine Hat, wreaking similar destruction. A few buildings were left standing on the western edge of Calgary, only to be blown apart like sand castles by the sonic boom that followed moments behind. In another eight seconds the asteroid thundered across the border with the United States and just fourteen seconds later, now less than 15 miles above the surface of the threatened planet, it reached Billings, Montana.

The asteroid's tail stretched over 300 miles, flailing objects picked up all along its path like the tail of a child's kite. Among the smaller debris was an ever-growing number of formerly living, breathing creatures — both human and otherwise — who had not been close enough to the asteroid to be incinerated by its heat, but who instead were picked up, slammed about, and ripped apart. Their soon-lifeless forms, looking remarkably like rag dolls formed of too-often-washed fabric, were subjected alternately to unimaginable pressure and then swept into areas of near total vacuum, crushing them like grapes and pouring out their blood like wine to the vengeance of the alien stone. Wild animals including deer, elk, moose, caribou, and bear, whole herds of cattle and sheep, flocks of assorted fowl, domestic animals, and entire populations of towns and villages surrendered their blood to the mix of rain and hail as they were picked up and carried along for scores or hundreds of miles in mere seconds. Also among the human debris were many who had died in recent weeks, pulled from their newly covered graves by the violent turbulence and added to the asteroid's cortege.

Imperceptible except to weather satellites that watched its path from above, and unimportant to anyone within hundreds of miles of its path below, the asteroid's speed was slowly deteriorating against the resistance of the earth's atmosphere. By the time it reached Billings, its speed had dropped to about 15½ miles per second. Thirty-one seconds and nearly a million human lives later, as the asteroid passed 11¾ miles above Ft. Collins, Boulder, Denver, and Aurora, Colorado, the speed had dropped another quarter of a mile per second. The Rocky Mountains offered no break to the winds and heat which swept across them, repeating the destruction that had befallen the forests, lakes, and towns farther north.

Mile after mile, city after city, the asteroid held to its merciless course, destroying everything in its path. Colorado

Springs, Pueblo, and Trinidad, Colorado; Raton and Tucumcari, New Mexico; Lubbock, Sweetwater, Abilene, and San Angelo, Texas. By the time the asteroid reached Austin, Texas, only five minutes and seven seconds had passed since it had entered the earth's atmosphere. The asteroid's speed had been cut to 14.834 miles per second (53,402 miles per hour) and its altitude to only 7.48 miles above sea level. There was no counting the cost of the damage done or the number of lives lost.

Twenty-four seconds later, after devastating San Antonio and Corpus Christi, the asteroid passed over Brownsville, Texas and Matamoros, Mexico and headed southeast across the Gulf of Mexico. Its altitude was now only 5.2 miles above sea level and its speed had dropped to 14.6 miles per second. Once again over water, the tail of the asteroid became rich with moisture, which fed and sustained the storms created by its wake.

Seconds after leaving land, at an altitude of just under 4 miles, an event occurred which by itself would have been a point of some interest for scientific inquiry, but under the circumstances would draw little attention. From the moment the asteroid first entered the atmosphere, it began to build up a static charge from friction with the air. As its tumbling brought the asteroid to within 20,000 feet of the earth's surface, it released an electromagnetic charge in the form of a massive bolt of lightning so immense and powerful that it literally vaporized the water where it struck, momentarily creating a huge crater, 1,800 feet in diameter and 260 feet deep.

It took the asteroid just forty-two seconds to span the 580 miles across the Gulf of Mexico, coming back over land 18 miles west of Paraiso, Mexico at an altitude of just 6,864 feet (1.3 miles) above sea level. To this point the asteroid's altitude could best be stated as an average of the lowest and highest point above sea level of its bottom-most point during any one rotation. Now, however, such averaging would no longer be appropriate. Because of the asteroid's shape and tumbling, the distance between it and the earth varied by more than a mile during any one eight and a half second rotation, depending on which part of the asteroid was down at that particular moment. The asteroid was now so close to the earth that the significant issue had become not altitude, but rather the distance between the two bodies at any particular instant.

One other element was quickly becoming a factor. As the asteroid traveled inland across southern Mexico toward the Sierra Madre Mountains, the hilly terrain rose rapidly to meet it.

As the asteroid drew closer to the surface, it no longer required so powerful a static charge to span the distance to the earth, and it began to release bolt after bolt of lightning, fulminating the scraps of timber and debris which defied the winds preceding their host. No sooner did it discharge than the static charge from the friction with the atmosphere began to build again and in less than a second it discharged again with similar destructive effect. As it came closer to the earth, the interval between bolts continued to decrease until, so quickly was the static charge replaced after each discharge, that to the naked eye (had anyone been alive to witness it), it would have appeared as if a solid "sheet" of lightning spanned the entire 12-mile breadth of the tumbling titan, obliterating everything in its path milliseconds before sweeping them along in its wake.

Thirty miles ahead of the asteroid, the earth reached up her mountainous terrain as if to receive the oncoming celestial visitor. Row upon row of mountains, each one seemingly higher than the one before, stood only seconds away, waiting in silent challenge in the asteroid's path. Impact was imminent.

The asteroid just brushed the surface of the first mountain, cutting out a pass about 60 feet deep and 1¾ miles across. The contact slowed the asteroid so imperceptibly that even the weather satellites watching from above could not measure the difference. It would not make it past the next mountain so cleanly.

The top of the second mountain stood in defiant stillness before the asteroid, rising more than a half mile above the asteroid's lowest point. It was not nearly large enough to stop the asteroid, but it would slow it noticeably.

A fraction of a second later the asteroid met the mountain 3,200 feet below its peak. The collision sheared off the top of the mountain, throwing millions of tons of rocks and chunks of asteroid up to 1,200 miles, and was detected on every seismic monitoring device in the world. A millisecond later the asteroid's tumbling motion brought the largest lobe slamming down on the top of the next, slightly lower mountain peak, pulverizing the peak under the pressure, and bringing down an avalanche of crumbling rock into the valleys below. A village of 300 people on the mountainside slid into the valley below, where it was buried beneath tons of rock and dirt. Neighboring mountains shook, causing landslides up to 30 miles away. Later, scientists would estimate the force of the collision at five megatons of TNT, or about 250 times the force of the bomb dropped on Hiroshima.

The tumbling impact against the top of the lower mountain vaulted the asteroid skyward, causing it to pass just above the largest of the mountains directly ahead and throwing it in a slightly more easterly direction. Less perceptible but far more important — the impact had changed the asteroid's rotation. The change was slight but it was enough to reduce the coefficient of drag sufficiently that inertia became the greater force, thus altering the asteroid's aerodynamics. The result was that instead of being pushed slowly and relentlessly toward the ground, the asteroid now traveled in a nearly straight line. Because of the curvature of the earth and the fact that the asteroid's speed was still more than sufficient to overcome the earth's gravity, the asteroid actually began to rise above the earth's surface. It was very slight — approximately 37 feet of rise per mile — but by the time the asteroid reached Guatemala City, 208 miles farther south, it had risen 7,696 feet, to an altitude of just over 2 miles, well above any mountains in the asteroid's way.

The point was academic to those in the asteroid's path. The destruction was just as severe regardless of the asteroid's exact position above the earth. The people of Guatemala City suffered the same fate as the people of every other city in its course.

The asteroid took just thirteen and a half seconds to span Guatemala and cross the border into El Salvador, passing halfway between San Vicente and San Salvador, heading for the Salvadoran Pacific coast. Over the Pacific, the asteroid stayed within about 160 miles of the Central American coast except where the coast turns northward past Punta Mariato, Panama. Throughout its ocean passage it continued to rise, reaching an altitude of 10.814 miles by the time it reached the coast of Columbia. Seven seconds later, at a speed of 11.412 miles per second (41,083.2 miles per hour), the asteroid passed 11.374 miles over Popayán, Columbia.

Below the asteroid, the Columbian Pacific coast rainforest, called the 'Choco' by the inhabitants, and the great Amazonian forests of the eastern lowlands were tinder before the winds and fires brought by the asteroid. Hundreds of species of flora and fauna indigenous only to the South American jungle were destroyed at a single stroke, as literally millions of acres were instantly set ablaze.

Four minutes and twenty-eight seconds later, at an altitude of 31.6 miles, after destroying the coastal cities of Itabuana and Illheus, Brazil, the asteroid reached the Atlantic Ocean. It had spanned the broadest part of the South American continent in just six minutes and eight seconds. Seventy seconds later, at a speed of 9.622 miles per second (34,639 miles per hour), it passed 36.46 miles over Trinidad Island in the Atlantic. As the asteroid's altitude became greater and the air grew thinner, the resistance decreased rapidly, which allowed its course to become increasingly true, thereby putting it at a sharper angle away from the earth's surface and reducing the time required before it exited the atmosphere.

At 7:53:27 a.m. GMT, 309 miles above Bethanie, South Africa, Asteroid 2021 KD returned to space. The entire passage through the earth's atmosphere lasted just over twenty minutes and covered 14,210 miles. It had passed through fifteen time zones and had caused more destruction than all of the pre-atomic wars combined. When it entered the atmosphere, the asteroid had been traveling 18 miles per second; by the time it left, it was traveling only 8.43 miles per second (30,362 miles per hour).

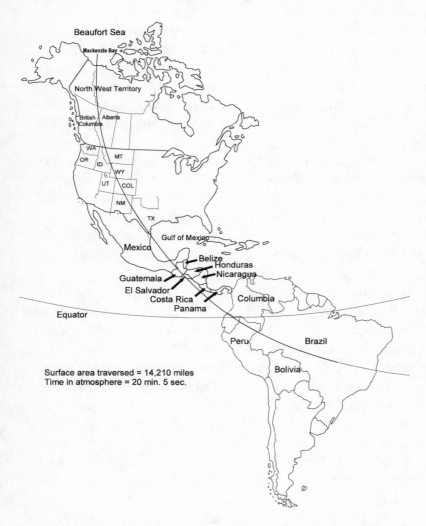

While that was still fast enough to escape the earth's gravitational pull, as a result of its earthly encounter the asteroid's new course sent it hurtling directly toward the sun. In the void of space and pulled by the tremendous gravity of the sun, the asteroid would continually accelerate. Six days after leaving the earth, after reaching an incredible speed of 360 miles per second (1,296,000 miles per hour), the asteroid would pass inside the orbit of the planet Mercury. Two minutes later it would begin to melt from the sun's heat, and in a few minutes more, would become a gaseous cloud before finally being absorbed by the sun.

The event would have provided an unprecedented observational opportunity for the scientists at the solar observatory atop Sacramento Peak, New Mexico. That, however, was impossible. There no longer *was* an observatory at Sacramento Peak: it had been destroyed. All that remained was a bare mountain top, stripped of all vegetation and man-made structures. The Tower Telescope building had been sheared off at ground level, leaving only a 220-foot hole in the mountain to mark where it had been.

Even after the asteroid exited the earth's atmosphere, its destructive influence was far from over. Later, searches through the ruins would reveal that no one for 160 miles to the east or west of its path had survived. Beyond that distance, up to 600 miles away, the few who did survive the initial blast and the fires and storms had been struck deaf as their eardrums were ruptured by the tremendous sonic boom. The sound violently shook walls as far as 800 miles away, and some reported hearing the boom for up to 1,800 miles, making it second in intensity only to the explosion of Krakatoa in 1883, which was heard for up to 3,000 miles. And while the initial storms and fires cut a swath 800 to 1,400 miles wide across the North and South American continents, the fires would ultimately rage uncontrolled in many areas for several months and would destroy, in total, about one-third of the earth's total forests.

Hours after the asteroid, as winds began to subside, hundreds of millions of tons of debris fell to earth along with the rain and hail and blood: twisted pieces of automobiles, tree roots, branches and trunks, building materials of all sorts, broken glass, miscellaneous rubbish too mangled to identify, rocks, offal, and other assorted wreckage. Bodies, most stripped bare of their clothing, many stripped of their limbs, fell from the sky.

In Gila Bend, Arizona, nearly 550 miles from the asteroid's path, a family of four, lucky enough to have survived the storms, emerged from their basement to find their home gone, destroyed by the storm. A second floor bathtub, suspended in air by its plumbing, offered scant evidence of what had stood just two hours earlier on this now-barren plot. Unable to comprehend what had occurred, the family walked in the still-falling rain around what had been their home, too muddled by disbelief to cry. On the pavement that had served as the driveway of their small single-family home, the nude blood-drained head and torso of a woman lay face down where it had fallen after being released from the grip of the storm. The father told his wife and two daughters to turn away as he quickly found something to cover the body. Gritting his teeth and trying not to vomit, he turned her head in an attempt to determine who the woman was but the bones of the her face were so crushed that she was unrecognizable. He assumed it was a neighbor. Certainly, he would never have guessed that the body had been carried 400 miles by the storm, or that for a brief moment, the woman whose body had fallen here had been known around the world for the discovery of three asteroids.

One additional tribulation brought on by the asteroid's passage would not be apparent for another two weeks. When the asteroid entered the atmosphere it created a great turbulence in the upper atmosphere, causing a massive disruption in the earth's ozone layer. This was compounded when the asteroid returned to space, pulling with it millions of cubic miles of atmosphere. That lost atmosphere would quickly be drawn back by the earth's gravity, but over a period of a few days the combined disruptive effect to the ozone layer would stretch around the world. It would take only a few weeks before the ozone layer would begin to settle back into place and would again provide its protective blanket to the earth's surface. But this would not come before the earth had been bathed in sufficient ultraviolet light to severely damage the enzymatic pathways of plant life throughout the world.

Of the two major varieties of plant life (broad leaf plants and grasses), grasses — distinguished by their long, slender leaves and including not only the numerous varieties of grass but also such plants as corn, wheat, rye, oats, barley, and sugar cane — are far more dependent for life on the synthesis of aromatic amino acids which takes place in the plant's enzymatic pathways. If the enzymatic pathway is blocked by damage from herbicides or ultraviolet light, grasses will immediately stop growing. About a week and a half later, when the plant's storehouse of aromatic amino acids is depleted, the plant turns reddish-yellow, then yellow and then finally brown, dying completely in about three weeks. Thus it was that three weeks after the asteroid all of the grassy plants — burned by the ultraviolet rays of the sun — shriveled and died throughout the world. In some areas the grass would return before the fall and the grain crops would be replanted the next year. But in the interim, famine would claim the lives of millions.

In the parts of the world unaffected by the immediate results of the asteroid, the rest of mankind looked on in disbelief at the incredible destruction that had befallen their planet. Satellite videos of the asteroid's course were pieced together to provide a complete depiction of the path of slaughter and destruction.

No one who watched was unaffected. Those who did not have relatives or friends in the affected areas had their own fears to trouble them: two more asteroids were still out there, heading toward the earth. Scientists and government officials tried to reassure people, pointing out that the first asteroid's change in course had been a highly unusual quirk and that there was nothing to fear from the second asteroid. Someone came up with a 'best guess' to explain why the first asteroid had changed course and it quickly caught on with the media, who were desperate for some sort of explanation. The theory was that, just as a bantam black hole or chunk of white dwarf had originally pulled the three asteroids from their normal orbits, so a similar phenomenon had affected the first asteroid when it came closer to the earth; perhaps it was the same black hole or chunk of white dwarf that had pulled the asteroids out of their orbits in the first place. For the public, however, that explanation only evoked more questions: Was it still out there? Would it have a similar affect on the second asteroid? Would the object itself threaten the earth? And most menacing of all: would it somehow prevent the missiles headed for the third and largest asteroid (which scientists had said could destroy *all* life on the planet) from reaching their target?

To the last question the answer was relatively certain. The missiles, now five days and nearly three million miles into their journey, had already passed beyond the distance from the earth at which the first asteroid had been diverted, and the telemetry from all missiles indicated they were still precisely on course. As to whether the bantam black hole or chunk of white dwarf or whatever it was, was still out there and whether it threatened the earth — either by altering the course of the second asteroid, or by colliding with the earth itself — the possibility was almost as unlikely. "Bodies in space are constantly in motion," one of the interviewed scientists said. "The possibility that a similar set of circumstances could occur, causing the second asteroid to be pulled off course in the direction of earth, is simply too astronomical to be imagined."

July 3, 2021 — The United Nations, New York (4:25 a.m. local time, 9:25 a.m. GMT)

Ambassador Christopher Goodman stared blankly as those around him in the emergency meeting of the Security Council discussed providing relief to the survivors of the asteroid's devastation. It had been less than two hours since the asteroid had made its pass. The first logical order of business was to dispatch teams to assess the situation and report back with recommendations. Beyond that, all that could be done was to discuss contingencies for providing relief.

It would not be an easy matter. The U.N. was still struggling to provide relief to the survivors of the China-India-Pakistan War, and it was in large measure the benefactor nations of that effort which now found themselves needing aid. For the moment this fact went unmentioned but certainly not unnoticed by the Primary members of the Security Council who represented those war-torn countries. They realized that the countries of North and South America would be turning their attention to their own needs, which would cause an end or at least a dramatic reduction in aid to the east.

Their only real hope was to obtain increased aid from Western Europe and Northern Asia. But diplomatically this was not the right time to bring up the matter of aid to China and India. North and South America had suffered greatly and it would not be well received if other members were too focused on their own problems before the smoke even began to clear. Better to wait and discuss this with the Primaries from Northern Asia and Europe in private later on. Besides, the Primary from Europe (Christopher) seemed distracted by his own thoughts at the moment.

Had the ambassadors from China and India known what Christopher knew, they would have realized that the problems for their countries were about to become much worse. John and Cohen had proven their ability to make good on their threats. The first prophecy had been fulfilled to the letter. If the remaining prophecies were carried out as literally, the suffering was only beginning.

Chapter 6

Cat Strike

Kiso Mountains, Japan (6:35 a.m. local time, 9:35 p.m. GMT)

As they went about their work observing the approach of the second asteroid, the astronomers of the Tokyo Astronomical Observatory outstation 200 kilometers west of Tokyo kept one eye on the television and the graphic depictions of destruction in the Americas from the first asteroid.

As scientists they realized the incredible odds against a repeat of what had happened with asteroid 2021 KD. Even so, they each watched carefully, as did the rest of the world, for any deviation in the second asteroid's course. When it actually began to happen no one said anything. At first it was only enough to be detected by the most sensitive equipment, and the most sensitive equipment is, by its very nature, most susceptible to error. Besides, it was so incredibly unlikely that the second asteroid could be off course that no one wanted to be the first to say anything and risk causing a panic over some minor computational error. But with each passing second the deviation in course grew and it became obvious to the observatory team that there was no error; the asteroid's course was changing. Soon it would be apparent even to a novice.

Dr. Yoshi Hiakawa, Director of the Kiso outstation of the Tokyo Astronomical Observatory, looked over at the television crew and motioned to the lead reporter to come over. In the most business-as-usual presentation he could summon, he told the reporter, "We've detected a slight deviation in the asteroid's course."

The reporter waited for additional information but none followed. "Is it headed toward us?" he prodded.

"On its present course it will still miss the earth," Dr. Hiakawa said. "But if the angle of deviation from its original path continues to grow, that possibility does exist."

"If that happens, where will it hit?"

"As I said, at this time there is no indication that it will hit the earth at all; only that its course is presently undergoing an unexplained deviational anomaly."

"What shall I tell the public?" the reporter asked.

Dr. Hiakawa shook his head. "I don't know," he answered. "I've provided the information. What you do with it is up to you." Hiakawa had no desire to start a panic which itself could cost lives, but neither did he want to bear the responsibility for withholding the information. Leaving the decision to the press was the safe way out and he took it.

It took nearly a half hour to determine whether the asteroid would strike the earth. It took only a few minutes beyond that to determine with some certainty where it would hit. Asteroid 2021 KE would score a direct hit on the earth somewhere in or near the Philippine Basin in the Pacific Ocean. Emergency broadcasts began immediately to warn residents to seek high ground in preparation for the tsunami (often incorrectly called tidal waves) and earthquakes that would certainly result.

□   □   □

At 10:47:18 a.m. GMT, asteroid 2021 KE pierced the earth's atmospheric skin. Unlike its predecessor, the second asteroid's path left no doubt that collision with the earth was certain. Twelve seconds after entering the atmosphere, traveling at 67,280 miles per hour, the temperature of the asteroid's surface rose above 1,525 degrees Celsius, the melting point of iron. Quickly an oblation shield formed as the molten droplets of iron peeled away, taking with them much of the heat and thereby keeping the core of the asteroid cool. The red hot trail of liquescent iron gave the asteroid the eerie appearance of a huge flaming mountain.

Just eighteen seconds after entering the atmosphere, as sea birds flying nearby were roasted alive in the tremendous heat emanating from the asteroid and the scorched feathers filled the air with a putrid incense, the asteroid reached sea level. Four hundred and seventy miles south of *Kōchi*, Japan, in the southern-most portion of the *Shikoku* Basin, asteroid 2021 KE slammed into the Pacific Ocean, creating an initial splash which reached 42 miles above the earth.

Despite the tremendous resistance of the water, it took just a third of a second for the asteroid to reach the sea floor, 3.6 miles below the surface. So quickly did the asteroid pass through the water that it reached bottom well before the surrounding waters could rush in to fill the void, and thus created a two-mile-wide open shaft the full distance from the surface.

The asteroid struck the sea floor with an explosive force equal to 90,000 megatons (90 billion tons) of TNT, or nine times the total destructive power of the world's combined nuclear forces at the height of the Cold War, or four and a half million times that of the atomic bomb dropped on Hiroshima. The center of the impact, which was three times hotter than the surface of the sun, vaporized the sand and rock in the asteroid's path and caused the sea for 18 miles around to erupt and boil violently, filling the surrounding air with scalding steam and cooking the entire 157-man crew of a Japanese Navy frigate like lobsters in a pot.

Continuing down like a bullet into soft wood, the asteroid

created a massive crater 22 miles in diameter and 12 miles deep. Had the asteroid struck dry ground or in shallower water, the debris from the impact would have been sent flying into the atmosphere and created a dark blanket of dust over the entire planet. Within weeks, such a blanket would have eliminated all or nearly all life on earth. Instead, because it hit in one of the deepest parts of the ocean, in water more than 3½ miles deep, only about 2 percent, or 96 billion tons of the debris, was ejected above the ocean's surface. Of that material, the vast majority consisted of large pieces of iron and massive tektites formed by the impact, which fell back to earth over a 1,600-mile radius. Only a very minute amount of material was small enough to be kept aloft.

But while the water's resistance stopped most of the smaller debris from reaching beyond the surface and thus spared the atmosphere from filling with dust, the sea itself bore the brunt as over 3.8 trillion tons of debris small enough to be suspended in ocean currents, including more than 720 billion tons of iron particles from the asteroid, were carried across the ocean by the giant waves which radiated out from the impact.

In the seabed, the shock of the initial impact and the subsequent fracturing of the earth's mantle set off massive earthquakes which were felt for thousands of miles throughout the Circum-Pacific Belt and the Eurasian, Philippine, and Fiji tectonic plates. On land, buildings crumbled, killing tens of thousands, and in the sea the quakes set off additional tsunami hundreds of miles in advance of the waves from the actual impact.

The first tsunami created by earthquakes in the Pacific off China's coast threatened Asia's shores within two minutes of the impact. The tsunami, rippling out from the actual impact, would take another two hours to reach the continental shelf.

In the bay of *Wangpan Yang*, south of Shanghai, China, the waters of the Pacific suddenly and without warning began to recede with incredible speed toward the open sea, pulling with them nearly everything afloat that was not securely tied or anchored. With a terrifying roar of hissing, sucking, and gurgling, the water as far inland as the mouth of the *Fuchun River* was drained out in less than five minutes, leaving tens of thousands of acres of sea bottom suddenly exposed. On the Wangpan Yang seabed, well-anchored boats and ships of all sizes were left foundering on dry ground. All but the flat-bottomed vessels had tipped over and lay on their sides, their crews forced to climb out among stranded sea creatures left by the retreating waters. On the surrounding shores, startled onlookers, seeing fish and booty from long forgotten wrecks laying there for the taking, rushed out to take advantage of nature's apparent boon, completely unaware that what nature had relinquished, it would just as quickly reclaim, along with their lives.

At the mouth of the bay, the crews of ships which had been pulled toward the sea watched helplessly in awful fear as their vessels, large and small, were sucked into the churning trough of death beneath the oncoming wave which rose like a foaming mountain, 220 feet into the air.

Within the next few moments the event was repeated at every bay and the mouth of every major river along the Asian coast, as Pacific waters swept over China as far inland as four miles. Along the *Yangtze* river, flooding reached as far inland as *Nanjing*.

The coastal regions and cities of Taiwan were completely covered, killing four million and causing untold economic loss.

As large as they were, these first waves were merely a pale foreshadowing of the waves to come. Two to three hours away — depending on the geography of the Asian coast — a train of waves sent out like ripples from the point of the asteroid's impact and expanded outward in rings which sped through the open ocean at over 450 miles per hour — waves so large they dwarfed the one which struck the bay of Wangpan Yang. The Ryukyu Islands, Okinawa, the Philippines, Malaysia, Indonesia, the Northern Marianas and Guam, the Sunda Islands, the Palau Islands, Micronesia, the Caroline, Solomon, Marshall, Santa Cruz, Gilbert, and Phoenix Islands, New Zealand, the Cook Islands and hundreds more, all lay helpless in the path of the immense killer waves.

In Siberia, Korea, China, and Vietnam, those on land who had survived the earthquakes and the first tsunami struggled inland to reach higher ground. Ships at port which had not been scuttled by the initial waves and that could muster sufficient crews on short notice headed out to sea, hoping to reach deep water before the waves grew to an unmanageable height. Their efforts would be futile. As the waves began to climb Asia's continental shelf, the lead wave in the train had already reached 180 feet in height. By the time the tsunami were within 20 miles of shore the lead wave had grown to more than 1300 feet. Those ships which had left port hoping to reach safety in deeper water, instead found they were sailing into certain death as a wall of water that no ship could survive sped to meet them. Ships of all sizes were thrown about and swallowed up like mere toys by the leviathan waves. The same scene was played out throughout the Pacific basin countries, with some waves topping 2800 feet by the time they reached shore. The Chinese and Japanese Navies were reduced to fewer than a half dozen ships each. Thousands of cargo ships carrying goods to and from Japan, China, and the other Pacific Basin nations and islands, more than a hundred supertankers fully loaded with oil, others returning empty, literally millions of commercial fishing boats, and untold smaller crafts and their crews, all fell prey to the waves.

An hour later the wave ring reached New Guinea which, because of its location directly between the point of impact and Australia, took the full force of the waves and largely blunted the tsunami's impact on the island continent to its south.

Owing to their volcanic origins, on the islands of Hawaii there was no shortage of high ground, and with eight hours' warning to escape the tsunami, most islanders loaded cars, trailers, trucks, and carts with everything they could carry and headed for the safety of the nearest dormant volcanic mountain. From there, they watched in disbelief as 300-foot walls of water washed the islands clean of their homes and businesses.

On the rim of the *Kilauea Caldera*, the scientists of the Hawaiian Volcano Observatory had their hands full with another matter. Using seismographic data and satellite telemetry to monitor the effects of the earthquakes caused by the fracturing of the earth's mantle, the scientists found evidence that volcanoes from New Zealand to Mexico and everywhere in between showed early signs of new activity. It would not happen immediately, but it was becoming nearly certain that over the next few weeks or months scores of volcanoes would erupt as a direct result of the asteroid's impact.

On the other side of the Pacific, on the west coast of North and South America, there was much more time to prepare. The tsunami train took sixteen hours to travel the 6400 miles to Cape Mendocino California, which was first on the coast of the Americas to be hit. It took an additional nine hours to reach *Iquique*, Chile, the most distant point on the Americas' Pacific coast. Having been warned of the tsunami's strength, residents had ample time to reach higher ground, and most ships reached deeper water. Ships in drydock and smaller vessels were abandoned.

In every country there was one group — the looters — who defied the tsunami's approach, hoping to escape to higher ground with as much plunder as possible, just ahead of the wave. A few were shot by police and property owners. Most of the more conservative looters survived. Others who waited too long or foolishly sought refuge on the top floors of tall buildings were drowned or crushed to death as the buildings turned to rubble in the onslaught of the crashing waves.

More than a week passed before the seas began to calm, for great tsunami do not strike once and dissipate, but reflect back like radar off the land masses they encounter, returning again and again across the sea to repeat their destructive impact. Because of the extent of the destruction, an exact accounting of the dead would never be possible. Most estimates put the final number between 110 and 120 million. Perhaps five to six percent of that number died aboard the millions of boats and ships which traverse the seas and sail among the thousands of Pacific Islands.

And yet despite the magnitude of the disaster above the surface, a much greater disaster was brewing beneath the waves. For a full week the tsunami reflected back and forth across the Pacific, not only from Asia to the Americas, but also from Siberia and Alaska to the Antarctic, bringing with them dramatic shifts in ocean temperature, wreaking havoc on the ocean's fragile ecosystem, and killing fish and other marine life by the billions. Even greater was the damage wrought by trillions of tons of debris, carried across the ocean from the site of the impact, which clouded the waters and turned the Pacific's surface a bloody red as 720 billion tons of iron particles from the asteroid turned to rust. The murky waters blocked out much of the sun's light, preventing photosynthesis by the phytoplankton — the delicate sea plants which serve not only as the bottom link in the food chain, but which also provide the oxygen needed by all sea life. As the phytoplankton died, so did the sea animals which depend upon it for food, followed quickly by each higher level of the food chain. Soon too, the oxygen level of the ocean dropped. Within two weeks nearly all sea life in the Pacific perished.

◻   ◻   ◻

And so, like the first, John and Cohen's second prophesy had been brutally fulfilled. Two more prophesies remained.

Chapter 7

Wormwood

August 2, 2021 (2:27 a.m. GMT)

Deep in the void of space, at a point 113 million miles from the sun, three clusters of warheads, propelled forward by inertia, sped through space at just over 25,000 miles per hour headed toward the asteroid designated 2021 KF. Twenty million miles away, the frightened people of a devastated planet waited in anxious anticipation for word on their attempt to destroy the menacing form. Failure would mean almost certain death of all remaining life on their planet.

At 2:27:32 a.m. G.M.T. the first group of forty cone-shaped twenty-megaton warheads began to deploy in a predetermined pattern, preparing to intercept the 30-mile-wide asteroid, which was advancing toward the earth at 65,000 miles per hour. So far everything was going according to schedule, but the biggest test was just ahead. In ten minutes, as they came to within 100 meters of the speeding asteroid, the warheads would detonate in a first attempt to destroy the target. With a combined head-on speed of

90,000 miles per hour, the window of opportunity for detonation within 100 meters was less than one five-hundredth of a second.

On earth, all humanity waited. Now only about half the distance between the earth and Mars, the massive asteroid shone in the night sky like a great star. If there was a total or partial failure, a second and third group of warheads launched after the first at intervals of thirty-five minutes would provide two more chances. Among the second and third volleys of warheads, infrared sensing devices would monitor the success of the preceding volley and provide telemetry to target the warheads in the later group on any remaining large pieces of the asteroid which were headed toward earth.

Because of the distance, it took a minute and forty-eight seconds after the first cluster's interception of the asteroid for the signal to travel back to earth. To everyone's great relief and many people's surprise, the interception was a complete success, far more successful than even the most optimistic estimates had been. The largest portion of the asteroid's mass had been reduced to pieces ranging in size between dust and chunks no larger than a few cubic feet. And of the pieces larger than that, none were now headed toward the earth.

As information of the interception's success reached earth, there was brief consideration given to using the warheads of the second and third clusters to further disperse the material that remained on a course for earth, but after careful analysis it was determined that the remaining material posed no threat and that detonation of the warheads would only serve to further irradiate it. The remaining pieces headed for earth were all determined to be small enough to either burn up harmlessly in the atmosphere or sift through as tiny particles of dust.

The decision was made to disperse the warhead clusters and, once they were fully clear of the asteroid debris that remained headed toward earth, they were detonated. Scientific review of the interception would conclude that the unanticipated success of the first volley was due to an unusual feature of the asteroid's composition. The asteroid's predominantly iron mass was apparently honeycombed with veins of stone or of a metal much more brittle than iron.

That day huge celebrations were held to mark the successful destruction of the third asteroid. To a visitor from another planet it would have seemed the strangest of festivals, for as celebrants drank to their success, forest fires smoldered across two ravaged continents, the largest of the planet's oceans lay barren, and widespread volcanic activity spewed plumes of steam, carbon dioxide, sulfur gasses, ash, and cinders into the atmosphere.

August 15, 2021

Despite the growing cover of ash in the stratosphere, the skies provided an unprecedented display of fireworks which lasted for two nights as millions of tons of dust and small debris from the third asteroid plunged through the atmosphere. The warheads had done their job exceptionally well, leaving very few fragments large enough to survive the trip through the atmosphere and reach earth in identifiable pieces. Like most meteorites, the small chunks of the asteroid began to melt as soon as they reached the stratosphere, each providing a brief streak of fire in the darkened sky as they disintegrated into tiny molten dust particles which cooled and fell harmlessly and unnoticed to the earth's surface.

August 17, 2021 — Villa Valeria, Argentina

Juan Perez held his grandfather's hand in eager excitement as they walked together in the cool night air just before dawn toward the nine-acre lake and adventure. In his other hand Juan held his brand new fishing rod. Today was Juan's sixth birthday and it was to be marked by his first fishing trip. His head was filled with anticipation of the enormous fish he imagined he would catch and of the look that would come over his mother's face when he returned home and showed the fish to her.

The cloud of volcanic ash which hung high above them blocked out much of the starlight, and the moon appeared as if in a deep, black fog. His grandfather held the flashlight under his arm so they could see the path as they made their way toward the lake, and though they were still twenty yards from the shore, Juan walked on tip-toe as he remembered his grandfather's admonition to be careful not to scare the fish.

A light breeze at their backs shifted and as it did it brought with it the unmistakable stench of rotting fish. Juan reached up to hold his nose and nearly poked his grandfather in the eye with his fishing rod.   Ducking to avoid his grandson's pole, Juan's grandfather released his hand and then walked slowly toward the lake, leaving Juan where he stood, still holding his nose. Juan was happy to stay behind, suddenly not so sure that fishing was as wonderful as he thought it might be.

Lifting his flashlight to illuminate the surface of the lake, Juan's grandfather found the source of the smell. As far as he could see, bloated fish floated belly up, covering the surface of the lake.

Mt. Gretna, Pennsylvania

The alarm clock rang and Betty Overholt reached to turn it off and then buried her face in her pillow as she groped for the switch to turn on the lamp. It was 4:15 a.m. Slowly she peeked out from the pillow to let her eyes adjust to the light and her nostrils filled with the delightful aroma of fresh coffee and bacon from the kitchen. As usual, her husband Paul was already up and had started breakfast. She had always envied his ability to get up every morning at the same time without an alarm. It was in his genes, she guessed. The son, grandson, and great grandson of dairymen, Paul Overholt had never known anything else. When he was in high school he had thought of becoming a lawyer, but on the day after he turned seventeen his parents and two older brothers died in the Disaster and left him alone with the farm.

When Betty got to the kitchen Paul had already started eating. With one exception, it was the same breakfast he always had: three scrambled eggs from their hens, six strips of bacon from the hog they had butchered last month, a large glass of milk fresh from the cow the night before, and a double-sized cup of coffee. The only thing missing from his normal fare was four pieces of toast. Bread had become extremely hard to find and very expensive since the blight on grassy plants, including wheat, rye, and corn. At Betty's place at the table were smaller portions of the same, except the coffee; she had never gotten used to coffee made with the sulfur water from their well.

Paul left the house and started toward the barn while Betty cleaned up from breakfast and put the dishes in the dishwasher. It would be another hour until dawn but Paul Overholt had walked the path to the barn so many times there was usually no need for him to carry a flashlight. Besides, there was the light at the barn which he turned on from the porch as he left the house. For the past month, however, the combination of smoke from the fires in the west and volcanic ash in the upper atmosphere had so darkened the night skies that Betty insisted he carry a light, lest he trip over something. It was cool; it had been for the past couple of weeks. The television news said the temperature was averaging 14 degrees below normal because of the ash cover.

It really wasn't necessary that Paul begin milking so early. He had thinned his herd by about one-third in order to conserve the hay he had from the previous year. But it was what he was used to, and what the cows were used to as well. Like Paul, the cows needed no alarm clock to know when it was milking time. Every morning they'd be there waiting when he arrived.

Paul was luckier than most. The previous winter had been very mild and the Overholt farm still had a silo full of corn and a barn full of hay from the previous year. That and the fact that Paul had planted most of his fields in clover, which was not affected by the blight, meant that he could keep most of his cows and continue milking. Despite everything — actually, because of everything — it was a good year for the Overholts: milk prices were sky high; beef was low as farmers thinned their herds, but that was sure to change later in the year.

Paul was only halfway to the barn when he first sensed that something was wrong. The cows were too quiet. It was not that cows are noisy animals, but with sixty cows in the loafing area outside the barn, there was usually a moo to be heard here and there, and the sound of manure or urine as it hit the ground in the holding pen was almost a constant. As he got closer, Paul could see by the light from the barn that there were no cows waiting.

It was not that unusual for a few of his cows to be missing, and on occasion none would be there, but that was rare. Paul Overholt cupped his hands around his mouth to form a mini-megaphone and called out, "Sook, cowwww! Sook, sook, sook, sook, cowwww!" It was the same call that his father and grandfather had used. Most everyone he knew called their cows the same way. He didn't even think to question the fact that it sounded silly.

The cows would be there soon enough; their late arrival would just give him a chance to get ready. Paul walked into the cooler room and checked the 1,500-gallon stainless steel cooler to be sure everything was operating correctly. The temperature of the milk in the cooler from last night's milking was precisely 39 degrees Fahrenheit, just right. The next thing to do was to run a strong chlorine solution through the pipes of the system to kill any bacteria. Having completed that, Paul thought that at least a few of the cows should have gotten to the barn.

At that moment his wife walked in. "Where are the cows?" she asked.

"Aren't they out there yet?" Paul asked.

"Not a one," she answered.

"I called them."

"I know. I heard you."

"I don't know," he said. "I guess I must have left the gate

closed last night. I don't think so, but I'll go check. Go ahead and fill the feeders with silage and mix up some iodine dip."

Paul left the milk barn and walked down toward the field by the creek. He couldn't remember closing the gate but it would not be the first time he had done something without thinking about it, especially when he had something else on his mind. Last night he had been thinking about a conversation he had had with his brothers on the night before the Disaster and . . .

Paul Overholt stumbled and fell to the ground. He had tripped over something — a cow. It didn't move as Paul fell over it, so it was unlikely it was just asleep. Paul wished he had brought the flashlight. He looked closely and even in the dark could see it was dead and well bloated, meaning it had been dead for at least several hours. Quickly he went to the barn, got the flashlight, and headed back. He found the dead cow and shone the light on it. There was no sign of a predator; no blood anywhere, so it wasn't some crazy hunter; the cow's belly wasn't discolored so it hadn't been struck by lightning; and the cow was not a 'new milker,' so it couldn't be milk fever. He'd have to check closer when it was light and call the vet to find out what had killed her. He didn't want something spreading among his herd. Depending on what it was, they might also have to dump the previous night's milk.

For now there was still another puzzle that needed to be solved. Paul continued toward the gate he thought he might have left closed. It was wide open. He called the cows again. Paul brought his light to bear on something lying on the path. It was another cow, bloated and stiff. Paul had no idea what was happening. He ran toward the creek at the end of the field. There was another cow and it was dead, too. And then another, and another. Paul froze and lifted the light above his head and shone it over the field in front of him. All around him and especially down by the creek, cows lay motionless and bloated.

Gdansk, Poland

Dr. Alexander Zielenski carried his five-year-old daughter, Anna, in his arms to the emergency room at St. Stanisława Hospital. She had gotten sick during the night with what seemed like a common stomach ache but as time passed the symptoms grew worse instead of better. He tried to treat the illness himself but after she had several fits of uncontrollable vomiting, followed by severe purging, he had decided to bring Anna to the hospital. The parking lot was full, which was unusual for this time of day, so he drove around to the physicians' lot and parked in his reserved spot. Entering the emergency room, he discovered why the lot was full. All around him men, women, and children waited to be seen. The few who were well enough sat in chairs or on benches. Others lay on the floor, comforted by family members. The air reeked with the fetor of vomit.

Dr. Zielenski scanned their faces. Their features were sunken, as if they had suffered severe malnourishment.

"Thank goodness you're here, Alexander," he heard a familiar voice say from behind him. "We need all the help we can get."

Turning, he saw it was his colleague, Dr. Josef Markiewicz. "Oh, my," Dr. Markiewicz said as he saw Anna in her father's arms. "It's hit poor Anna, too."

"What is it?" Zielenski asked.

"We're not sure, yet," Markiewicz answered, leading Zielenski into an empty office where they could talk privately. "Based on the symptoms, we're guessing its cholera, but we're running tests to be sure. The onset is marked by burning in the stomach and throat, followed by severe vomiting and then diarrhea. The stools are all fecal at first, but later take on a rice-water appearance, and often contain blood. The patient suffers from extreme thirst and dehydration, but anything they drink comes back up within minutes. There is weakness and physical collapse; the features become sunken; the skin moist and cyanosed; and additional pain comes from cramping in the calves. The pulse is increasingly weak and irregular, and respiration becomes more and more difficult. Death . . ."

"You've had deaths!" Zielenski interrupted, instinctively holding his daughter more tightly to him.

"Three so far here. I spoke with Lech at St. Tadeusz. They've had two so far and I understand there's been more than a dozen in Warsaw."

"I had no idea. How could cholera strike so quickly over such a widespread area?"

Dr. Markiewicz shook his head.

"I've got to get Anna cared for," Zielenski said, satisfied he understood what was happening, though he didn't know the cause.

"Let's get her checked in and we can start her on an IV right away to restore her fluids."

At that moment the door opened and in stepped Dr. Jakob Nowak. "Good," he began, "One of the nurses said you were in here."

"I've got to get my daughter started on an IV. Can this wait?" Zielenski asked.

"This will only take a minute," Nowak insisted. "We were wrong. This isn't cholera."

"Then what is it?" Zielenski asked, not giving Nowak a chance to finish.

"All these people have been poisoned," Nowak said. "It's arsenic," he continued before Zielenski could interrupt again. "It's all over Poland."

"But how?" Zielenski asked in disbelief.

"It's in the water."

Chapter 8

God Amok

August 18, 2021 — The United Nations, New York

"We've received reports of thousands of cases of arsenic poisoning from all over the world," Dr. Sumit Parekh of the World Health Organization told the special meeting of the U.N. Security Council. "With the cloud of volcanic dust continuing to spread and worsen, at first we thought that the arsenic was from the cloud. But atmospheric samples from the cloud taken at various altitudes in different parts of the world showed no significant levels of arsenic — certainly not enough to cause widespread poisoning. That's when we made the connection to the dust of the third asteroid.

"You're saying the asteroid was made of arsenic?" asked Ambassador Clark, who represented North America.

"Not all of it, no. But enough to create a problem, yes. It's unusual for an asteroid to contain sufficient levels of arsenic to cause what we're experiencing; most tested meteorites contain only trace amounts of arsenic, usually less than .1 percent of their total composition."[7]

"Has this theory been tested?" asked Ambassador Rashid, who represented the Middle East.

"Yes," Parekh answered. "Of the pieces of the asteroid that reached earth in identifiable fragments, most are no larger than a softball. A few of the recovered pieces have been turned over to museums and universities, but most have been kept as souvenirs by the people who found them. Luther College in Decorah, Iowa, has one of the larger pieces, weighing 288 pounds. Working with the college we have confirmed the hypothesis: running through the asteroid fragment are veins of a dull gray brittle material which, when chipped, reveals a tin-white color with a distinct metallic luster. Further tests have verified it. The third asteroid was apparently honeycombed with arsenic. We believe this is what caused the asteroid to shatter so completely when it was hit by the first volley of missiles. Now, as the dust of the asteroid settles to the earth, it has entered the water table, polluting lakes and rivers and reservoirs and poisoning the drinking water of thousands of communities."

"But the poisoning seems so random," Ambassador Clark said. "It hits one city and skips another altogether."

"We believe this is due to a number of factors, including the weather patterns. Like rainfall, some areas have received heavy amounts, while others have been passed over completely as prevailing winds blow the arsenic dust safely past. Where it falls, shallow rivers and reservoirs are more affected because the smaller volume of water creates a greater concentration of the arsenic. The deeper the river or reservoir, the less the concentration. Because they are fed by underground springs and generally have very limited exposed surface area, most wells have been unaffected. Other factors such as water temperature and pH levels dramatically affect the dissolution of arsenic into the water.

---

[7] *The Merck Index*, Ninth Edition, (Rahway, N.J.: Merck & Co., Inc., 1976), p. 107, item 820.

Because arsenic is colorless, odorless and tasteless in water, each water source must be tested."

"Will the water supply stay like this?" Clark asked. "Is there something that can be done to purify it?"

"With seasonal changes, temperature and pH balance shifts, and settling of the arsenic, eventually — perhaps in six months — most water supplies should become potable again. Until then, affected areas will have to ship in their water."

Nine months later: May 9, 2022 — Jerusalem

No one saw them arrive. No one had seen them at all since before the first asteroid. Then suddenly, they were back — the prophets, the lunatics, as unwelcome as the message they would certainly bring. Slowly and purposefully they walked through the streets of Jerusalem, again and again repeating in Hebrew, "Woe! Woe! Woe to the inhabitants of the earth, because of the trumpet blasts about to be sounded by the other three angels!"[8]

The sky over Jerusalem was as gray as the ash-covered sackcloth that hung on their bodies, yet no rain cloud could be found. For two and a half years the fields of kibbutzim lay parched and barren. Only those fields irrigated by water from Israel's desalinization plants produced any crops. Instead, the gray that filled the sky was the slowly-thinning but ever-present shroud of volcanic ash. The last volcanic eruption had been five months before, but the shroud remained, darkening by as much as a third the light of the sun by day and of the moon and stars at night.

All that the two men had foretold had been fulfilled and now they were back; and though much of the rest of the world had ignored the connection between the prophecies of these men and what had befallen the world, the people of Jerusalem knew.

A local news team was dispatched to follow the men to

---

[8] Revelation 8:13.

report on what they foretold. But again and again they repeated only, "Woe! Woe! Woe to the inhabitants of the earth, because of the trumpet blasts about to be sounded by the other three angels!" A strange energy seemed to surround the two men, causing those nearby to shudder with fear. No one dared approach them. Soon police arrived, but even they held back and only watched.

The situation remained unchanged for several hours. The prophets walked, repeating their message; the police surrounded them and the cameras and reporters followed. Then the situation changed. The men moved toward the Temple Mount.

The United Nations, New York

When Decker arrived at Christopher Goodman's office he found Robert Milner already there. The television was on and it was obvious they had already heard the news from Jerusalem. Christopher pointed without speaking to a large leather chair next to his and Decker sat down, joining them in front of the screen. Decker recognized the setting immediately. It was a street near the Temple Mount in the old city of Jerusalem; he had been there more than once. A British reporter described the action.

"The two men continued without incident until it became clear to local police that they intended to approach the Temple, Judaism's most sacred shrine, and Israel's most popular tourist attraction. Concerned that the two fanatics would disrupt worshipers and visitors to the Temple, police ordered the men to stop, but they ignored the order. At that point, a squad of police moved in to arrest the men. As the twelve-man squad of police approached, the two finally stopped repeating their single message, and, as you can see from the video from our local affiliate, apparently warned the police to stay back, calling out in Hebrew, 'Stay back or taste the wrath of God.' The police continued to advance, and then . . ."

As Decker, Christopher, and Milner watched, the entire

squad of Israeli police began to convulse and cry out in pain and then suddenly burst into flame. It was not that their uniforms were set afire; rather the fires came from inside their bodies, burning outward and only coincidentally igniting their clothing. It was a horrible sight but the camera stayed with it, catching every gruesome minute as the two men in sackcloth stood surrounded by screaming and burning flesh. Decker was not certain — the picture through the flames was not that clear and the screams covered all other sounds — but he thought he saw the two men weep.

"Additional police then opened fire on the men," the British reporter continued, "with equally disastrous effect." A round of shots rang out but it was as though the bullets never reached the men. Rather, like their colleagues before them, the police who fired the shots were incinerated. After a moment of the grisly display, the reporter continued.

"With the police dead or dying and reinforcements nowhere in sight, no one tried to stop the men as they walked in silence past mounds of charred human flesh toward the Temple."

The scene changed, indicating that a few moments had been edited out. In ash-covered sackcloth, John and Cohen now stood before the broad stone steps leading up to the Temple. Temple Police stood back, their rifles at the ready, seemingly keeping the crowds of worshipers and tourists from venturing too near the men, though no one would have dared to approach. Halfway up the steps, alone except for a few assistants standing behind him, stood a bearded man dressed in elaborate robes and head covering. The reporter continued:

"When they arrived at the steps to the Temple, the Jewish High Priest, Chaim Levin, a man rarely caught on camera, was waiting midway down the steps. It is unclear whether he intended to confront the men or had come to see the disturbance for himself. Whether out of fear or respect of the High Priest, or whether getting Chaim Levin's attention was their only intent, the two men went no farther. Instead, they simply repeated their message so that all could hear, adding that the first woe would come soon; then they turned and simply walked away. Our affiliate's cameras followed the men as they moved away from the Temple, followed by police and some of the more venturesome onlookers."

The scene changed again, showing John and Cohen on the northern edge of the modern city.

"Outside the city, Israeli military awaited the men's approach. They were obviously uneasy, perhaps fearing the same fate as had befallen the police. But at the city's edge, in the plain view of hundreds of people and of our cameras, as you can see in this incredible footage, the two men stopped and then simply vanished."

As the reporter spoke the words, John and Cohen disappeared, leaving a crowd of police, reporters, soldiers, and others gasping and staring at one another in disbelief.

"That these men, known as John and Cohen, have unusual powers is now undeniable," the reporter said, now appearing on the screen himself for the first time since the report began. "Many in Israel attribute the long Israeli drought to these men and point to the striking similarities between their predictions last January and the devastation brought on by the three asteroids. Some in Israel firmly believe that these men and their followers are responsible for causing the asteroids to leave their orbits and head toward the earth.

"Whoever they are," the commentator concluded, "considering what they have done here today, the questions must be asked: do these people represent God as they claim? Are they latter-day prophets? Or does their power come from somewhere else? And if they do represent God, one more question seems reasonable to ask: Has God gone amok?"

Milner reached over and turned off the set.

"Can't you do something to stop them?" Decker pleaded.

"It's still not time," Christopher answered, shaking his head. "The world is not yet ready to receive the truth."

"But can you be sure?" Decker insisted.

"In the desert in Israel, my father told me that only when I fully understand what I am to tell the people of the world — only when I understand the full truth about myself — only then will it be time."

"And?" Decker pressed.

Christopher shook his head in obvious frustration.

"But we can't let this go on," Decker pressed. "You've got to do something! Someone has to stop them!"

Christopher dropped his head and put his hands on his temples as if to keep his head from exploding from the pressure. He appeared to be in pain. Decker had never seen Christopher like this.

"Decker," Milner said, "there's nothing he can do."

Decker knew that if there was anything Christopher could do, then surely he would have done it already. It was just the frustration, the pain, the anger. The world was collapsing, millions had died, half the world was struggling to find enough food to survive, and yet there was nothing they could do. Decker put his hand on Christopher's shoulder. "I'm sorry, Christopher," he said. "I know this hurts you, too. It's just so damned frustrating!"

"I know, Decker," Christopher said quietly, not looking up.

"So for now we just wait?" Decker asked.

"At least they won't do any more harm to the earth." Christopher raised his head, letting his fingers glide down the side of his face where they intertwined into folded hands. "Now they will turn their attention strictly to injuring the people."

The thought was not consoling.

Chapter 9

Swarm

July 1, 2022 — Jerusalem

It was almost two months before John and Cohen were seen again and their return was much the same as their previous advent, except that this time the police had strict orders not to interfere or attempt to apprehend the pair unless they clearly threatened the public safety or government property. Again they walked through the streets of Jerusalem repeating their message, and again they went to the steps of the Temple. This time their message was much more lengthy. As translated in the papers the next day, the message read:

> *Hear O nations of the world what the Lord, the God of Israel, who made the heavens and the earth says: "Cursed are they who trust in their own flesh and whose hearts are turned away from the Lord. They will be like a bush in the land that the locusts consume." Listen! The fifth angel sounded his trumpet and a star*

that fell from the sky to the earth was given the key to the shaft of the Abyss. When he opened the Abyss, smoke rose from it like the smoke of a huge furnace. The sun and sky are darkened by the smoke. And out of the smoke locusts swarm down upon the earth and are given power like that of scorpions. They have been told not to harm the grass or any plant or tree, but only those people who do not have the seal of God on their foreheads. They have been forbidden to kill men, but are given power to torture them for five months. And the agony shall be like the sting of a scorpion when it strikes. So great shall the agony be that men will seek death, but they will not find it; they will long to die, but death will not take them.

As before, after John and Cohen delivered their message at the Temple, they left and walked to the northern edge of the city. With witnesses all around and cameras broadcasting the live scene around the world, they once again vanished. There were no deaths this time, which made for dull television, but it gave the networks a chance to rerun their footage of the fiery deaths during the duo's previous appearance.

July 11, 2022 — New York

Decker Hawthorne tipped the driver and got out of the cab in front of the U.N. Secretariat Building. It was a hazy, dreary day as were most days, but it was getting better. Much of the volcanic ash had settled and the temperature was now only eight degrees below the normal average, but only infrequently was the sun seen clearly. Grass was growing again: there was that much to be thankful for. And while the diminished sunlight had stunted the growth of grain grasses, there would be at least a modest harvest.

As Decker approached the revolving doors into the

Secretariat's lobby he heard what sounded like a helicopter approaching and looked up. But instead of a helicopter it seemed as if the volcanic ash cover had suddenly become a thick gray liquid, slowly pouring out upon the earth. He squinted, hoping to get a clearer focus, but to no avail. As the darkness descended, the sound intensified. Decker ran and ducked for protection under the overhang of the building in front of the door and then looked up again. The sound was now a roar that seemed to fill the sky over the entire city. The bulk of the dark mass was a hundred feet above the ground, but parts of it had already reached the tree tops. Around him Decker heard sudden shrill screams and then he saw what it was: an immense swarm of insects of a type he had never seen before. They were as large as small birds and there were millions of them.

Decker ran for the door but a dozen of the insects had already landed on him. He made it inside, but in doing so he allowed a hundred more to fly past him into the building. Most of the insects clung to his clothes but one climbed up his collar to his neck. Decker reached up to knock it away but it was too late. Searing pain nearly knocked him off his feet as the creature simultaneously stung him with a stinger in its tail and bit into the soft flesh of his neck to feast on his blood. In the lobby people screamed and swatted desperately as the insects bit and stung their exposed flesh.

The pain seemed unbearable but Decker tried again to grab at the one on his neck, hoping to crush it in his hand. It was larger than he expected, nearly filling his palm. Unable to crush it, Decker ripped it from his neck and flung it to the floor and stepped on it. He put his full weight on the creature before its exoskeleton finally gave way, spitting guts and blood — some of it Decker's — onto the floor.

Outside, people ran through the streets, vainly hoping to escape or to get to an open door. Those inside the building, fearing the insects would enter along with the fleeing people, locked or blocked the doors, leaving the unfortunates to fend for themselves. True to the prophecy, only those who had 'the seal of God on their foreheads' — the members of the Koum Damah Patar with their bloody sign of membership written above their brow — were spared. A pair of KDP members who had been across the street from the U.N. when Decker arrived stood watching the attack, completely untouched by the insects.

All around Decker the screams and swatting increased as more people from the plaza area in front of the Secretariat came in the revolving doors, each time letting in more of the insects. In his agony, Decker was totally unaware of the additional insects which still clung to his clothing. Then suddenly he felt another fiery sting on his left ankle just above his shoe, and then immediately another on his left thigh, and then another on his right calf near the back of his knee. They were all over him, chewing and thrashing at the fabric of his suit with their teeth and spiny legs, digging their heads and stingers down into his flesh. As each one stung he grabbed at it and threw it to the floor, but the pain had become too excruciating for him to step on them. As they hit the hard tile floor the insects lay stunned for a few seconds and then reoriented themselves and either flew to another victim or reattached themselves to Decker. Finally Decker fell to the floor, writhing in pain as two more insects crawled inside the back of his suit coat and began tearing at his shirt. He was in too much pain to continue to fight, but with all the strength he had left he managed to roll over on his back, hoping to smash them. It only drove the stingers deeper.

There was a stampede to get away from the lobby: people were pushing and shoving and climbing over each other. Those who could find an open door ducked into offices, locking the door behind them to keep others out.

Lying on his back unable to move, another insect landed on Decker's face. As it was about to sting him, Decker passed out. When he did, the insect strangely seemed to lose interest and flew away. The others on him did the same. The two on his back beneath him released their hold and scratched and squirmed along his back trying to get out from under him. As entomologists would discover later, the insects would not attack a victim that had already been driven into unconsciousness by their stings.

Outside, thousands of the insects flew into the plate glass, trying to reach the people inside. The collision only seemed to stun them and the sidewalk below the window became alive with the wobbly insects attempting to regain their bearings and fly away.

Perhaps the insects' greatest weakness was their persistence; once they had landed on a victim they would not cease their attack until they had drunk their fill of blood or until the person fell unconscious. This persistence added to the fierceness of their attack but it also made them 'sitting ducks.' By the time additional security personnel from all over the building began to reach the lobby, most of the insects had already attached themselves to their selected victims, and except for those withdrawing from unconscious victims, few were left to interfere with the security personnel's efforts. As one group of the security force ensured that no more insects would get in the doors, others attempted to help the victims and quickly found, as Decker had, that the best way to kill the creatures was to pull them from their host, throw them to the hard floor, and then to step on them with their full weight.

Soon afterward teams from the U.N.'s medical facility arrived and began helping the victims. Scores lay unconscious on the floor while others screamed in pain from the welts that rose where they had been stung. A security guard who had captured two of the insects alive held one in each hand by the backs of their strange trunks as they squirmed and struggled in his hands, trying in vain to reach some part of his flesh with their stingers. He had pulled the insects from the face and leg of an elderly woman as they sucked the blood from their nearly unconscious victim. Someone would no doubt want to have a look at the peculiar creatures. Standing there, he began to wonder where he would find a glass jar large enough to put them in.

Outside, the rumbling of the insects' wings suddenly grew louder as millions of them began to fly away. Within thirty seconds they were all gone: headed for another part of the city and fresh victims. The sidewalk and street were littered with unconscious people lying in crumpled heaps.

□   □   □

There was no consensus and not even very many guesses among entomologists as to the particular species or even genus of the insect. Whatever it was, it was something no one had ever before reported — a strange mutation without explanation. The insects ranged from two and a half to three inches in length and were approximately three-quarters of an inch across the back, and slightly less than that thick. Their wings were sturdy but transparent with a wingspan of a little more than six inches. They were covered with a thick dark gray exoskeleton over most of the body, giving the appearance of heavy armor. It was this aegis that made crushing the insects so difficult. Over the head of the insect the exoskeleton was spiny and luminous gold with perhaps a hundred inch-long soft fibers extruding from beneath that looked remarkably like human hair. The insect's face bore an eerie resemblance to a human face but was somewhat flatter. Its mouth, which, relative to a human face was easily twice as wide, exhibited fearsome-looking fangs which it used to rapidly chew through clothing and then bite its victim. The tail of the insect carried a large stinger, used to inject its victim with an unidentified poison.

The insects traveled in immense swarms up to fifteen miles across, and stayed in one place just long enough to feed off conscious victims before moving on. The swarm that descended on the United Nations Plaza was now moving northeast, but it was just one of hundreds of swarms that had appeared suddenly throughout the world. In areas of the world where shelters were constructed of materials less substantial than concrete, steel, and glass, far more people were bitten and stung by the creatures than had been in New York.

Laboratory dissection revealed an additional feature that added to the entomologists' confusion about the origin of the insects: they had absolutely no identifiable reproductive organs.

□   □   □

Five hours later Decker regained consciousness. In his arm, a needle fed his vein with saline solution to prevent dehydration. He was in the U.N. medical facility surrounded by other victims, some conscious, others not. Like Decker, those who were conscious wished they were not. The shrill cries of agony had yielded to sorrowful moans, not because the victims had obtained relief from the anguish but because they were too exhausted to cry out. The U.N. medical facility was not designed to handle anywhere near this many patients, but the New York hospitals were all filled beyond capacity with other victims. There was simply nowhere else to put them.

All around him there was moaning and weeping, but Decker didn't care. A few were pleading for termination, but Decker was in too much pain to be distracted by someone else's problems. Huge welts, six to eight inches in diameter, covered his body in sixteen places from his neck to his ankle. His temperature had risen to 103 degrees as his body fought the poison. Never had he experienced such pain. Decker was whimpering and tears rolled down his cheeks but he didn't even know it. The doctors had tried the maximum dosages of a dozen different pain killers but nothing provided any relief. Every second was like an eternity. Torment was all he knew.

Beside his bed, amidst the forest of IV stands with their clear plastic vines, a familiar face looked down upon him, but Decker could not see it. Christopher Goodman looked around to be sure there were no doctors or nurses nearby and then reached down and touched Decker on his forehead. As he did, a wave of sweet relief immediately swept over Decker's body. He was exhausted but in that instant the pain and fever were entirely gone.

"How are you, old friend?" Christopher asked with a smile.

Now Decker wept with relief. "Thank you," he cried as he reached out to touch Christopher's arm.

"I came as soon as I found out," Christopher answered.

Decker looked around at the others who still lay there, and then looked up at Christopher. Christopher nodded and left Decker. Quickly he moved among the other patients but, unlike he had done with Decker, as he touched each person, Christopher softly whispered "sleep," and they slipped into a quiet peaceful rest, unaware of the gift they had been given.

Decker struggled to keep his eyes open and watched as Christopher left the room to go to other patients. Then he fell asleep.

Chapter 10

Naorimashita

July 13, 2022 — New York

Decker awoke to find a team of U.N. doctors examining the places on his body where he had been stung. His welts had disappeared, as had the welts on the other patients. The doctors could not understand it. Everywhere else in the world, the victims from the first day of the insects' attack were still suffering. The research on the insects' poison indicated that it could take five days to a week for the pain to subside. But here was a single isolated group of patients for whom the norm mysteriously did not hold true. Not only were they no longer suffering; they were entirely recovered, some reporting that they felt better than they had in years.

Decker sat up. Some of the other patients had already left. "How long have I been here?" he asked the doctor in charge.

"Two days," she answered.

"And the, uh . . ." Decker struggled, not sure exactly what to call the insects that had attacked him.

"Locusts?" the doctor said, completing Decker's question. Decker nodded, a little surprised at her choice of terms. "They've moved on for now but they're still with us."

Decker found his clothes and shoes in a cabinet and started to dress. It was a new suit and he was distracted by the holes made by the insects. He dressed and looked in the mirror. Between the two-day growth of beard and the ruined suit he looked pretty unkempt. He could clean up and change clothes later, though: right now he wanted to see Christopher.

□   □   □

"I'm so glad you're all right!" Jackie Hansen said as she ran to hug Decker when he arrived at Christopher's office at the Italian Mission. "I visited you in the medical facility, but you were in so much pain, I don't think you knew I was there."

"I don't remember much of anything except pain," Decker said, returning the hug. "Is Christopher in?"

"He just stepped out. I expect him back any minute. You can wait in his office if you like," Jackie offered.

"Thanks," Decker said, and started toward Christopher's door.

"Secretary Milner is waiting for him as well."

"Oh," Decker responded. It seemed anymore that Milner could almost always be found near Christopher.

"By the way, nice suit," Jackie added with a smile, as she put her little finger in one of the holes left by the locusts.

Decker rolled his eyes.

When Decker entered, Milner was at Christopher's desk on the telephone. Milner looked up at him and seemed to be inspecting him unapprovingly; it wasn't just the holes in his suit or the two-day growth on his face. There was something more.

Decker nodded in greeting, not quite sure what caused the strange reaction from Milner, and then walked over to look out Christopher's window. The street below was nearly deserted.

There were fewer than a dozen cars and only a couple of quickly-moving pedestrians. A moment later Christopher walked in. "Decker, how are you?" Christopher asked with some excitement in his voice.

"I feel wonderful," Decker answered. "Thank you for what you did. I guess I shouldn't be surprised, but I didn't know you could do that."

"I didn't either," Christopher answered. "It just seemed like the natural thing to do at the time."

Robert Milner got off the phone and was about to join the conversation, but Christopher spoke first. "Welcome back," he said, looking in Milner's direction. "I thought you were in Spain."

"I was," Milner answered, "until I heard about what happened at the U.N. medical facility."

"You mean people know what happened!?" Decker interrupted.

"No," Christopher answered calmly. "Not exactly. They just know that for some unexplained reason the people in the facility had an unusually quick recovery."

"Christopher, you cannot be taking this kind of chance," Milner said. "What if someone had seen you?" Milner's voice was raised but it was clearly out of concern, not anger.

"When I heard that Decker had been stung I couldn't just leave him there," Christopher insisted.

"No," Milner said, frowning and shaking his head as he looked over at Decker. "I guess you couldn't. But did you have to heal everyone else while you were there? It would be a lot easier for doctors to overlook one person who had a miraculous recovery, but a whole facility?"

"They were in so much pain. I had to do something."

"Christopher, people are in pain all over the world. Over 400 million died in the China-India-Pakistan War; hundreds of millions more died because of the asteroids. China is starving because millions of acres of farmland along the coast are ruined by the salt left behind by the tsunami. The west coasts of North and South

America are wastelands. What's left of Japan, the Philippines, and all the other countries that used to depend on the Pacific for fishing, are having to ration food and are deep in economic depression. The crop harvest all over the world is a fraction of what is needed . . ." Milner discontinued the list, though he could have gone on. "But you know as well as I do," he concluded, "this is part of the process. It's like labor pains. It's a necessary part of the birth of the coming age. If you subvert that mechanism of change, you may remove the pain but you also risk undermining the birth process."

"Bob, it was only a few people," Christopher reasoned.

"From what I hear, it was over a hundred."

"But that can't possibly make any difference in the overall scheme of things."

"It might, if anyone saw you."

"I was very careful."

Milner sighed; he had made his point and didn't care to argue specifics. "Well," he said, and then sighed again, "I guess there's nothing we can do about it now anyway."

"It'll be okay," Christopher said.

"But you can't let this happen again. I know it's hard when you see the suffering up close, but you cannot let your heart rule your head."

"I know, Bob, I know," Christopher answered. "Thank you for being here to remind me."

"And you're sure no one saw you?"

"I was very careful."

There was a pause and Decker took the opportunity to try to get answers to some questions he had. "The doctor at the medical facility called the insects 'locusts.' Was that just a coincidence or do people realize that John and Cohen are behind all of this? I mean, I assume that those things are the 'locusts' that John and Cohen prophesied."

Robert Milner pulled a copy of *The New York Times* from his briefcase. Nearly the entire front section was filled with articles about the 'locusts' — where they had attacked, estimates of how many people had been stung, protective measures to seal homes and other buildings to keep the locusts out — and an international poll showing that 66 percent of those polled said they thought John and Cohen were responsible for the locusts. Milner pointed at an article titled "Search for 'Prophets' Continues in Israel."

"They won't find them, of course," Milner said.

Decker sat down and quickly scanned one of the articles. The swarms of locusts had struck throughout the northern hemisphere and the tropics. The only areas of the world that were spared were in the southern hemisphere where it was late winter. Apparently the locusts were sensitive to cold climate. The swarms were so large that they were easily tracked by satellite and radar, enabling the World Meteorological Organization to provide some advance warning to inhabitants when a swarm was approaching a city. However, it was never really safe to be outside because smaller swarms of stragglers became separated from the larger swarms and their movements were impossible to track and predict. So far the use of U.N.-approved pesticides had been unsuccessful on the insects.

In addition to the agonizing pain it caused, the locusts' poison also caused the victim's kidneys and liver to go into overdrive, and though this did little to eliminate the poison, it rendered painkillers of no benefit. Ironically, it had the same effect on the U.N.-approved thanatotopic (death inducing) drugs, and for an as-yet-unknown reason, even sodium potassium ATPase inhibitors were ineffective. So it was that, though many victims would have gladly chosen life completion rather than enduring the pain, none of the drugs approved by the World Health Organization for completion assistance was of any use to them.

"I have a meeting in Barcelona in four and a half hours," Milner said, as he closed up his briefcase. "I need to be on the next supersonic out of Kennedy."

Decker looked up from the paper. "Be careful getting to

your car."

"My driver is picking me up out front. It's relatively safe as long as you're not out for more than a few minutes. Besides, they tell me you can hear the locusts coming."

"Well, yes," Decker said from experience, "if they're in a large swarm."

"It will only take me a few seconds to reach the car. I'm sure I'll be fine."

"Okay," Decker said. "But believe me, you do **not** want to get stung by one of those things!"

"I'll keep that in mind," Milner said.

Decker went back to the article he was reading while Christopher walked out with Milner. When Christopher returned, Decker offered, "Well, I understand what you did. And I appreciate it."

"He just wants what's best," Christopher responded. "He's looking at the big picture."

"Sure, but I don't know how he can expect you to just stand by and do nothing if you can stop someone's suffering."

Christopher shrugged. There was nothing more to say on the matter. "What are your plans?" he asked.

"Well, I'd like to go home and get cleaned up and change clothes but I'm not too excited about going back outside. It was bad enough running over here from across the street," he said, referring to his route from the U.N. to the Italian Mission. "I'm not real comfortable about running three blocks and up a long flight of stairs to the Hermitage." Decker's apartment in the Hermitage was conveniently close to the U.N., but it meant he had no need for a car, and there were few cab drivers willing to risk going out with the locusts. If Decker wanted to get home, it would have to be on foot.

Christopher's phone beeped, indicating an intercom call from Jackie Hansen. "Mr. Ambassador, Ambassador Tanaka is here to see you," she said, referring to the ambassador from Japan who served as the Primary member of the Security Council from the

Pacific Basin countries.

"I wasn't expecting anyone," he said, but it would have been a serious breach of etiquette to keep the Ambassador waiting. "Send him in," he said after a moment. Ambassador Tanaka was a slender man in his mid-seventies. He had been a Primary member of the Security Council for the past seven years and an Alternate member for two years before that.

"Mr. Ambassador," Tanaka began when he came in. "I apologize for the intrusion, but I . . ."

"It's no intrusion, Mr. Ambassador," Christopher assured him politely. "What can I do for you?"

The Japanese Ambassador looked uncomfortable, as though either he didn't know how to begin or that what he had planned to say now seemed inappropriate and more difficult than he had anticipated. Christopher waited.

"Mr. Ambassador, as you know, I have long been a supporter of the fine work of Secretary Robert Milner and the Lucius Trust. For many years Secretary Milner has talked of the coming of a '*Krishnamurti*,' the Ruler of the New Age." Ambassador Tanaka was obviously uncomfortable talking about this, but even more he was intent upon completing the mission he had begun. Decker tried not to show his own discomfort at where it appeared Tanaka might be going with this. "It was said among those at the Trust," Tanaka continued, "that both Secretary Milner and Alice Bernley would see the Krishnamurti before their deaths." Tanaka paused again and then continued. "Director Bernley is dead." Ambassador Tanaka stopped and looked down at the floor. Decker looked at the ceiling and bit the inside of his lower lip, now certain he knew where Ambassador Tanaka's soliloquy was leading. "Please," Tanaka pled, "my granddaughter has been stung by the locusts. She is near death. She was here visiting from Japan and . . ."

"Mr. Ambassador, no one has actually died from the locusts' stings," Christopher said, but the interruption did not deter Tanaka.

"Ambassador Goodman, are you the Krishnamurti, the Ruler of the New Age?"

Decker dropped his head into his hand. He was glad that Ambassador Tanaka was not looking at him. He was sure the look on his face would have given away the truth. Peeking through his fingers he was relieved to see that Christopher was handling the question more calmly.

"Ambassador Tanaka," Christopher responded, "Secretary Milner has told me of this prophesied ruler as well, but I'm afraid that . . ."

"I know that you healed the people in the U.N. medical facility," Tanaka interrupted.

Christopher fell silent. Tanaka continued. "Ms. Love told me that you were seen leaving immediately after the healings occurred," he said, referring to Gaia Love, who had taken over as director of the Lucius Trust after Alice Bernley's death. "Please, if you are the Krishnamurti, you must heal my granddaughter. She is very young, only eight years old. She was stung eleven times."

At that moment the door opened and Decker and Christopher saw Jackie Hansen attempting to block the path of a Japanese man in his early thirties. In his arms he carried the limp body of a young girl — the ambassador's granddaughter — tightly wrapped in a thick blue cotton blanket because of her fever. "Sir," Jackie Hansen was saying, "you cannot go in unannounced."

"It's all right," Christopher said after a moment. "Let him in."

Jackie let the man enter and closed the door behind him. "This is my son Yasushi and," Tanaka lovingly pulled the blanket from his granddaughter's face, "this is my granddaughter Keiko."

Christopher looked at the girl for a moment and then pulled his gaze away, turning sharply to look out his window. "I'm sorry," he said finally, "there's nothing I can do. She should be in a hospital."

"The doctors say there is nothing they can do," Tanaka countered. "But you can heal her."

"I'm sorry," Christopher said again.

A look of defeat slowly replaced the look of hope that had been on the ambassador's face. For a moment Tanaka just stood there as Christopher continued looking out the window. Finally, Tanaka looked at his son and then down at the floor. "I'm sorry to have bothered you, Mr. Ambassador," Tanaka said, and motioned toward the door for his son to exit. Christopher continued to look away as Ambassador Tanaka, his son, and granddaughter left, shutting the door behind them.

Christopher turned and looked at the door and then at Decker. Then suddenly, he went to the door and opened it. "Mr. Ambassador," he called after them. "Ambassador Tanaka," he called. "Please come back."

Tanaka was back in the office immediately, followed quickly by his son and granddaughter. Christopher stood by the door and closed it as they came in. "Mr. Ambassador, you have put me in a very awkward position," Christopher said.

"Then you will heal her?" Tanaka asked, hoping to secure a positive response before Christopher could change his mind.

"I will heal her," Christopher answered. "But I must have your word, and that of your son, that you will not reveal any of this to *anyone*. Especially not to Secretary Milner or Ms. Love," he added almost under his breath.

"Yes, of course. Anything," Tanaka said, and then turned to his son, who also agreed.

Christopher walked over to the little girl. Carefully, he pulled the blanket back from her face to look at her. One of the welts was on her right forehead, causing the whole side of her face to swell and horribly distorting her tender features. Touching her where the locust had stung, he whispered in Japanese, "*Naorimashita*," meaning 'you are healed,' and immediately the swelling was gone. Decker looked at Christopher and was struck by what appeared to be a momentary look of foreboding that swept over Christopher's face. He had seen that look before.

Ambassador Tanaka pulled the blanket back to see his

granddaughter. All of the welts were gone, as was her fever. The look of astonishment was obvious on Ambassador Tanaka's face. It was clear that even though he had come to Christopher asking for a miracle, he did not entirely expect to see one. Dropping to his knees and bowing at Christopher's feet, he began repeating something in Japanese which Decker took to be as much worship as it was gratitude.

Christopher bent over to raise him up. "Please, Mr. Ambassador," Christopher said, "this is not necessary. Just do as you have promised. Take her somewhere for a few weeks where no one will ask any questions."

"Yes. Yes. Of course. Just as you say. She will return to Japan today with my son."

"Decker," Christopher said, "would you please have Jackie — as nonchalantly as possible — clear the office of any of the staff, then escort the ambassador, his son, and granddaughter out. Make sure that no one who might have seen them come in sees them leave." Decker nodded and left the office to do as Christopher had asked. A moment later he returned and led them out with the ambassador's granddaughter covered as she had been when they came in. As they reached the door, Christopher stopped Ambassador Tanaka. "Mr. Ambassador," Christopher said, "one question:"

"Anything," Tanaka responded.

"Do you have any idea who it was that saw me leaving the U.N. medical facility after the patients there were healed?"

"I believe it was Ms. Hansen," Tanaka answered.

"Hmm. Okay. Thank you," Christopher said. "I assume I'll be seeing you at the Security Council meeting next Thursday?"

"Yes," Tanaka said and then bowed to Christopher. It was a very low bow, especially respectful considering that Ambassador Tanaka seldom kept with the Japanese tradition of bowing when he was out of his country.

When Decker returned, Christopher had already called Jackie into his office. Decker assured Christopher that the departure had gone well, and then Jackie continued her explanation.

"I was at the facility trying to comfort Decker," she said. "I had been there for about a half an hour and I left for a moment to go to the rest room. When I returned, I saw you leaving and assumed you had been to see Decker. But when I got to his bed, he was well — they all were. The welts and fever were gone. I didn't know what to think. And then I found out the poison was supposed to take a week to wear off. I was going to ask you about it, but I wasn't sure exactly what to say, so I just kept putting it off. Then yesterday, I went to the Lucius Trust, as I often do to meditate during lunch. While I was there — I guess I looked like I had something on my mind — Gaia Love asked me what was troubling me, and I talked to her. I tried to be vague but I guess she figured it out. I hope I haven't caused too much trouble," she concluded, with a great look of concern on her face.

Christopher shook his head. "No, it's all right," he said reassuringly. "Just don't say anything to anyone else. And, please, if you have any more questions, ask me first."

Jackie nodded agreement and then started to leave but turned before she opened the door. "I do have something I'd like to ask," she said hesitantly.

"Yes?"

"Did you heal the people in the U.N. medical facility?"

"Yes," Christopher answered directly.

"And Ambassador Tanaka's granddaughter"

"Yes."

"Then . . . are you the Krishnamurti, the Messiah of the New Age?"

"Yes."

Jackie threw her arms up then covered her mouth with her hands. "I knew it. I knew it," she said.

"Jackie," Christopher said firmly. "You must not repeat this to anyone."

"No, sir, I won't," she promised. It occurred to Decker that having known him since he was only 15 years old, Jackie had never called Christopher 'sir' before, except in public.

"Thank you, Jackie. Now see if you can get things back to normal with the rest of the office."

"Yes, sir."

Decker waited until Jackie left. "I hope that was the right thing to do," Decker said once the door was shut.

"I don't think I had any choice," Christopher answered. "I was going to have to tell her sooner or later. If I had told her sooner, this would not have come up in the first place. Besides, I'm certain I can trust her."

Decker moved on to another matter that concerned him. "When you healed the Ambassador's granddaughter, there was something, I don't know, just a strange look on your face, almost like something frightened you."

"Oh, I uh . . . I'm sure it's nothing really. It's just that . . . Do you remember I told you about the strange feeling I got when I used astral projection?"

"Yeah. You said it felt like you were walking through a field, and that even though everything around you seemed peaceful, it was as though somewhere nearby there was a battle going on."

"Exactly," said Christopher. "And somehow I sensed that I was the subject of the battle. And every time I traveled by astral projection, even though I couldn't see or hear the battle, it felt like it was getting closer and fiercer. It was as though someone or something was trying to get to me, and someone or something else was trying to prevent it." Christopher shrugged and shook his head. "I don't know."

"And you experienced the same feeling when you healed the girl?" Decker asked.

Christopher nodded. "And when I healed the people at the U.N. medical facility."

"I've seen that same look on your face before: when we went to visit Secretary Milner in the hospital."

Christopher nodded again. "That was the first time I experienced it since I traveled by astral projection."

"Well, then," Decker responded, "except for that time, it seems that every time this feeling occurred has been when you were doing something that might be considered supernatural."

Christopher paused for a second and then agreed with Decker's analysis. "But what does it mean?" he asked.

Decker thought for a moment, then shook his head. "Oh, well," he said after a moment, "there's another matter we need to work on as well: What about Gaia Love?"

"I guess I'll have to call Secretary Milner on that," he said as he reached for the phone. "She'll do whatever he says. I can probably catch him before he gets to the airport, and he can call her from the plane."

"Are you going to tell him about Ambassador Tanaka's granddaughter?"

"No. There's no reason to worry him about that now. Besides," Christopher said as he began dialing the phone, "Tanaka may not be our only worry. I 'neglected' to mention that two of the people that I healed at the U.N. medical facility were wives of Security Council members."

Chapter 11

The Source of These Powers

August 23, 2022 — The Italian ambassador's residence, New York City

Ambassador Christopher Goodman sat back in his favorite chair in his large wood-paneled study watching the news as he sipped from a glass of amaretto on ice. As had been the case since they arrived, the locusts were a major news story. In addition to media coverage of the locust attacks, weather forecasters followed their movements from space by satellite. According to the report Christopher was watching, based on computer simulations, there was about a 90 percent chance that New York City would be hit again within the next two days by one or more of three nearby swarms. If this happened, the city had already made plans to shut down all but the most essential operations to keep people in their homes and off of the streets.

The doorbell rang and Christopher switched the television to the monitor at the front door. His butler was already there. It was Ambassador Toréos of Chilé, the Primary member on the Security Council who represented South America. It was unusual enough for him to be calling without an appointment, but to be here after nine o'clock and to be alone without an aide was singularly peculiar.

Christopher turned off the television and went to greet him.

"Good evening, Mr. Ambassador," Christopher said. "Come in, come in."

"Good evening," Toréos responded, a little uncomfortably. He knew it was not good protocol to call without an appointment but he was determined to speak to Christopher.

"Would you like to join me in the study?" Christopher asked, politely. "I was just enjoying a glass of amaretto. Would you care for something to drink?"

"Yes, thank you," he answered.

"What would you like?"

"Uh . . . amaretto would be fine."

Christopher looked at his butler. "Carl . . ."

"Yes, sir," the butler responded. "I'll bring it to you in the study."

"Thank you," Christopher responded. "Mr. Ambassador, if you'd like to follow me."   Ambassador Toréos followed Christopher to the study and the two men sat down. "Well, Mr. Ambassador, to what do I owe the honor?" Christopher asked, but before Toréos could answer, Carl arrived with the ambassador's drink.

"Mr. Ambassador," Toréos began after the butler left and closed the heavy double doors, "may I speak with you frankly?"

"Certainly, Mr. Ambassador," Christopher responded, and then volunteered: "Mr. Ambassador, if this is about the reforestation project for your region, let me assure you that you have my complete support."   Christopher was referring to a massive long-term project to reforest the nearly 2¼ million square miles of South American rainforests that had been destroyed by the first asteroid. It was an important project to South America but not a high priority for most of the other regions, who had problems of their own.

"Thank you, Mr. Ambassador," Toréos said. "I'm very glad to hear that, but actually this involves a far more personal matter."

Christopher tilted his head slightly to the right and raised an eyebrow. "Well, then . . ." Christopher shook his head in puzzlement, "what can I do for you?"

"Mr. Ambassador, my wife has been diagnosed with an inoperable brain tumor. The doctors say she will die within three months. Mr. Ambassador, I have never been a religious man, but in these days, who can deny there are greater powers?" Ambassador Toréos paused and took a deep breath. Christopher didn't interrupt. "I have heard that you have the power to heal. I have been told that you were responsible for the unexplained recoveries at the U.N. medical facility after the first attack by the locusts, and that you healed Ambassador Tanaka's granddaughter." Christopher let out a barely audible groan; obviously the healing of the girl had not been kept entirely secret. "If you have this power," Toréos continued, "I plead with you, I beg you . . . heal my wife. She is a good woman. I could not live without her. Please, if you have the power, do not let her die." Ambassador Toréos stopped and waited for a reply. A full minute passed. Christopher would have to answer.

"What would you have me do, Mr. Ambassador?" Christopher responded finally. "Where is your wife?"

"She is at our home in *Valparaiso*."

"Can she travel?"

"No, Mr. Ambassador."

Christopher frowned and sighed at the same time. "That's a long trip. I don't know how soon I can get away. I'll have to check my schedule."

"Oh, forgive me, Mr. Ambassador," Toréos interrupted. "I did not mean to make you travel all the way to Chile." Christopher's expression became puzzled. "If you have the power to heal," Toréos continued, "just say the word and she will be healed."

Christopher stopped, leaned back slowly in his chair, folded his hands and smiled, more to himself it seemed that at Ambassador Toréos. "You are right, Mr. Ambassador," he said after a minute, "there *are* greater powers. But they are not off in the great beyond somewhere. You say you are not a religious man, but I tell you, these powers are not a bunch of religious mumbo jumbo. The source of these powers dwells in each of us. You do not need me. Your faith that your wife can be healed though we are thousands of miles apart is power enough. Go home to your wife. She is well and she is waiting for you."

October 3, 2022

Ostensibly the purpose of the meeting was to share dinner and evening prayer. But Ambassador Jeremiah Ngordon, the Primary from East Africa, had another reason for inviting to his home his Muslim colleague, the new Primary from the Middle East, Ambassador Abduhl Rashid of Yemen. He wanted to know how Rashid intended to vote on the Consolidated Aid Package that would be presented to the Security Council the next day. Rashid was the newest Primary member of the Security Council, having taken that position when the former Primary from the Middle East, Ambassador Fahd, had retired a month earlier for health reasons. Rashid was a swing vote and although Ngordon thought he could count on his vote, Rashid had never definitively declared his support.

The Consolidated Aid Package was a major funding project to provide extended assistance to the regions hardest hit by the effects of the asteroids as well as to areas impacted by the China-India-Pakistan War. Drafted by a committee of three Primary members chaired by Christopher Goodman, its intent was to combine and expand two previous aid packages and to modify the size of contributions to be made by each of the regions. The first aid package, known as the Asia-India Relief Program, had covered only the areas affected by the China-India-Pakistan War. As serious as that war had been, the damage was, relatively speaking, localized to a single part of the world. Then had come the first and second asteroids and with them an additional U.N. aid package known as the Natural Disasters Aid Program. But no sooner had the second aid package been passed than the third asteroid caused the worldwide poisoning of one third of the world's fresh water. With the ash-filled skies only now beginning to clear, and with swarms of locusts wreaking havoc on any type of production which required working outside, there was sharp dissent among the nations and regions that had originally voted for the aid packages. As long as the problems had been localized the argument could be made that those regions that were least affected should help the regions that were most affected. Now that the problems were worldwide, the individual regions wanted to keep their money at home. Added to the difficulty of getting the package adopted was the necessity of forging an agreement among the individual nations in each region as to exactly what percentage of the region's contribution each nation would be responsible for. This had required particular diplomatic skill when working out a compromise agreement among the nations of Western Europe which, together with the Middle East, would provide the greatest portion of aid for the other regions.

The meal that Ambassador Ngordon and Rashid shared included traditional middle eastern fare: roast lamb, rice, chicken, bread, feta cheese, *doukh* (a watered-down yogurt), and Coca Cola. After sufficient polite conversation, Ambassador Ngordon broached the subject. "Have you reached a decision on how you will vote on the Consolidated Aid Package tomorrow?" he asked.

"I have decided to vote *for* the package," Rashid answered. Ngordon smiled and nodded his satisfaction with Rashid's decision. Ngordon could now be certain of the support needed to adopt the Consolidated Aid Package. "I must add, however," Rashid continued, "that public opinion is split nearly evenly among the nations of my region. And I must confess, I have my own reservations." Ngordon's expression prodded Rashid to explain those reservations. "I understand the reasons for supporting the Consolidated Aid Package," Rashid said. "Ambassador Goodman has gone to great lengths over the past few weeks to point out how the package will benefit the Middle East in the long run. And it is not that I am opposed to the aid package — far from it. But does it not seem odd to you that Ambassador Goodman is so eager to get this package adopted? After all, his region will bear much of the burden of funding the measure. How curious that he should be so involved in urging its passage." Rashid took another drink of Coke, and then added, "I have never seen a man so intent upon giving away his region's wealth."

"But you say that *you* support it," countered Ngordon who then added the caveat, "at least I suppose you do in principle. And yet clearly the plan calls for your region to contribute every bit as much as Western Europe. Are you not, therefore, in a similar position to Ambassador Goodman — eager to give away a part of your region's wealth?"

"Indeed," Rashid answered. "But with one important distinction: It is in the Middle East's interest that the rest of the world recover. The world depends on my region for its oil, and we depend on them for goods and services. And, of course, there is also," he noted the obvious with only a little reluctance, "that when the world suffers, oil prices suffer. But what is the interest of Ambassador Goodman? Europe does not need to have India or China or the Americas recover in order for Europe to prosper. Western Europe has nearly all that it needs: natural resources, industry, agriculture, a skilled workforce, and a ready market for what it produces. And they stand to benefit most from cheap oil. What little they do lack can be bought at a **far** lower price than the amount Ambassador Goodman offers to give away. Western Europe is poised, if it chooses, to become the predominant technical and economic world power and yet their representative on the Security Council not only refuses to take the power, but is doing all that he can to give it away." Abduhl Rashid took another bite of roast lamb, and then concluded. "I do not understand such a man and therefore I do not trust him."

"I understand," Ngordon said, "but I believe that you will find Christopher Goodman to be exactly as he appears. He is one of those rare men in the government who places the good of all before the benefit of his own region."

"Well," Ambassador Rashid said, gesturing freely with his hands, "we shall see." The mention of Christopher Goodman's character gave Ambassador Rashid an opportunity to ask Ngordon about another matter. "But tell me," he began, "I have heard some very strange stories about Ambassador Goodman. Curious things. That he has the power to heal."

"Merely rumors," Ngordon answered, brushing off the suggestion authoritatively. "I have known Christopher Goodman since he was no more than twenty, and I have never seen him do anything unusual. Who knows how such stories get started? I just ignore them."

Ngordon looked at his watch. It was ten minutes until six o'clock. In twelve minutes the sun would begin setting — one of the five times each day when devout Muslims face *Qiblah*, the direction of the *Ka'bah* in Mecca, and offer *Salah* (prayer). Ngordon and Rashid left the table and after performing the ceremonial ablution or *Wudu*, Ngordon showed his guest to a room on the eastern side of the apartment which had a balcony overlooking Central Park. The temperature outside was in the upper 40s and while the warmer areas of the northern hemisphere were still plagued by attacks from the giant swarms of locusts, the cooler days had kept the insects away from New York for nearly two weeks. Ambassador Ngordon was therefore confident that it was safe to open the double balcony doors which faced east toward Mecca. Placing their prayer rugs on the floor, the two men knelt down to pray. The prayer would last about fifteen minutes, until the red glow of the sun disappeared from the western horizon. Being in the middle of New York City and on the eastern side of the building, Ngordon would, of course, have to depend on his watch to know when that occurred.

Unnoticed by the men as they spoke the prayers of the Salah over the sounds of the city below, a small swarm of about fifty locusts flew into the open balcony doors.

October 4, 2022 (9:00 a.m.)

Italian Ambassador to the United Nations, Christopher Goodman, walked into his office. He was late after having had breakfast with Decker Hawthorne. "Will you get Ambassador Ngordon on the phone?" he asked Jackie Hansen as soon as he had entered the room.

"Both Ambassador Ngordon and Ambassador Rashid were stung by locusts last night," Jackie answered. Christopher's face registered shock.

"How bad was it?" he asked.

"I haven't heard yet."

"Well, find out for me, will you — as quickly as you can. Oh, and find out where they're being treated."

"Also," Jackie added, "you've had three calls from Secretary Milner. He asked that you call back. He said it was urgent."

"Okay, get him on the phone," Christopher said, and then walked into his office and closed the door behind him.

"Good morning, Bob," Christopher said when Jackie put the call through. "What's up?"

"Good morning, Christopher," Milner responded in a rushed manner — there was obvious concern in his voice. "I assume you've heard about what happened to Ambassadors Ngordon and Rashid."

"Jackie just told me."

"What does this mean for the vote on the Consolidated Aid Package?" Milner asked.

"I'm afraid it's not good." Christopher said. "Ambassadors Khalid and Khaton are both resolutely opposed to the package," he explained, referring to the Alternates representing the Middle

East and East Africa who would be standing in for Ngordon and Rashid. "I'm certain they'll vote against it."

"Can the vote be delayed until Ngordon and Rashid return?"

"No. It's definitely set for this afternoon's session."

"We must do something," Milner said. "The Consolidated Aid Package must pass."

"I agree with you, of course," Christopher said. "But the vote cannot be delayed."

There was a pause of about ten seconds and then Milner spoke again. His voice conveyed either inspiration or that he had come to a difficult decision — it was hard to be sure which. "Where are Ngordon and Rashid?" he asked. "Are they in a hospital?"

"I don't know. I've asked Jackie to find out."

"You've got to go to them."

There was another long pause and then Christopher asked for clarification. "What? . . . Why?"

"They must be there for the vote."

"But . . ."

"I know what I said before, but we're going to have to make an exception."

□   □   □

Four hours later, as the meeting of the Security Council was called to order, German Ambassador Hella Winkler, who served as the Alternate from Western Europe, found herself unexpectedly filling in for Ambassador Christopher Goodman of Italy. He had not indicated that he planned to miss the meeting, and it seemed unimaginable that he would do so with such an important vote scheduled to take place. But the rules of procedure were clear. If a Primary was not in attendance, the Alternate was to fill the Primary's position until the Primary either returned or until such time as a new Primary was elected. So it was that, of those who sat in voting positions around the table today, three were

Alternates, including Winkler, the ambassador from Uganda who served in place of Ambassador Ngordon, and the ambassador from Syria who served in the place of Ambassador Rashid.

A few minutes after the meeting was called to order, Christopher quietly entered the room. Ambassador Winkler did not see him enter and so remained in her place until Christopher came and tapped her on the shoulder. Looking around, she gave Christopher a smile and relinquished her place. "Just keeping your seat warm," she whispered to him.

"Thanks," he said and returned the smile.

Fifteen minutes later, as the Security Council listened to a summary report on agricultural production, Ambassadors Ngordon and Rashid entered the room together. Their entrance did not go nearly so unnoticed as had Christopher's. Nor were their Alternates nearly so quick to give up their positions at the inner circle, but their stalling could only last a few seconds. Ngordon and Rashid took their places and the vote on the Consolidated Aid Package was guaranteed. More than a few eyes stole a glance at Christopher when the two men came in, but Christopher showed nothing except pleasure that Ngordon and Rashid were there for the vote, and Ngordon and Rashid gave no hint that Christopher had anything to do with their presence. Christopher's powers were becoming a poorly kept secret but it was not yet to the point that anyone wanted to openly question him in public about the strange stories.

Chapter 12

What He Must Do

December 11, 2022 — U.N. World Meteorological Organization, Washington, D.C.

"Come look at this," Ed Rifkin called to his supervisor as he rechecked the orientation of his equipment.

"What is it?" asked Jeff Burke, Rifkin's supervisor.

"I'm not sure. A moment ago I was tracking swarm 237a over Northern Africa. Now they've simply vanished. It was as if they suddenly just fell out of the air."

"They're probably feeding," Burke responded.

"No, sir. I don't think so. I've seen them drop to feed too many times. This was different."

"I've got the same thing over *Mar del Plata*, Argentina," said another tracker.

"Ditto that over Sydney, Australia," said someone else.

"Same over Miami."

Another dozen reports came in the same way.

"What the hell's going on?" Jeff Burke demanded. "Give me a check on every swarm and trackable sub-swarm. I want to know what's going on now!"

What was going on was that all over the world the locusts were dying and falling from the sky. The swarm that fell over Sydney, Australia was so large it would take two weeks to clean it up. Other areas had similar accumulations, which clogged gutters and sewers in the cities. In all, the plague had lasted five months. Now, as quickly as it had come, it was over. It was a time to celebrate. But the celebration would not last long.

February 2, 2023 — Jerusalem

It was the last thing anyone wanted to hear. They were back. And again they brought with them a message of wrath on the people of the earth. As they had before, again they walked the streets of Jerusalem shouting their message until they came to the Temple. Then, as they stood before the steps of the Temple, John and Cohen declared their newest prophecy.

> *The sixth angel sounded his trumpet and I heard a voice coming from the horns of the golden altar that is before God. It said to the sixth angel who had the trumpet, 'Release the four angels who are bound at the great river Euphrates.' And the four angels who had been kept ready for this very hour and day and month and year were released to kill a third of mankind. The number of the mounted troops was two hundred million. I heard their number.*[9]

As John and Cohen left the Temple they were again followed by police, press, and curiosity seekers. This time the crowd was stopped by police as they neared the edge of the city. The military

---

[9] Revelation 9:13-16.

was ready. They had cleared the street and evacuated the buildings surrounding the spot where the men had disappeared on their two previous visits. They were prepared to do whatever was necessary to capture or kill the two.

John and Cohen walked straight ahead. In front of them a huge nylon net spanned the width of the street. John and Cohen continued walking as though they did not even see it. When they came within a few yards of it, the netting simply dissolved into vapor and they passed through. A moment later a helicopter descended, carrying a ten-foot-square cell of iron bars with no bottom. Had they split up, John and Cohen easily could have evaded such a ridiculous trap, but just as the designer of the trap had hoped, the two men refused to vary from their set course and walked straight ahead as the trap was lowered over them. But a moment before the bottom of the cage reached the street the bars crumbled into dust and the prophets continued walking, undaunted. The sudden loss of weight threw the helicopter out of control and it crashed with explosive force into a nearby building, setting it and two other buildings ablaze and ultimately killing eleven people.

The military ground troops stepped in. With no one else in the line of fire, four squads of soldiers simultaneously opened fire on the two men. The bullets had no effect. Instead, as had happened seven months earlier, each soldier was instantly consumed by fire.

At the city's edge, the two men again disappeared, leaving behind the dead and dying.

February 22, 2023 — The United Nations, New York (5:58 p.m)

It had been a long day and the meeting of the Security Council was finally coming to a close. Christopher Goodman, whose turn in rotation it was to be President of the Security Council, was about to adjourn when Ambassador Yuri Kruszkegin, the Primary member representing Northern Asia, sought to be recognized. Kruszkegin was one of the most senior and respected people in the entire United Nations, having served in the U.N. since the days of the old Russian Federation.

"Mr. President," Kruszkegin began, "in this, the 77th year since the founding of the United Nations, I am reminded that for over four years this body has functioned in a manner other than that which was envisioned by its founders. Specifically, I refer to the fact that for the past fifty-two months we have been without the benefit of a Secretary-General. For a while — after the untimely death of Jon Hansen — this body tried, without success, to fill that post, but we were too divided to reach a consensus on a nominee.

"Since that time, we have attempted to operate on a rotating basis with the current President of the Security Council carrying out most of the functions of an acting Secretary-General. I am certain, Mr. President, that we would all agree that this body and the United Nations as a whole operates in a far more productive and efficient manner when those responsibilities are carried out by a single person serving as Secretary-General for the prescribed five-year term. Too often, important matters have been delayed or simply fallen through the cracks as the responsibilities of Secretary-General are handed off each month from one member of the Security Council to another.

"I believe that we would also all agree that the recent tragedies throughout the world, as terrible as they have been and continue to be, have nevertheless acted to unify the members of the Security Council into a more cohesive body. Mr. President, I believe that this body has now achieved a level of mutual trust and cooperation such that we should again set about the business of selecting a person to fill the post of Secretary-General.

"Admittedly, the position of Secretary-General requires the talents and attention of a very uncommon person — someone who will not place the needs of his own region above the needs of other regions. Jon Hansen was such a man. I believe that another man of similar disposition has emerged as a leader of this body.

"Mr. President and fellow members of the Security Council, I therefore wish to place into nomination for the position of Secretary-General a man who has repeatedly shown himself to be a selfless servant of the United Nations and the people of the world; a man who single-handedly forged a consensus among the nations of his region to provide the lion's share of the financial and technical support needed to implement the Consolidated Aid Package and then worked with every other member of the Security Council to ensure not only its passage but its optimum functionality for all regions; a man who would bring to the position of Secretary-General a rare insight and ability as well as wise judgment; a man who exposed the heinous intentions of Albert Moore, thus sparing the world the rule of a dictator on par with Adolph Hitler and Joseph Stalin.

"Mr. President, I place in nomination for Secretary-General the distinguished Ambassador from Italy, the man who has served his region and the world so well, Ambassador Christopher Goodman."

Ambassador Toréos of Chile, the Primary member representing South America, and whose wife Christopher had healed, quickly seconded. Ambassador Ngordon called the motion without debate and it appeared the matter would be brought to a vote before Christopher could even say anything. Finally, however, even though it was not entirely in accordance with rules of order, Christopher had a chance to speak.

"I'm not sure what to say. I appreciate this show of support but I'm not sure I agree that . . . Well, could we just take a brief recess so I can have a few minutes to think this over?"

The Security Council agreed to a thirty-minute break and Christopher went very quickly to his office to make a phone call. He could have made the call from his seat at the Security Council but he wanted the privacy offered by his own office. The meeting of the Security Council was carried live on closed circuit television, so news of the nomination was already spreading throughout the United Nations. As he made his way out of the

U.N. and across the street to the Italian Mission, people offered their congratulations. Jackie Hansen applauded when he arrived at his office.

"Oh please, Jackie. Not you, too."

"Sorry, Mr. Secretary. I just couldn't help myself," she responded.

"Don't start calling me 'Mr. Secretary' just yet," he said. "I haven't even decided to accept."

"But you can't refuse. It's your rightful place. It's your duty; your destiny."

Christopher shook his head. "I don't know," he said. "I'm not sure the timing is right. Look, I need you to get Decker and Secretary Milner on the phone for a conference call immediately."

Decker Hawthorne had been in a meeting when Christopher was nominated and was informed of the nomination by a member of his staff. He quickly excused himself and went to a closed circuit television to watch the proceedings. When the recess was taken and Christopher left the Security Council Chamber, Decker had guessed correctly that he would be going to his office. Decker went to meet him there, arriving just as Christopher was telling Jackie to call him.

"Decker," Christopher said, "thank you for coming. I assume you have heard about the nomination."

"I saw it on the monitor in my office. This is great!" Decker hugged Christopher and patted him on the back. "I am so proud of you!"

"Well, thank you. But I'm not sure about it at all. According to what Secretary Milner has told me, this wasn't supposed to happen for at least a few more months." Christopher and Decker went into his office and closed the door while Jackie tried to locate Milner and get him on the phone.

"Decker, I need your counsel on this. What should I do?"

"I appreciate that you would ask me," Decker said, "but I'm not much of a substitute for the likes of Secretary Milner when it comes to matters of prophetic timetables."

"No, but you have something that Bob Milner lacks. You look at things from a real life perspective that Bob Milner can't." Decker was justifiably flattered. "I don't want to know what you think about prophecy; I want to know what your gut instinct is."

"Well," Decker replied, taking a deep breath and raising his eyebrows as if to see more clearly into the future, "I think you should accept." Then he added with a grin, "And do it quickly before they change their minds."

Christopher smiled. "Of course, it's not even certain that I'll be nominated. Remember, it takes a unanimous vote by the Security Council for the nomination to pass, and then I'd still need to go before the General Assembly for a vote."

"Well, I think the fact that there was no discussion on the matter is a good sign; no one appeared to have any objections. And the fact that there was unanimous consent for a thirty-minute recess is also a positive sign. If someone intended to vote against you they could have saved themselves and the rest of the Security Council some time by just indicating they intended to vote 'no.' That would have kept the matter short and sweet. I think you have a pretty good shot at it. But as you said, you still have to be approved by the General Assembly."

"Yes, and there could be the rub."

The phone rang and Christopher answered as Jackie transferred the call with Robert Milner.

"Bob, something unexpected has just happened here and I need your guidance," Christopher began.

"Go ahead, Christopher. What's the matter?"

"The uh . . ." Christopher stammered. "I've just been nominated to become Secretary-General."

There was silence on the other end of the phone.

"Bob, are you there? What should I do? Should I accept?"

"Well, this is coming a little ahead of schedule," he said finally, "but hell, yes! Accept! Accept!"

"Great!" Christopher responded.

"I just wish Alice Bernley could be here to see this day."

"So do I, Bob," Christopher said sympathetically. "When will you be back in New York?"

"I'll have to change a few plans but I'll be there as soon as I can."

"Great. I'll see you then." Christopher hung up the phone.

"What did he say?" asked Decker.

"He said to do it."

□   □   □

Christopher returned to the Security Council Chamber and as acting President called the meeting back to order. The vote was unanimous. Decker, who had accompanied Christopher, looked around the inner circle and considered what had prompted each of the members to vote for Christopher. Christopher had told him about each of the healings; that explained at least some of the votes. To Christopher's right was Ambassador Ngordon, whom he had healed from locusts stings. Next to Ngordon was Kruszkegin. From working with Kruszkegin in the past, Decker surmised that he simply felt as he had stated in his nominating remarks — that the U.N. needed a full-time Secretary-General and that Christopher was a qualified candidate upon whom his colleagues could agree. Two of the other Primaries were closely associated with the Lucius Trust, which no doubt figured into their support. Then there was Ambassador Rashid, who, like Ngordon, had been healed by Christopher, as had the wife of Ambassador Toréos, and the granddaughter of Ambassador Tanaka. Still, that left two for whom Decker had no clear explanation for their vote beyond the fact that Christopher had worked with each of them and was highly regarded by all.

There was, however, one other factor involved: the most recent prophecies of John and Cohen. There was no denying the magnitude of their threat, and no explanation for the dramatic scenes of the unsuccessful attempt to detain or eliminate the two men. Still, men and women of authority have difficulty accepting and therefore dealing with anything which conflicts with the perception of reality upon which their power is based. So it was in the U.N. Security Council. Certainly no one would openly acknowledge that in part their decision to nominate Christopher was based on fear of the two Israeli madmen's prophecies, nor would they admit to making a decision based on a non-rational feeling deep inside that only Christopher could lead the world out of — or at least through — what it faced. But neither could they deny that the prophecies to this point had been entirely accurate, and therefore, would probably continue to be so.

"Fellow members of the Security Council," Christopher began when the room finally quieted after the vote, "it seems to me that the problem with nominations is that the honor is accompanied by the opportunity to fail and to come out looking like an ass when the vote is put before the whole body." The comment drew appropriate laughter from the members and observers. "Given that fact, and the late hour, I believe I should save any speeches for the General Assembly. Therefore, in the simplest of terms: I accept your nomination."

7:55 p.m.

Gerard Poupardin sat alone in his apartment, consumed by rage. The television news reports of Christopher's nomination to become Secretary-General echoed tauntingly in his mind. Following Albert Moore's death, Poupardin had remained on the staff with the new French ambassador, but it was not the same. He missed the excitement of serving a member of the Security Council. The new French ambassador, in his position as just one of more than two hundred U.N. members, seemed sickeningly impotent compared to Moore. But that was the least of it.

The committee investigating Albert Moore's participation in the events leading up to the tragic conclusion of the China-India-Pakistan War had discovered no evidence that implicated Gerard Poupardin. Indeed, beyond Moore's own confession just before he died, very little hard evidence could be found even to implicate Moore. Still, it was painfully clear to Poupardin that the new French ambassador was uncomfortable about having Albert Moore's former chief-of-staff serving as his own.

Poupardin was not concerned about his job; that, at least, was secure. International labor laws made it extremely difficult to fire *anyone* without being able to prove either gross incompetence or a definitive pattern of flagrant negligence. Instead, the new French ambassador had diffused Poupardin's power by shifting many of his responsibilities to other staff members. In the end, Poupardin was chief-of-staff in name only. All important decisions were made either by the ambassador himself or by staff committee.

Poupardin also missed the closeness he had shared with Moore. From the very beginning of his relationship with Moore, Poupardin had known that Moore was basically heterosexual. At first that had even made having sex with Moore more exciting: he wanted to do for Moore what he believed no woman would ever, or perhaps, could ever do. Poupardin had no doubt that Moore enjoyed the sexual part of their relationship, but as time passed he had hoped for more. He wanted Moore's love. He wanted to feel the warmth of Moore's embrace, the comfort of his caress, not just the strength of his unyielding control when he was aroused. But that had never come. Poupardin had hidden his disappointment from Moore and, as much as possible, from himself. At times he had suspected that Moore used the relationship simply to buy his loyalty, but Gerard had never dared confront him with the suspicion.

When Moore died that suspicion became moot and in the intervening months Poupardin forgot it entirely. Now, two years later, as he looked back at their relationship, he was fully convinced that Moore *had* loved him deeply, in his own way. The thought of Christopher Goodman — the very man who had caused Moore's death — rising to the post that Albert Moore had coveted for himself, and that Poupardin had so coveted for him, filled him with rage.

For a moment Poupardin thought back to a fantasy he had played through his mind time and again. Actually, it was more a plan than a simple fantasy, which had made it all the more arousing. He had worked out every detail. It would be on the night after Moore took office as Secretary-General: a sort of private party of mutual congratulation. Poupardin would lock the door to the office as he had so many times before, but this time it would be the office of the Secretary-General of the United Nations. And then . . . Just the thought of having sex with the most powerful man in the world seemed to Poupardin the ultimate fantasy. Under his clothes he would be wearing the most seductive outfit Moore had ever seen him in. That part he was sure of: he had already bought it.

Now it hung, unused in his closet.

And instead of Moore, the very one who had caused Moore's death would now be taking that office.

Slowly Gerard Poupardin began to understand what he must do.

Christopher Goodman must die.

Chapter 13

The Avenger of Blood

March 3, 2023 — New York

The vote by the General Assembly was set for March 8, 2023, two weeks after Christopher's nomination, to allow sufficient time for the nominee to meet with the caucuses of each of the world's ten regions. Immediately before the vote, Christopher was to address the United Nations and the world from the Hall of the General Assembly at U.N. headquarters in New York. At Christopher's request, Decker worked extensively with him preparing his speech. Decker wouldn't have had it any other way. Christopher had his own speech writers who participated, but for something this important it just made sense to take advantage of Decker's experience and skill. However, Decker's availability was limited by his own responsibilities.

Decker's staff was certainly capable of handling the media requests for background information on Christopher as well as questions on the process and procedures of electing a new Secretary-General. But because Decker had raised Christopher since he was fourteen, the media insisted on talking to Decker directly. After all these years working with the press, Decker was surprised to find it a heady experience. He had been in literally thousands of press conferences over the years, but this was different. Except for the time after he and Tom Donafin had escaped from Lebanon, he had always been writing about, or a spokesman for, someone else.

Decker had returned to his office after completing just such a press conference when Christopher arrived with a stack of papers under his arm.

"Good morning, Mr. Secretary-General," Decker said.

"I wish you wouldn't call me that," Christopher said. "You're liable to jinx it for me."

"Just getting in practice," Decker responded.

Christopher rolled his eyes and let it pass. "I just got the most recent revision of the speech," he said, holding up the pile of papers. "Are you available to go over it with me?"

"Absolutely," Decker answered, though he already had as much work as he could possibly handle. "Let's take a look." They sat down and were just about to begin when Decker noticed Christopher yawning.

"You want some coffee before we start?" Decker asked.

"Yeah, that would be great."

Decker opened the door to his office and asked Jody MacArthur, one of his secretarial staff, to bring coffee. When he returned, Christopher was yawning again. "Have you been getting enough sleep?"

Christopher was already starting another yawn, so Decker had to wait for an answer. "It's been pretty tough the last several nights," Christopher answered. "Ever since the nomination, actually."

"You don't want to drive yourself too hard. You need your rest."

"Yeah, I know. But that's not it. I've been getting to bed, just not getting much sleep."

"You're not nervous, are you?"

Christopher shrugged. "I don't know; maybe that's it."

"Well, there's no reason to be. The latest poll of the membership indicates a very strong vote in your favor."

"That's good, but I don't think getting elected is what's got me bothered."

"Well, what then?"

"I suppose it's dealing with the responsibility of the position after I win. I told you that while I was in the desert in Israel, my father told me that only when I understood the full truth about myself would it be time for me to rule." Christopher shrugged, indicating confusion. "I don't think I know anymore now than I did then. Maybe we jumped the gun on this. Maybe Bob was wrong; maybe I should have refused the nomination until I was sure it was the right time."

Decker thought for a moment; it was not easy to offer meaningful encouragement in such a situation. "Maybe the election will act as the catalyst to reveal whatever it is that you don't yet understand." It wasn't a very convincing suggestion, but it was something. "Anyway," Decker continued, "it won't do you any good to lose sleep over it."

"Yeah," Christopher agreed, "but how do you control your dreams?"

"What do you mean?" asked Decker.

Christopher exhaled audibly. "Oh, it's that crazy dream about the box. You probably don't remember it. I think the last time I had it was the night that the warheads exploded over Russia. That was nearly twenty years ago."

Decker shook his head. "I remember that you had a dream that woke you up that night, but you're right, I don't remember much about it."

"Well, it's a strange dream; it has a very odd feeling about it. It's as though I dreamed it long, long ago, perhaps even when I was Jesus. And yet at the same time, the memory seems clear and fresh. When the dream starts I'm in a room with immense curtains decorated with gold and silver threads hanging all around me. The floor of the room is made of stone and in the middle of the room is an old wooden box, like a crate, which is sitting on a table. I can't explain why, but in the dream I feel compelled to look in the box, but at the same time I know that what's in it is something quite terrifying. When I approach the box to look inside and I'm just a few feet away, I look down and the floor has disappeared. I start to fall but I manage to grab onto the table that the box is sitting on. I try to hold on but after a minute my hands slip. Then I hear terrible hideous laughter."

"And you dreamed this again last night?" Decker asked.

"I've had the same dream every night since the nomination."

There was a long pause as Decker tried both to find some clue as to the dream's meaning and to think of something comforting to say. "There's one other thing," Christopher added. "Though I wonder if we might have acted too soon on the nomination, I'm also concerned that we might have already waited too long." Christopher shook his head, conveying not puzzlement but distress. "Whatever it is that John and Cohen have in mind for their next curse will occur very, very soon — within days. And I am absolutely certain that whatever it is, it will be far worse than anything they've done so far.

Wednesday, March 8, 2023 — Gerard Poupardin's apartment, New York City (11:39 a.m.)

It was the day of Christopher Goodman's address to the General Assembly and Gerard Poupardin had called in sick. Flipping through the news channels on television, he watched the stories about Christopher through the stale cigarette smoke that filled the air. Around him on the floor of his usually immaculate apartment were dozens of articles about Christopher that he had cut from newspapers or torn from magazines. Poupardin hardly moved as he smoked the cigarette nearly down to the filter and then snuffed out the butt in a saucer which served as an ash tray.

These days the art of smoking was lost to all but a few devotees of old movies, and ash trays were sold primarily as novelties in antique shops. Poupardin had not tried smoking since he was a teenager and was shocked to find that the price was now about fourteen international dollars a pack. Still, it was a small price to pay to soothe his nerves. And besides, he would soon have little use for money.

He easily could have gone to a drug store and picked up something stronger, and certainly cheaper than the cigarettes — almost everything was legal as long as a doctor or med-tech had authorized it and it wasn't used while driving or operating heavy equipment. With a diplomatic passport, even these obstacles disappeared. But Poupardin needed to be alert, in full control of his faculties. He would have only one opportunity to accomplish the task he had set for himself.

Poupardin took another cigarette from the pack. It was his last. His calculations were a bit off: the pack should have lasted at least another twenty minutes. Now he was left with only one cigarette and he still had twenty minutes to kill. He decided to take a long hot shower and start getting ready. He would save the last cigarette for later. For now, he returned it to the package and set it down on the endtable next to the .38 caliber snub-nosed pistol he had purchased two days before.

The United Nations

Decker sat in his office re-reading Christopher's speech for the umpteenth time. He felt a little like a novice again, worrying about each word, going through his old, worn thesaurus, reading the speech aloud to make sure the words flowed easily off the tongue and gently into the ear of the listener while conveying both sincerity and conviction. He hadn't made any changes to the speech in the last three times he had read it, but decided to read it one last time just to be sure.

As he began the *final*-final read of the 18-page speech, the intercom line on the phone rang. "Mr. Hawthorne," said a woman's voice.

"Yes?" Decker answered without looking away from the speech.

"I'm sorry to disturb you."

"That's all right, Jody. What is it?"

"There's a call from Security in the visitors lobby. There's a man there asking to see you. I explained that you were busy and that he'd need to make an appointment, but he says he's a friend of yours. He was pretty insistent."

"I'm not expecting anyone. What did he say his name is?"

"Mr. Donovan."

Decker thought for a moment. "I don't think I know anyone by that name. Did he say what he wanted to see me about?"

"No, sir. Just that he was a friend of yours and he wanted to see you. Shall I tell him you're not available?"

"No," he answered, reluctantly. "It's possible I met him at some party or official function somewhere. Go ahead and patch the call in here to me."

"Yes, sir," she answered, and a second later the phone rang.

"Hello," he said. "This is Decker Hawthorne."

"Yes, sir. This is Johnson with Security in the visitors lobby. There's a Mr. Tom Donafin here to see you."

Decker fell suddenly silent.

"Sir?" the guard said after a moment, not sure Decker was still there.

"Dona**fin**?" Decker asked. His secretary had said 'Donovan.'

"Yes, sir," the guard responded.

"Would you spell that, please?" Decker heard the security guard ask the man to spell his name, and in response, heard a voice which nearly stopped his heart.

"D - O - N . . . the security guard began to echo.

"I'll be right there," Decker interrupted and hung up the phone. He reached the elevator at a full run. It was only then, as he tapped his foot nervously on the floor while he waited for the elevator to arrive, that he realized this could not be happening. Tom Donafin was dead! He died in Israel on the first day of the last Arab-Israeli war. The elevator arrived and Decker stepped on, utterly confused by what was happening. He was too deep in thought to do anything but that to which his momentum compelled him.

As the elevator descended the thirty-eight stories to the ground, Decker quickly tried to consider every possible explanation. It couldn't be a relative. Tom didn't have any. It might be someone with the same name, but that wouldn't explain the voice or why the man identified himself as a friend. If Decker had met someone else named Tom Donafin, he surely would have remembered. Could his mind be playing tricks on him? Or could this whole thing be just a dream? Could someone be playing a sick joke? No, he decided, no one he knew now had even known Tom Donafin. Besides, no one he knew would be that sadistic. In rapid succession Decker ran through every possibility, speeding toward the conclusion he desperately wanted to reach, but fearing his hopes would be dashed by some completely logical explanation he had overlooked along the way. Soon he realized it was simply not possible to summarily eliminate all of the other explanations, and so he took another approach. Could it really be Tom Donafin? Decker replayed in his mind the circumstances of Tom's death. The car Tom was in was hit by a stray air-to-air missile; there were no survivors. The force of the explosion, coupled with the resulting gasoline explosion, had so completely demolished and incinerated the car that it was impossible to recover much that even resembled any recognizable part of a human body. . . . Could Tom have escaped the explosion?

Just as the elevator stopped on the first floor and the door opened, Decker was hit with one solid piece of evidence that he had thus far overlooked: it had been nearly twenty years. If Tom was alive, he would have contacted Decker before this. The conclusion was clear: despite the visitor's name, despite the apparent similarity to Tom's voice, Tom was dead.

Decker took a deep breath and stepped from the elevator. For a moment he just stood there, unsure of what to do. As he did he realized he was shaking and his heart was racing. He thought of going back but the momentum was still there to go on, and he was still curious. Besides, Johnson at Security was expecting him.

Walking through the halls from the Secretariat Building to the General Assembly Building, Decker tried to put the brief confusion behind him and hoped only that this would not be a total waste of his time. As he came to the visitors lobby he forced his thoughts back to the wording of Christopher's speech. There were still a couple things he thought might be said more compellingly. There was the issue of . . . Decker scanned the faces and profiles of those near the front security desk in the middle of the lobby near the doors. There was no one there he recognized except Johnson, who had just looked up and had seen Decker coming toward him.

Johnson, having made eye contact, and without speaking, turned and pointed toward a man who stood looking out the glass doors of the building toward the North Garden. As Decker got closer, the man turned around.

It was Tom Donafin.

Despite the call Decker had received in his office, despite thinking that he had heard Tom's voice over the phone, despite the torrent of emotions and thoughts he had had on his way to the lobby, seeing his old friend alive was so completely unexpected that he may just as well have bumped into him on a deserted street somewhere.

For a moment Decker just stared. Tom looked back and allowed himself to smile just a little as his eyes scanned the changes of twenty years: the wrinkles and gray hair, the added pounds, and the unmistakable look of success. He had missed Decker perhaps even more than Decker had missed him. For Decker, Tom had been dead; there had never been any possibility of seeing him again. But Tom had always known the truth; for him, the exile had been self-imposed, a matter of the will rather than of fate. Now — for a brief moment anyway — they were together again.

Neither Decker nor Tom were aware they had moved but somehow the two came together, falling with great tears of joy into each others' arms.

For a long time there were no words. No words could have satisfied.

Neither man wiped his eyes; neither would release the other from his embrace.

"I thought you were dead," Decker said at last through his tears.

"I'm sorry, Decker. I'm sorry," Tom wept in reply.

A moment passed before Decker could speak again. "What happened? Where have you been? Are you all right?"

"I'm sorry, Decker. I'm really sorry," Tom said again, but he offered no explanation. Around them people watched, some unabashedly staring, as the two men hugged and cried. It didn't matter. Finally Tom managed to ask if there was somewhere they could go to talk.

"Yes, of course, of course," Decker answered, as he wiped away some of the tears and Tom did the same.

Decker spotted Johnson, the security guard. "It's all right," Decker told him. "He's with me."

"Yes, sir," Johnson responded.

"Please, Tom," Decker pleaded, as they walked, "tell me what happened. Where have you been? Why didn't you ever try to contact me?"

"I did," Tom answered. "But then . . . Look, let me just start from the beginning." Decker nodded his agreement. "When the fighting started in Israel I was in the hospital in Tel Aviv. In the midst of the battle, the British embassy sent a driver to get me. I think that must been Ambassador Hansen's doing." Decker didn't interrupt to mention his own involvement in that episode, but nodded in confirmation. "I packed up my stuff and went with the driver, a young fellow named Połucki." Tom had never forgotten the driver's name. "On the way to the British embassy we came upon an Israeli jet that had crashed into a building, so I asked Połucki to stop and I got out of the car to take some pictures." Tom's words conjured up a mental image in Decker's mind of their days together: Tom was never without his camera. Decker smiled nostalgically as they stepped onto the elevator. Tom continued, "There was a dogfight overhead. The Israeli fired a missile, but the MiG managed to dodge it. When I turned back toward the car the missile hit it. Poor Połucki was killed instantly. I remember the flash but before I could even blink I was hit by debris from the explosion.

"The next thing I knew, I woke up in a doctor's apartment in occupied Tel Aviv. The doctor, a woman named Rhoda Felsberg, told me that her rabbi had found me and carried me there on his back. If he hadn't found me and brought me to her, I'm sure I would have died there on the street."

Decker and Tom stepped from the elevator and Decker showed Tom to his office, pausing just long enough to introduce him to Jody MacArthur, his secretary. They were about to go into Decker's office when Christopher arrived.

"Decker," Christopher began as soon as he walked in, "did you have any more changes to the speech?"

"No. Not since the last copy I sent to your office."

"Great. So does that mean you're happy with it?"

"Yeah," Decker said with a contemplative nod. "I feel pretty good about it, though you know me; I'm never entirely satisfied."

"I think it's one of your best ever," Christopher said.

"Well, it was really a joint effort," Decker replied, though he agreed with Christopher's overall assessment. "Christopher," Decker said, changing subjects, "I have someone I'd like you to meet. He's an old friend of mine."

"Sure, Decker, but can we make it a little bit later? Maybe after the speech."

"Uh . . . yeah, sure," Decker answered. Decker was a little

taken aback by Christopher's response. It seemed rude to just ignore Tom who was standing right there beside them. Jody MacArthur was surprised as well, but Tom didn't seem to mind.

"Okay, well, wish me luck," Christopher said as he left Jody's office.

"Good luck," Decker and Jody obliged in unison.

As soon as Christopher was gone, Decker turned his attention back to Tom. "Tom, I'm sorry about that," he said. "I'm sure he was just in a hurry. It's a big day, you know."

"Sure, Decker. No problem," Tom answered.

When they were settled into Decker's office, Tom continued his story. "Apparently after I was brought to Rhoda's apartment, I was in and out of consciousness for the next couple of weeks, but I don't remember any of that. It was nearly a month before I really had my wits about me. Shortly after that I tried to call to let you know what happened, but because of the Russian occupation it was nearly impossible to get a call out to the United States. The times I did get through no one was home. When the occupation ended, I called your house over and over again but I never got an answer."

"I had already moved to New York by then," Decker explained. "But you could have written."

"Decker," Tom said, and then almost in a whisper to emphasize the sincerity of what he was saying, "I was blinded in the explosion that killed Połucki."

Decker sat up straight. His raised eyebrows, cocked head, and the intense scrutiny of his expression asked the question long before he could form the words to speak it.

"The flash from the explosion burned my corneas," Tom continued, "and I was hit in the face and eyes by flying glass. The ophthalmologist who treated me was surprised that I could even sense bright light."

"But you can see now."

"Decker, God healed me . . . miraculously. For six months I was blind and then, just as quickly as I had been blinded by the flash and the flying glass, I could see again — better even than before the accident."

Decker looked at Tom and it was clear that Tom believed what he was saying. Decker had no reason to doubt his friend's earnestness, but almost reflexively he examined Tom's expression for several seconds, looking for any sign of deception. He saw none. Decker sighed and shook his head and sat back again. "If you had told me that a few years ago," he said, "I would have thought you were crazy. Now, I'm not so sure."

"Believe it, Decker. It's true. I was completely blind for six months. You can still see some of the scarring if you look close." Tom pointed to his eyes and Decker suddenly noticed the wedding band that had thus far escaped his attention.

"Wait a second. Wait a second. Wait a second!" he said excitedly with steadily increasing tempo and volume. "What is this?!" he asked, as he reached out and grabbed Tom's left hand.

"Oh, yeah," Tom answered, almost blushing. "Well, I was getting to that."

"Who? When? Is she here in New York? Is she with you?" Decker asked with obvious excitement.

"No, no," Tom answered, responding to the last question first. "She's still in Israel."

"Oh, too bad. But I'll meet her later?"

"Yeah, she wants to meet you, too."

"Tom, this is really great!" Decker said, looking back and forth between Tom's smiling face and the wedding band on his hand. "Well, who is she? What's her name? Where did you meet her?"

"Her name is Rhoda."

Decker made the connection immediately. "You mean Rhoda what's-her-name? The doctor who took care of you?"

"Rhoda Felsberg," Tom said. "Yeah. Only now, of course, it's Rhoda Donafin."

"Man, this is great! You just don't know how happy I am for you. That's really wonderful? So how long have you been married?"

"Nineteen years."

Decker's arms went limp and dropped to his sides as he shook his head, his face revealing both joy at his friend's good fortune and anguish at all the years the two friends had missed. "So, is that where you've been living — Israel?" he asked after a moment.

"Yeah," Tom answered. "We've got a place outside of Tel Aviv. That is, we *had* a place outside of Tel Aviv. We just sold it."

"Any kids?"

"Yeah, three," Tom answered. "Two boys and a girl."

Decker smiled so broadly it almost hurt. This day was too wonderful to be believed. Tom didn't say anything but just sat and shared the smile with Decker. Finally he continued his story. "After the Russian occupation but before I was healed, when I thought I'd never see again, I contacted *NewsWorld* to turn in my resignation, get my back pay and to try to collect on the insurance for an injury sustained while on duty. Of course I never got the insurance money because like most insurance companies they had gone bankrupt from paying claims after the Disaster. I asked about you at *NewsWorld,* but no one seemed too eager to talk about you."

"I don't think they were very happy with me when I left," Decker admitted, "which I can't blame them for; I did act like a bit of a bastard. But I can't believe they wouldn't tell you that I was working at the U.N."

Tom shrugged.

"But still, in all these years, after you were able to see again, surely you could have contacted me."

Tom didn't answer. Decker knew that with the blindness and then the healing and then the marriage, all of which fell right on the heels of the captivity in Lebanon, it was possible that Tom had simply put his past behind him . . . and Decker with it. It was possible . . . but not likely. They had been too close for that; they had been through too much together. And then too, it seemed to Decker that Tom was holding something back.

Gerard Poupardin's apartment

Gerard Poupardin stepped from the shower and dried himself. As he did, he became aware of a feeling that he had had for some time, but had never really noticed before now. In a way, the feeling had come on in much the same manner as a headache, which until it is of sufficient strength to cause substantial discomfort, goes unnoticed against the background of other thoughts. The feeling had now crossed the threshold of what could be ignored, and upon breaking that barrier, seemed to grow rapidly.

In the beginning, when the idea had first come to him to kill Christopher, it was just a wild angry thought, but for the sake of argument, he imagined how it might be done. It didn't take a lot to clear that initial hurdle; it all seemed so hypothetical. But then, imagining had become thinking, and thinking, considering. Considering had become contemplating, and contemplating, planning. And now, finally, planning was on the verge of becoming the act itself. Through each of these steps, Poupardin had continued to believe he could stop at any moment the course which he had begun. What he found, however, was that at each step the force which had carried him past the previous hurdles had subtly but significantly intensified, pushing him toward the next step and making it easier to take because of how far he had already come. The last hurdle that lay before him was certainly the biggest, but he felt compelled to continue.

Part of him wanted to just forget about the whole thing and he still believed he might. But for the present, momentum won out. Caught up in the current against which he could not swim, Poupardin could only tell himself that it carried him in the direction he wanted to go.

Besides, he reasoned, he didn't really need to make a decision right now; not yet. The logical thing to do, he thought, was to simply leave his options open. Perhaps as the time drew nearer he might still change his mind. If so, he could simply abort his mission and no one would ever know. It was probably even best to wait before deciding, he thought; to give himself as much time as possible to think it through. He didn't want to do anything he wasn't sure of, but then again, he didn't want to miss the opportunity because of fear.

In reality his decision to put off a decision would not allow time for further thought, but rather would only serve to stifle his thoughts for a while longer.

Poupardin folded his towel, hung it neatly on the rack, and went to the walk-in closet. Hanging by itself, away from the shirts and pants and suits, was a single item, still covered by the bag in which it had come from the store. For over two years it had hung there, awaiting the day when Albert Moore would become Secretary-General. But that day would never come.

Poupardin took it down and uncovered it, running his fingers across the white lace. His mind went back to the day he had purchased it in the men's department of Harrods. He had gone there during lunch for a fashion show of men's lingerie with some friends, and though he really went just to watch, when he saw it on the model he was determined to have it. It had cost him dearly but he felt it was well worth it.

How different, he thought, that occasion had been from the experience of purchasing the gun at the seedy little pawn shop.

The silky material sliding down over his nude body had an erotic effect which brought back and aggrandized many fond memories of Moore. Checking his appearance in his dressing mirror, it would have been easy to get lost in the distraction, but he refused to be drawn from his intent. Turning away, Poupardin selected a charcoal gray suit and quickly finished dressing.

The United Nations

Decker decided not to press Tom any further. If there was more to tell about why Tom had not tried harder to contact him, Decker would let him tell it in his own time. What was important was that Tom was alive and they were together now. He decided to ask Tom more about his family. "You say you just sold your house near Tel Aviv?"

"Yes," Tom answered. "Rabbi Cohen said it was time to sell our assets and get cash."

Cohen — it is a common Jewish name but Decker had to ask. "That's not the same Rabbi Cohen who's been making all the prophecies and causing people to explode in flames and everything, is it?" Decker asked the question almost as a joke, sure that his old friend could not possibly be associated with such a lunatic.

To Decker's horror, Tom nodded. "Rabbi Saul Cohen is the one who found me and brought me to Rhoda. If he hadn't, I would have died out there on the street. And it was by Cohen's hand that God healed my eyes. He even performed the ceremony when Rhoda and I were married," said Tom.

Suddenly the tenor of the reunion changed dramatically. Tom's attachment to Cohen was obviously strong. Decker could see that it might take intensive and extended deprogramming to break the hold that Cohen had on his friend. "Tom," he said, "I am aware that Cohen has many unusual powers. But the issue is the source of these powers and what he uses them for."

"The source of his power is God," Tom answered. "And what he and John use their power for is to perform God's will."

If it had been anyone other than his old friend Tom Donafin making that assertion, Decker might have raised his voice in vociferous argument. Instead, his thoughts were only of helping Tom to see reason. "Tom, was it God's will that Cohen and John use their powers to send three asteroids hurtling toward the earth?" Decker asked rhetorically, but with compassion. "Was it

God's will that the locusts be released on the people of the earth? Is it God's will that people all over the world are starving? Is it God's will that when anyone tries to stop John and Cohen they burst into flames?"

"Yes, Decker, it is," Tom answered confidently.

Decker nearly fell out of his chair. The correct answer was so obviously 'NO' that he had not expected Tom to answer at all. "But how can you say that?!" he demanded, his temper slipping from his grasp for a moment.

"Decker, it's just like in the movie *The Ten Commandments*."[10] Decker had forgotten how Tom always used movie plots to make his point, and he was tempted to laugh at the reference but the matter at hand was far too serious.

"You remember," Tom continued, "how Moses and his brother Aaron called down the plagues on Egypt?"

"Yeah," Decker responded. Tom's expression seemed to say that he thought Decker should have caught his point, which Tom apparently believed was obvious. But all that was obvious to Decker was that Tom had been brainwashed.

"Don't you see?" Tom continued. "Rabbi Cohen and John are just like Moses and Aaron."

Decker was shocked at how complete the brainwashing had been but this was neither the time nor place to try to begin deprogramming — best to leave that to the professionals. As soon as Christopher's speech and the vote were over, he would make some calls and arrange for a psychiatrist to talk to Tom. He'd have to find some way to set it up without Tom's knowledge. If Tom knew, he would try to leave and Decker might never see him again. Decker would not allow that to happen. Tom was his friend and he needed help. He'd have him locked up in an institution if necessary until he came to his senses. Decker had enough influence to do whatever was necessary, and he would not hesitate to use it to help Tom — whether Tom

---

[10]   1956, Paramount.

wanted his help or not.

"Well," Decker said, trying not to show how disturbed he was at what Tom was saying and at the same time intending to bring the subject to a close, "I'm glad to see at least that you didn't brand your forehead like some of the others."

"The mark is only for the Koum Damah Patar — male virgins selected by God to serve as his priests."

"Well, I guess that leaves you out," Decker said, seizing the opportunity to bring the conversation back to a more agreeable topic. "So, when can I meet this Dr. Rhoda of yours?"

"The next time you're in Israel, I guess."

Decker nodded. "Good," he said. "I'll look forward to it."

"Where are you staying?" Decker asked.

"I don't really have any plans."

"You'll stay with me then," Decker said in a way that indicated he wouldn't take 'no' for an answer. He had no intention of letting Tom out of his sight.

Tom smiled and nodded his agreement and appreciation.

"Right now I have to go over to the General Assembly. It will be extremely crowded, but I want you to come with me as my guest. Too bad you don't have a camera with you," Decker said. "You're about to witness history in the making."

□   □   □

Gerard Poupardin looked around nervously as he walked into the men's room on the third floor of the U.N. Secretariat building. Under his arm he carried a sealed diplomatic pouch. The restroom was empty. Stepping into a stall, he locked the door behind him, opened the pouch, removed the pistol and put it in his pocket.

□   □   □

The Hall of the General Assembly was filled to capacity. The delegations of 226 countries were present. Many heads of state who had come to hear the speech and to be seen in the presence of power had also managed to get seats. There were no empty seats anywhere. The visitor's gallery was closed to the public to make room for other dignitaries and the heads of U.N. agencies who had flown in for the occasion. The press gallery could not have held another reporter. Staff members from the many U.N. offices packed the back of the hall and were overflowing into the aisles.

Decker looked over at his regular seating area and noticed that the seats were already taken by friends of the American ambassador. Decker could have asked them to surrender the seats but it would not have been good politics. "I hope you don't mind if we stand," Decker said.

"No, that's fine," Tom answered.

"Come on. At least we can move near the front." Tom followed as Decker led.

In the back of the room Gerard Poupardin entered, nervously holding his hand over his right-hand jacket pocket in an effort to conceal the bulge from the gun. Christopher would be stepping up to the dais soon, and despite the fact that he felt in control of his emotions, Poupardin could feel the sweat begin to bead on his forehead.

It took a couple of minutes for Decker and Tom to get near the front of the hall and it was another five minutes before the session got underway. The first order of business was to read the nomination of the Security Council to the General Assembly. A moment later Christopher got up to speak. From his position near the front of the hall Decker watched with fatherly pride as Christopher walked to the lectern before the assembled members of the United Nations. The sound of applause was thunderous. Christopher nodded appreciation but the applause continued for several minutes.

From the back of the hall Gerard Poupardin pushed his way through the crowd toward the front of the room. The point of no return was now only seconds away and Poupardin felt more like a spectator to the events than a participant. There was no longer any thought of 'if.' Now it had become only a question of 'when.' The time for thought which he had assumed he would gain by putting off a decision, had been spent in the mere process of coming to this point, not in any additional contemplation of a final decision. Now all that he could do was follow through, pushed along as if in a dream, mindlessly watching and seemingly unable to alter the course he had laid out. Without planning it or even thinking about it, he felt his hand drop into his pocket. With disinterested abandon he grasped the butt of the pistol as his thumb began to play with the safety. He did not notice the faces around him, but his course had now brought him within three feet of where Tom Donafin and Decker Hawthorne stood.

Unnoticed, Tom pulled a handwritten note from his pocket and slipped it into Decker's jacket pocket.

The applause finally subsided and Christopher moved closer to the microphone to speak. "My fellow delegates and citizens of the world," he began, using the greeting that had been Jon Hansen's trademark opening — that had been Decker's suggestion, and from the applause that followed, it had been a good one. Christopher looked down from the dais to where Decker stood. Decker was pleased but surprised that Christopher had been able to spot him among the throng. Decker clapped and smiled his approval but Christopher did not smile back. Instead, Christopher's face was covered again with that same strange look of foreboding Decker had seen before, only now it appeared as sheer terror.

From the corner of his left eye Decker saw a flash of movement. In front of him on the dais Christopher suddenly raised his hands in a strange motion which seemed to Decker an attempt to protect his face. An instant later, from near Decker's left ear, a thunderous sound ripped through his head. With the sound still echoing through the room, Decker saw an explosion of red from Christopher's left forearm as he fell backward behind the lectern and out of Decker's view.

Wincing from the sound so near his ear, Decker turned toward the direction of the sound. Someone . . . a man . . . stood there, his arms still extended in front of him and his hands wrapped tightly around the butt of a revolver. In statuesque pose his finger still held the trigger. Decker wheezed in disbelief.

It was Tom Donafin.

As he let his arms drop he looked back at Decker.

"Why?" Decker gasped in horror. The sound of cheers around them had faded and turned to screams and cries of disbelief.

"He was going to leave me . . ." Tom began, but his explanation was cut short.

Decker watched as Tom's body was thrown violently to the right, his already misshapen head exploding in a cascade of red; spraying blood, pieces of brain, and bone fragments over those who stood nearby. An instant later the sound of the shot reached Decker's ears. On his left, he could see Gerard Poupardin tightly gripping the gun that had fired the shot.

Poupardin was lost: overcome by the drive to kill. He had turned his gun on Tom, who, having shot Christopher, seemed in Poupardin's insanity the obvious surrogate for his hatred. Poupardin's bullet had passed through Tom's brain and struck the steel plate left in his skull after his childhood automobile accident. The force of the bullet stripped the screws holding the plate out of their moorings and tore a gaping hole in the side of his head. Tom was dead even before he began to fall.

Blood gushed out from the massive wound, forming a large pool of red on the floor near Decker's feet. The screams of a woman nearby barely pierced the ringing in Decker's ears from the two shots. Then suddenly three more shots were heard, fired in rapid succession into the chest of Gerard Poupardin by a security guard, who, seeing Poupardin with a gun, mistakenly assumed that it had been Poupardin who had shot Christopher.

The large television monitor mounted in the front of the room focused on the lifeless, blood-streaked face of Christopher Goodman, who lay crumbled on the floor. From the socket where his right eye had been, blood spurted several times toward the camera and then stopped, along with his heartbeat. Another stream of blood issued from hole torn through his left forearm.

From behind him, Decker felt a wall of flesh push him to the floor. It had all taken only seconds, but as Decker fell under the throng of fleeing dignitaries, it seemed that a lifetime of loss accompanied him.

The crush bruised Decker's rib cage and badly twisted his left knee, tearing ligaments and popping the joint out of its socket. The panic was unnecessary. There was no danger to anyone else in the room. Tom had accomplished his hideous, unexplained mission and had made no attempt to escape or even to protect himself.

□   □   □

Later, when he was alone in his grief, Decker found Tom's note in his jacket pocket. "Do not weep for me," it said. "What I do shall not be held against me. I am the Avenger of Blood."

Chapter 14

Dark Legion

March 9, 2023 — Northwest Iraq (6:16 a.m. local time, 3:16 a.m. GMT)

From deep below the bed of the Euphrates river, between the Iraqi cities of *Ana* and *Hit*, and bordered by the four ancient river guard posts of *Baia Malcha*, *Auzura*, *Jibb Jibba*, and *Olabu*, a dark assembly crept eagerly toward the surface, its members fighting and clawing in the agitated hive to be among the first ranks to emerge. Their time was near. They knew it. This was the hour and the day and the month and the year for which they had waited since before the dawn of human history. Their manumission would not last long though, and each hoped to make the most of it while they could. Then, unheard by physical ears, a trumpet sounded and thunder rolled and chains were loosed and fell to the ground. John and Cohen's most recent prophecy was about to be fulfilled upon the people of the earth.

At last the time had arrived. The earth retched and the

waters of the Euphrates churned and boiled and then violently erupted, releasing an ooze of savage, shadowy, repulsive brutes into the world of men. Like lava from a volcano or pus from an inflamed abscess, the vile horde, imperceptible to human sight, spread out in all directions across the face of the earth, seeking out human life wherever it could be found. The foul stench of burning sulfur rose to the heavens and filled the air for a thousand miles as row upon hideous row of the ghoulish spectral mass emerged upon the earth.   Arrayed in ghostly armor, their otherwise gray hides covered with breastplates of fiery red, dark blue, and yellow, each of the sinister throng rode upon an aberrational mount which resembled nothing so much as it did a horse but which had a head and mane more like that of a lion and nostrils filled with putrid breath of yellow smoke and flame. The tail of each beast seemed to rise and move independent of the movement of the beast itself and on close examination appeared less like a tail and far more like a venomous serpent grafted to the beast's hindquarters. Scores of the malevolent legion rose above the earth on leathery wings and filled the sky with foul shrieks of glee as they eagerly scouted ahead of the dark army of 200 million, each bent on participating in the destruction of man.

Northeast of the city of *Ar-Ramādī*, a small village of Iraqi "Marsh Arabs" from the marshy areas around the Euphrates and Tigris rivers lay sleeping in the cool pre-dawn March air. Unaware of the approaching danger, an old man rose from his sleep and threw on his cloak in preparation for morning prayer toward Mecca. Outside his home the invisible legions advanced with incredible speed, bearing down upon his small village, eager to draw first blood. Unheard and unseen, one of the phantom riders passed effortlessly through the wall of the man's house, saliva dripping from the corners of his grotesque mouth as he spotted his first victim. Sensing only the faint odious fetor of burning sulfur, the old man's body shuddered as though he had tasted a bitter fruit as the invisible demon entered him and took control of his mind and body.

Quietly, so as not to awaken anyone else in the house, he walked to the kitchen area and picked up a large knife and brought it back to his bed. Then, nudging her a little so she would wake up to see it coming, he plunged the knife without second thought into the heart of his wife of forty years. The terror in her eyes was so great he had to cover his mouth quickly with one hand so that his laughter would not wake the others. He then repeated his act, sometimes stabbing and sometimes slashing throats until he had cut short the life of his two sons, their wives, and all of his grandchildren. Looking around him at the slaughter, he finally relaxed, found a chair, sat down, and broke into loud uncontrollable laughter.

After a few moments of basking in the self-satisfaction of his achievement, the old man ran from his house, howling in crazed revelry as he brandished the bloodied knife, looking for others to feed his blood lust. Throughout the small town the invisible army found other victims and murder reigned triumphant over every living thing. Both screams and laughter filled the air as the old man, still carrying the knife, found a young girl about three years of age playing by herself in front of her home. With the knife in his hand and lust in his eyes, he charged toward her, ready to spill her blood out onto the street.

Instinctively the child screamed with fear. Then suddenly a shot rang out and the old man fell, dropping his knife within a few feet of the girl. As he looked up to see who had shot him, the dark spirit left him.

Shaking with fear in the doorway of his home, the girl's father put down his rifle and went to comfort his terrified daughter. Then unexpectedly he caught a hint of the smell of burning sulfur. He looked first at the man he had shot and then at his child. Picking up the bloody blade the old man had dropped, he walked over to where the girl stood still screaming and picked her up. In a few moments she stopped crying and when she had, he looked deep into her loving brown eyes and held the point of the blade to the soft flesh of her stomach. Smiling broadly until she began to smile and then laugh with him, he shoved the knife into her small body, and with another thrust, pushed it the rest of the way through and out her back. Then, holding the handle of the knife with both hands, he lifted his daughter's impaled body up over his head like a trophy and began spinning about and caterwauling in a mad dance as the blood of the child ran down upon his head, soaking his hair and beard and clothing.

In a house nearby, a young woman worked in her kitchen preparing breakfast for her still-sleeping husband. Abruptly she stood up straight and dropped her cooking utensils to the floor. Looking around, she picked up a large heavy skillet, left her meal preparations, and went to the bedroom. Going to the side of the bed, she raised the skillet above her and brought it down with all her strength onto her husband's head. For just a moment his eyes opened and he looked up at her in agony and bewilderment as she laughed and raised the skillet and brought it down upon him again. Losing consciousness, he slipped away as his wife struck him again and again until his skull was crushed beyond recognition and his brains spilled out on the bed.

With his blood splattered all over her dress the woman dropped the skillet and, still laughing, walked back to the kitchen where the breakfast she had been preparing was now burned. Calmly she lifted the hem of her blood-splattered dress and held it up to the flame of the stove until it caught. With her dress in flames, she giggled as she swayed gently from side to side and the fire engulfed her.

With increasing swiftness the murderous mounted madness swept across farm, village, town, and city. The slaughter was unimaginable as people turned on one another, driven on by forces they could not see or understand. Seven and a half hours after it started, the insanity reached *Umm Qasr* and *Faw* and the other cities on the Persian Gulf, and people ran by the thousands like lemmings into the sea to drown.

As the madness swallowed the capital of Baghdad, all

communications with the outside world were lost. There was no one to report the story to the rest of the world because no one survived. Everyone was killed. For death's agents, the more violent the slaughters, the better. And when no one was left to kill, the last person standing would take his own life.

March 10, 2023 — London (6:03 a.m.)

Stan McKay spit out a pistachio shell and washed down the half-chewed meat with a quick swallow of his soft drink. The young journalist was still new on the job and so was quick to respond to the blinking light before him. Picking up the receiver of the phone, he answered simply, "McKay." No more answer than that was necessary since anyone intentionally calling that number would know they had reached the headquarters of World News Network in London.

"Let me talk to Jack Washington," the voice demanded urgently.

"I'm sorry, sir," McKay responded. "Mr. Washington is out of the office right now."

"Then let me talk to Oliver Peyton."

"I'm sorry," McKay said again. "He's with Mr. Washington. Can I help you?"

"Yeah, yeah," the voice said after a second's hesitation. "Look, this is James Paulson. I'm about to send you a live feed from the Riyadh office. I want you to make absolutely certain you're set to record and then I want you to be sure that the report gets to Jack Washington. Can you do that?"

"Yes, sir," McKay answered confidently.

"Okay, I'll start the feed in twenty seconds. Is that enough time for you?"

"Uh . . . yes, sir. I think so," he answered with less certainty.

"Okay, just do your best."

It took about thirty seconds for McKay to check his equipment. "All set, sir," he said when he returned to the phone, and switched on his own monitor so he could see what was coming across.

"This is James Paulson reporting from the WNN offices in *Riyadh*, Saudi Arabia," he said in the same hurried tone he had had on the phone. Stan McKay had no actual experience in front of the camera but he had studied it in school — which really didn't qualify him to have an opinion — but it seemed to him that this James Paulson character was talking much too quickly for television. "Outside the window of our offices," Paulson continued, "a scene of utter chaos is unfolding." The hand-held camera moved from Paulson to the WNN office window, revealing the grisly spectacle on the street, superimposed over the reflection of the camera and its operator in the glass of the closed window.

"It looks like a war zone out there," he said. And, indeed, it did. There were people throwing bricks and stones and other heavy objects at one another; there were a few people with knives and other sharp objects; and scattered around there were the bodies of those who had already fallen. "The violence seems to be totally indiscriminate," Paulson continued. "Shop owners killing customers and vice versa; men and women killing each other in the most brutal ways imaginable; and perhaps the strangest aspect to it all: no one appears to be doing anything to protect themselves. No one runs, no one hides. They just stand in plain view, without seeking cover, as they continue to assault and kill each other."

As Paulson spoke, the camera focused on an adolescent girl as she repeatedly stabbed a woman who may have been her mother with a short sharp object which appeared to be a writing pen. The blood made it impossible to be sure. As the camera pulled back, a man jumped from the eighth floor of an adjacent building, coming down head-first onto the pavement.

Paulson paused in stunned silence and then struggled to continue. "The melee appears to have begun about ten to twelve minutes ago when sirens were heard throughout the city as police, fire, and emergency medical teams responded to reports of random violence. Immediately following that, the sound of gunfire began and still continues sporadically. As you can see out our window, the sky is beginning to fill with smoke from hundreds of fires that have sprung up all over the city as savagery rules the streets.

"Here at the WNN offices we have sealed ourselves in, locking security doors and terminating all elevator access to the two floors . . ." James Paulson abruptly stopped speaking and looked somewhere off-camera, behind the camera operator. His right eyebrow raised in apprehension. His eyes shifted about the room. Something was obviously happening in the office, though Paulson didn't seem to know exactly what.

Stan McKay, watching the monitor in London, twisted and turned in his seat, instinctively looking at the screen from different angles hoping to get a better view, though logic told him it really wouldn't change his perspective of the office. The look on Paulson's face went from apprehension to sheer terror. The picture tumbled as the camera dropped and then the screen went blank.

Saudi Arabia (2:57 p.m. local time, 5:57 p.m. GMT)

The sound of air passing through regulators was entirely drowned out by the swirling blades of the United Nations helicopter as it hovered a few hundred yards from a camp of 80 to 100 Bedouin tribesmen camped a few miles south of the helicopter's destination of *As-Mubarraz*, Saudi Arabia. Inside the helicopter, a team of four men and two women plus the helicopter's pilot and copilot studied the actions of the tribesmen, while cameras recorded the event and transmitted the pictures via satellite to an aircraft carrier in the Indian Ocean. According to satellite photography, a rapidly-growing circle of death, inside of which no human life remained, extended from *Yazd*, Iran in the east, 1,050 miles to *Mahattat Al-Qatrānah*, Jordan in the west;

from *Nachičevan, Azerbajdzanskaja* in the north, 920 miles to *Al-Hulwah*, Saudi Arabia in the south. *As-Mubarraz*, 82 miles below the southernmost edge of the circle, thus far appeared to be unaffected and the Bedouin camp was the first sign of human life the team had spotted this close to the periphery of the circle.

The preponderance of evidence about the circle of death indicated the presence of some incredibly fast-acting, 100 percent virulent, rapidly-dispersing biological or chemical agent. There were two pieces of data that conflicted with that thesis. The first was that whatever the killing agent was, it traveled in all directions at about the same speed and was therefore unaffected by air currents, as would have been the case with any known nuclear, biological, or chemical agent. The second chink in the thesis was the macabre video report that had come from World News Network in Riyadh.

For protection, each member of the helicopter's crew and research team wore an entirely self-contained nuclear/biological/chemical suit which provided protection against any infiltrant larger than .005 microns. Gas masks were used until the helicopter came to within twenty kilometers of the city, after which point respiration was provided by individual tanks of compressed air carried by each member of the team and the crew members. Because of this protective encasement, communications among the team were carried out by means of short-range radio transmitters and receivers that were built into their masks and hoods. Anything said by a member of the team would be heard by all other members and transmitted back by the helicopter's communications equipment to the carrier in the Indian Ocean.

There was no indication of anything unusual when the helicopter reached the southern edge of the city. The residents were going about their daily lives. Hovering about 150 feet above the ground, the six cameras mounted below the helicopter recorded everything they encountered, providing a complete panoramic view from the chopper's belly. Inside, the team members scanned the vicinity for anything that seemed at all unusual, but found nothing. The team leader, Col. Terry Crystal, leaned through the doorway from the cargo bay to the helicopter's cockpit and signaled the pilot to proceed northward, stopping at each of the predetermined coordinates for subsequent inspection.

The helicopter was a flying laboratory with equipment on board to provide immediate analysis of all environmental data and the retrieval and collection of samples for further analysis on their return to their base in *Qal'at Bishna*. At each of the several stops made over the city, air samples were taken for immediate analysis but so far nothing unusual had been found.

Arriving at the northern edge of the city the helicopter slowed again, hovering while the team repeated its routine. If nothing was found, the itinerary would take them next to *Al-Hulwah*, a location within the known radius of the circle of death, where satellite photographs indicated no human life remained. The air sample from the city's northern border indicated the presence of no contaminants and there appeared to be no visual indication of anything out of the ordinary on the ground. Col. Crystal checked with each member of his team and then, leaning back into the cockpit again, motioned to the pilot to continue.

The pilot was about to carry out Col. Crystal's order when the copilot thought he noticed something. "What's that?" he asked, pointing to something on the ground.

Col. Crystal and the pilot looked where the copilot was pointing. "It's just a woman doing her laundry in a washtub," Col. Crystal said.

"No, look closer," the copilot insisted.

Col. Crystal picked up his binoculars and stepped into the cockpit for a better view. "What the hell?!" he gasped, still holding the binoculars. His response drew the attention of the rest of the team in the helicopter's bay. As the members of the team looked on in horror, a woman in her mid-twenties held a baby by its feet while its head dangled, submerged beneath the water of her washtub.

"There's something else!" someone said, pointing about a hundred yards from the woman. Shifting their attention, they watched as a man with a pitchfork ran up behind another man and drove the instrument through his body and out his chest.

"Quick! The woman!" someone else yelled cryptically, and pointed back to the previous scene, where a man with a rifle was approaching the woman, who still held the baby by his feet. A second later, at point-blank range the man put the rifle to the woman's chest and pulled the trigger, blowing a large hole where her heart had been. The body of the dead baby dropped into the tub, where it bobbed a few times and then floated face down.

"Get us out of range of that rifle!" Col. Crystal ordered quickly.

"Everybody hang on!" the pilot yelled as he pulled the chopper sharply up and to the left to take cover behind one of the city's taller buildings. He did so just in time, as the man turned and started shooting at them.

"Look! Over there!" one of the female team members called.

"And over there!" someone else said.

It quickly became apparent that there were more than enough atrocities to keep them all busy; no one needed to point them out. Even from a distance of hundreds of feet in the air, the slaughter was sickening to watch. The madness spread below them at incredible speed.

"Are we getting all this on camera?" Col. Crystal asked.

"Yes, sir," came the answer from the team member monitoring the cameras.

"Let's get our air samples and get the hell out of here," the colonel directed. Crystal stepped back into the cockpit. The cockpit's large windows provided a much wider angle of view than the observation windows in the helicopter's bay. Despite the horror on the ground, the attention of all three men in the cockpit was fixed on it, unable to conceive of such mindless slaughter. For a while no one spoke; they all watched in disbelief, struggling to comprehend what could be causing this.

"Sir," the pilot said, addressing Col. Crystal, "I don't know what's going on down there, but if your people have their samples I think we ought to get the hell out of here and come back for the other tests when things have calmed down. Right now we're a sitting duck for anyone with a gun. They've pretty much ignored us so far, but . . ." The pilot's sentence was cut short by a flashing light on the instrument panel, followed by a sudden shift in the helicopter's weight distribution. "Someone's opened the bay door!!" he yelled.

Col. Crystal turned on his heel and went back into the helicopter's bay. What he saw there defied logical explanation. The bay door was indeed open as the pilot's instruments had indicated, but the research team was gone.

After waiting a moment but hearing no word from Col. Crystal, the pilot decided to have a look for himself. "Take over," he told his copilot. "I'm going back to see what's going on."

The same scene greeted him as had met Col. Crystal. The door was open and no one was there — not even Col. Crystal. "No one's back here!" he reported in stunned disbelief to his copilot by way of the internal radio in their protective suits. "It looks like they've all jumped!"

"Oh, shit!" the copilot answered. It didn't take much to realize that whatever was affecting the people on the ground had taken its toll on the research team. "Let's get out of here, skipper."

"Roger that. Just let me get this door shut and we'll be gone!"

The pilot moved quickly to the rear of the bay and reached to pull the door shut. Behind him there was a flash of movement and someone lunged from behind some equipment. Hit by the man's full weight, the pilot flew through the open doorway of the helicopter along with his attacker. Tumbling through mid-air towards his certain death, he saw who had tackled him. It was Col. Crystal.

"Get back to base!" he yelled as loud as he could, hoping that he was still within range for radio contact with his copilot — it was imperative that the data gathered by the team be delivered. Two seconds later the pilot and Col. Crystal were dead.

Inside the helicopter, the copilot had heard the pilot's last order and was already making good its completion. Moving south as quickly as the chopper would take him, he retreated back the way they had come. Everywhere below him the killing progressed with amazing speed. The cameras were still rolling, capturing the details of the bloodshed and sending them back to a stunned analysis team in the Indian Ocean. Then unexpectedly, the copilot caught the smell of something like rotten eggs or burning sulfur.

The dark legions of the Euphrates River had not yet reached the Bedouin camp south of the city. Looking up from feeding his father's camels, a teenage Bedouin boy watched with great interest the return of the helicopter that had passed overhead about half an hour earlier. Curiously, it flew straight toward them and upon reaching their camp, hovered there, frightening the animals in camp and bringing everyone out of their tents. For a moment nothing happened, and then it seemed as though rain was falling but the rain burned their eyes. The 'rain' was fuel from the helicopter's tanks being dumped on the camp and blown about by the helicopter's blades. Many people took shelter in their tents, which soaked up the gas. With about a quarter of its fuel remaining, the helicopter shot straight up into the sky. At about a thousand feet up the copilot changed course and took the helicopter into a power dive, crashing directly into the heart of the Bedouin camp and turning the entire camp into a spectacular blazing inferno.

□   □   □

By the end of the second day there was not a person left alive within 1,200 miles of the Euphrates River and the murderous madness was continuing to spread, reaching as far west as Libya, as far east as Afghanistan, as far north as *Volgograd*, Russia, and as far south as the Gulf of Aden. Five hundred million men, women, and children had been killed and there was no sign of abatement. The following night the circle of death had reached *Timessa*, Libya, and the heel of the boot of Italy in the west; western India in the east; Moscow in the north; and *Burji*, Ethiopia in the south. Eight hundred million people lay brutally slaughtered; the populations of Iraq, Iran, Jordan, Saudi Arabia, Yemen, South Yemen, Oman, Afghanistan, Pakistan, Syria, Egypt, Turkey, Greece, Bulgaria, as well as most of Romania, Turkistan, Libya, Ethiopia, and the Sudan were dead. There was one exception: not one person within the borders of Israel had been killed.

Chapter 15

Avatar Dawn

March 11, 2023 — The United Nations, New York

Drawn curtains barred the light of the afternoon sun, reflecting the dark mood that permeated the room. Inside the stately chamber, under faint artificial light, silent guards stood vigil over the flag-draped, sealed coffin of the fallen leader. Decker was among the first to arrive for the memorial service in those final hours before the burial. Hobbling on crutches because of the injury sustained when he was pushed to the floor after the assassination, he stood beside the coffin in bitter grief and disbelief, tears flowing freely. After a few moments he moved away and sat alone in silence on the dais, from which he would later deliver Christopher Goodman's eulogy.

One by one the darkly clad dignitaries from around the world began to arrive for the solemn occasion of laying one of their own to rest. Most were ambassadors and other dignitaries whom Decker knew from his years at the U.N., but there were also others, many associates of Robert Milner — authors, college professors, actors, television and movie producers, religious leaders, people of influence from all walks of life. Soon the number grew and a line formed, stretching out into the hall as each of the mourners waited to pass slowly by the coffin, pausing to offer their last respects.

It was not the same as it had been with the funerals of Jon Hansen, where hundreds of thousands of people had waited in line to pass by the coffin. Within the United Nations Christopher was extremely popular, but except for Italy, which Christopher had represented in the U.N., his popularity did not extend to the general population of the world. Most people knew him as one of the ten members of the Security Council and knew that he probably would have become Secretary-General had he not been killed, so there was grief and certainly shock at his assassination, but not the sense of personal loss that had accompanied the death of Hansen.

Secretary Milner had taken responsibility for Christopher's body and had handled all of the arrangements for the funeral and the burial. Decker was relieved that he had taken that burden. He was a little surprised, however, by the number of press and cameras Milner had allowed at the funeral service. Most of the major networks and news services were represented, as were the all-news networks. With the incredible number of deaths in the east and the panic that was spreading all over the rest of the world, it seemed hardly believable that this much attention would be given to the funeral of one man. But as is almost always the case, the press tends to cover that which is most convenient — that which is either in its own backyard or some place where the reporter would like to take an expenses-paid sojourn — even when the world may be falling apart elsewhere. All of the major news media had offices in New York and so most were here to cover the funeral. There were, of course, reporters on the periphery of the horrific events in the east, and while their terrifying reports dominated the headlines, no one close enough to the story to report on it was long spared from becoming a victim.

Thus far all of the reconnaissance missions had ended in disaster, so most of the coverage was limited to stories based on satellite photography or of panicked masses attempting to flee the onset of the madness.

Perhaps the sense of business-almost-as-usual which filled the room was due to an inability to comprehend what was taking place on the other side of the world. Perhaps it was because it *was* on the other side of the world. Or perhaps it was the growing sense that crisis was becoming the norm.

Decker was as aware as anyone of the mayhem in the east, but after all the suffering and death he had seen in his life — from his tour of duty in Vietnam, to the murdered guards at the Wailing Wall, the death of his wife and children and hundreds of millions of others in the Disaster, the hundreds of millions more killed in the Russian holocaust and the China-India-Pakistan War, the countless loss of life and destruction from the asteroids and the resulting starvation in so many parts of the world, and most recently the torment of the locusts which Decker had experienced firsthand — he felt incurably numbed to it all. As long as Christopher was alive most of that suffering at least seemed to serve some purpose: the 'birth pains of the New Age,' as Milner and Christopher had called it. But with Christopher's death, nothing made sense.

Time after time Decker retraced the events in his mind. Most senseless of all were the circumstances that led to Christopher's death. He could not absolve himself of guilt for being the one who had given Tom Donafin access and opportunity to commit his heinous crime. When the connection between Decker and Tom had been made after the assassination, Decker was questioned by U.N. security. The news media were quick to jump on the story as well. There was probably no one who seriously thought that Decker had any intentional involvement in what had happened, but with so little known about the assassin, Decker's connection had become an angle which security and the media insisted on exploring in every detail. Decker and Tom had been friends, classmates, worked for the same magazine, and later both had been taken hostage and held for three years in Lebanon. The irony that Decker had been responsible for freeing Tom Donafin from his bonds in Lebanon and that now Donafin had assassinated Christopher, whom Decker had raised as his own son, was considered and reflected upon ad nauseam. Had it been known that it was Christopher who had actually freed Decker in the first place, thus allowing Decker to free Tom, the discussions of irony would have gone on even longer.

Later, after U.N. Security inspected the apartment of Gerard Poupardin and it became apparent from the many fouled and defaced news clippings and photographs that Poupardin's original target had been Christopher, there was at last something else for the news media to talk about. A number of commentators, perhaps motivated in part out of sympathy for Decker, argued that if Tom had not shot Christopher, then Poupardin certainly would have. 'Still,' they would conclude, 'it was ironic . . .'

So the 'official' verdict of the media was that Decker had acted innocently. That was also the conclusion reached by U.N. Security. Yet Decker could not help but blame himself.

Adding to his misery, Decker struggled with the grief he felt for Tom. The vision of Tom's violent death was not an easy one to forget. Still, there was a sense of guilt at the very thought that he could lament the death of Christopher's murderer. He had mulled over Tom's last words time and again. "He was going to leave me," Tom had said. Did it really mean something or was it just the ravings of a lunatic? And what did Tom's note mean about being the 'Avenger of Blood'? Whatever it was, it seemed clearly to have been the result of Tom's association with John, Cohen, and the Koum Damah Patar. Decker was sure they were the ones who had caused this. Somehow they had driven Tom to do it because they knew that Christopher was the one force that stood in their way. Their time was running out. Had Christopher lived and become Secretary-General, he certainly would have ended their reign of terror on the earth.

Decker stopped short and renewed his self-flagellation. *But it was still my fault that Tom got into the Hall,* he said under his breath. He never let himself get too far from that thought. His feeling of guilt, his suffering, even the pain of his twisted knee, were his penance, though he felt they were far from adequate for his self-supposed crime.

In the breast pocket of his jacket Decker had put a brochure from a nearby life completion center. He had always found 'life completion' to be a sickeningly sweet euphemism for suicide, but when the brochure had come in his mail two days earlier, sent by some aggressive life completion center's marketing manager, he had kept it. It was not the first time that he had received such a mailer — they were sometimes sent out in mass mailings — but this was the first time he had received a targeted mailer. The good marketers watched the papers for likely clientele, those who had recently lost a loved one, failed in a business, filed for bankruptcy, and the like. Actually, considering the circumstances, Decker was surprised to have received only one. The letter had offered consolation at "this difficult time" and had generously offered their services should he require them.

Decker still had a few matters to put straight, but soon after the funeral he planned to quietly slip away to the center's facility — not that he believed the letter claiming that the people at the center really cared about his suffering. It was simply the most convenient location and he imagined it far less painful than hanging himself or jumping from the top of a building.

Decker had read that most people considering suicide felt a great sense of relief once they had decided for certain on their course. He felt none of that.

Unnoticed by Decker, who was lost in thought, but conspicuous to the press and most others in the room, former U.N. Assistant Secretary-General Robert Milner had arrived. It was not that Milner was such a celebrity that so many should have taken notice — though those 'in the know' were certainly familiar with him. Almost everyone else was at least familiar by reputation with his work and his many books about the coming New Age. The reason for the present interest was caused instead by the way he was dressed. Centered between two of the honor guards who stood motionless at parade rest facing the opposite direction, Milner stood dressed not in his normal business attire but arrayed in a long flowing robe of pure white linen that touched the floor.

Silent and unmoving, six feet from the rear of the coffin with his head lowered slightly, Milner's eyes locked penetratingly on the casket. Decker knew that Milner had not been there a moment before, but now in his stillness, planted there like an oak tree, it seemed as if he had been there for hours. Then Decker noticed something else: it was almost imperceptible, but it appeared that the United Nations flag draped over Christopher's sealed coffin had begun to glow.

Soon there was no doubt, as every thread of the fabric became iridescent. Silence fell like a shroud as the attention of everyone in the room was drawn to Milner and to the coffin. In the absence of natural light, the coffin had become the brightest object in the room. Interest and curiosity quickly gave way to trepidation and fear as those nearest the coffin began to draw back into the crowd. On the dais from which he was to have given Christopher's eulogy, Decker struggled to his feet and stared in utter disbelief at the light emanating from the box which held his friend. Now even the guards had turned and began to inch away, leaving only Robert Milner still standing, totally immovable.

Anticipation filled the room as breathing stopped involuntarily and hearts pounded in near panic. Then suddenly Milner's hands flew upward. It seemed not so much that he had raised them, but that he could no longer hold them down. No sooner had his hands reached their zenith than light as intense as the sun burst forth from the seams of the coffin, muted only by the U.N. flag which still covered it. The light which streamed from the box was as hot as it was bright, causing the air to swell and resulting in a sound similar to the roar of an acetylene torch.

Decker immediately understood what was happening: Christopher was being regenerated — resurrected just as Jesus had been 2,000 years earlier.

The others in the room backed away and hid their eyes from the intense light. Then suddenly the coffin began to shake violently, causing the flag to slip off and drop to the floor and revealing the unfiltered light which had by now grown too bright to look at. Only Milner's eyes remained open. The television cameras stayed focused on the scene but the operators were forced to look away or close their eyes. The television picture showed only a bright flood of light which washed out everything around it.

Then the light vanished and there was silence.

In the center of the room the United Nations flag lay scorched in a heap. The lid of the casket had been thrown open and lay splintered on the floor, its latches and hinges ripped asunder. Beside the open coffin stood Christopher. His left arm hung by his side, rendered largely useless by the bullet which had pierced it, and the wound to his head had left him with an empty right eye socket. But he was alive.

Perhaps it was an illusion caused by the bright light that preceded, or perhaps it was caused by the blur of the tears of joy in Decker's eyes, but it seemed at least to Decker that an aura of light remained around Christopher. Immediately Christopher looked over and motioned to Secretary Milner, who had dropped to one knee in exhaustion. He then looked at Decker, who was leaning on his crutches. Christopher smiled. "Come, Decker," he said. "We have work to do." As Decker started toward him, Christopher stopped him. "You won't be needing those," he said of the crutches.

Immediately the pain left Decker's knee and he dropped the crutches where he stood. He was at Christopher's side in a moment. While the crowd maintained a safe distance, the three men made their exit from the hall.

"Where are we going?" Decker asked. He wanted to ask and

say a million other things.   He wanted to stop and hold Christopher in his arms and weep tears of joy, but he sensed from Christopher's quick pace and determined demeanor that only immediate issues should be addressed at present.

"Jerusalem," Christopher answered within earshot of most of the press.

"A helicopter is waiting to take us to the airport," Robert Milner added when they were a little farther away.   "The Secretary-General's supersonic is standing by at Kennedy."   It hardly seemed important that Christopher had never actually been elected to that position — under the circumstances, certainly no one would deny him the privileges of the office. Considering what had just occurred, Decker was a little surprised by the thought that Christopher would even need an airplane. He wasn't sure if he should ask, but Christopher seemed to anticipate the question. "There are certain limitations I must live with as long as I remain confined to this body," he said. "I'll explain it all on the plane."

Within seconds every news agency in the world had reported the astonishing story of Christopher's resurrection. The world stood paralyzed in wonder, stunned by the reports and television coverage of the actual event. No one was sure what it meant, but with so much violence and death in the world, it seemed that in this one victory over the grave, perhaps there was still hope for their threatened planet. Some wept, some celebrated, but most just stared in disbelief, wondering if it was all a cruel hoax. But in a world that had seen so much death and destruction, a world that even now was threatened by some unexplained annihilation and so longed for some sign of hope, most openly yearned for it to be true.

□   □   □

By the time the helicopter reached Kennedy Airport more than forty members of the press were already there with cameras and microphones poised. They were held back from the landing pad by United Nations Security forces — all prearranged by Milner — but they blocked access to the Secretary-General's jet.

As soon as the door of the helicopter opened, the reporters began to shout questions. Decker was the first off. He wondered how they could possibly make it past the reporters to the waiting plane. But when Milner and then Christopher, now attired in a long linen robe which matched Milner's, stepped from the plane, the reporters suddenly fell silent. Christopher's left arm hung useless and he wore a patch over the empty socket of his right eye. Seeing reporters silent was a unique experience, but Decker supposed it was appropriate for the circumstances. Pushed back by the U.N. Security forces, the reporters moved back out of their way, allowing Decker, Christopher, and Milner to pass.

As the three boarded the huge jet, one of the reporters finally found his tongue and shouted a question to Decker. "Where are you going?" he called. In the end it was the only question asked, which was just as well since it was the only one Decker could answer.

Conveying what Christopher had told him in the helicopter, Decker yelled back, "Jerusalem, to put an end to the killing!"

Chapter 16

The Origin of God —
The Destiny of Man

In minutes their plane was in the air. In the supersonic — one of three planes reserved for the Secretary-General — it would take seven and a half hours to reach Tel Aviv. Now there was time to talk.

"Decker," Christopher said with a great deal of excitement, "I've looked inside the box! The old wooden box in my dream: it was the Ark — the Ark of the Covenant stripped bare of its gold exterior," he explained.

"When Moses made the Ark he was instructed to build a wooden box as the form and then to cover it with overlays of gold. If you remove the gold covering from the Ark you'd find just a very ordinary box made of acacia wood. That's what the old wooden box was in my dream." Christopher paused. "And now I have seen inside it."

Christopher continued. "Decker, inside the Ark I was able to see into infinity past, and it has allowed me to also understand the future. I understand everything now: the meaning of life and death, the whole reason for my being here, now, at this precise moment. There *is* a purpose to it all. But accomplishing the task before us will be difficult — perhaps more difficult than anything you can imagine." Christopher paused in reflection.

"In a way," he said, "I think I'd rather face crucifixion again than to do what I have been called to do." Christopher's voice quivered as perspiration beaded up on his forehead. He seemed even to be fighting back tears of fear and pain, but his determination to go on was even stronger.

"It's all so clear," he said, shaking his head and running his hand through his hair. "But it's not at all like I believed it was! It's not what any of us thought." Christopher suddenly turned and looked at Milner as if he had just realized something that should have been obvious to him all along. "No one, that is, except you. You knew. Didn't you?"

Milner nodded. "I knew," he said. "But it wasn't something I could tell you. You had to find it for yourself — for all of us — for all Humankind.

"There is one thing that I was wrong about, though," Milner confessed. "I was wrong to ask you to not use your powers to heal people. I see that now. You could no more stop helping people than Decker or I could stop breathing. To ask you to do so was to ask you not to be who you were meant to be. And as it turns out, the healings led to your nomination as Secretary-General, which set things in motion for your assassination, which — as painful as it was for all of us — was a necessary step toward your realizing the full truth about yourself."

Milner turned to Decker, "You must not feel guilty for what happened. Christopher had to suffer and die," he said, "so that the world could live. He could not change the world if he was exempt from the cost of that change. To become the Ruler of the New Age, Christopher had to share fully in the world's pain. His death was analogous to the suffering endured by the earth from the plagues."

"But what about your arm and your eye? Will those be healed?" Decker asked.

"Yes," Christopher answered, "But I will not heal my own wounds until I have first healed the wounds of the rest of the world. Until then, my wounds will serve as a symbol to all of Humankind of what must be accomplished before any of us can truly rest."

The look on Christopher's face revealed the furious pace of the thoughts running through his mind. "I need your help," he said suddenly, looking at Decker.

Decker raised his eyebrows as if to say, 'What can I, a mere mortal, do?' After all, here was a man — if 'man' was even the right word — who had just returned from the dead, and he was asking for Decker's help.

"The task before us," Christopher continued, "requires a decisive act of the will, the will of every man and woman on the planet. We need not only their support and cooperation but their commitment to completing the course. To achieve that, the people must be fully informed of what is involved and what is at risk. The problem," Christopher said, "is that the truth is so fantastic, so contrary to what so many have believed for all their lives, that I don't expect even you to believe it!"

"Considering what I have just seen," Decker interrupted, "I think I'll believe anything you say."

"Don't be so sure," Christopher cautioned. "What I'm about to tell you will go against some of your most long-held traditions and beliefs. It totally shatters the foundations of the earth as many people believe them to be. But you've **got to try** to understand and believe, Decker, so you can help me to tell the world.

"That's why you're here. I know you're fond of thinking that you just have a knack for being in the right place at the right time, but your part in this is not just dumb luck. I'm sure of it. It's fate, it's foreordained. You alone have been a witness since the beginning, since even before my birth. Now I must reveal the truth to the world. And I need your help to find the words to make the world understand what I'm about to tell you."

"You know I'll do whatever I can," Decker assured him.

"Thank you, Decker. But before I explain what lies ahead, I need to tell you that there is another reason why you're here. I can't explain how it happened — there are some forces in the universe that are beyond explanation — but you have a very personal stake in all of this. Decker, this is not the first lifetime that we have shared together. This is not the first time that you have lived. I do not know how many other lives you may have lived, but I do know there was at least one other. Two thousand years ago you and I were as close as brothers. You were one of my followers, my disciples."

Decker blinked hard, his eyes growing wide and his brows raised halfway up his forehead, both in surprise and to keep from losing his eye contact with Christopher as he dropped his head and tried hard to swallow. Robert Milner smiled broadly, but Decker didn't see it.

"You were with me in Israel, and like me, you were betrayed. Now I understand why it seemed so natural for me to go to you when Aunt Martha and Uncle Harry died. We were drawn together in this life just as we were in the past."

"Decker, my dearest and closest friend, you were my disciple, Judas Iscariot! Like me, you were betrayed by John — Yochanan bar Zebadee — for his own gain."[11] Christopher put his hand on Decker's shoulder and gripped it firmly. "And now, together, we must face him to put an end to his wickedness."

Christopher released his grip. "But your history is not nearly so important as your destiny. It is not an accident, Decker, that you've never really fit in with people at the Lucius Trust or any of the other New Age groups at the U.N. I know that sometimes you have felt out of place with people like Secretary Milner and Gaia Love and the other leaders of the New Age movement. But you are more important to the movement — to the coming of the

[11]   See *In His Image, Book One of the Christ Clone Trilogy*, pp. 344-345.

New Age itself — than you can possibly imagine. You are the bridge that we must use to make all these things understandable to the people of the world."

"Decker," Robert Milner began where Christopher left off, "much has already been done to prepare for this moment. The work of the Lucius Trust is just the tip of a massive iceberg. It's just one small part of a worldwide network of similar groups which for the past several decades have been preparing the world for the coming of the New Age. Like the Lucius Trust, these groups have sponsored seminars and classes to teach meditation, channeling, visualization, self actualization, positive imaging, and the like, all preparing the world for what is to come. Some have written and published books and articles in popular magazines, or textbooks for the public schools. Others have written screenplays and music, all of which carry part of the message. Many of the popular political and religious movements and causes have at their heart men and women committed to our cause. In fact, it would be hard to find an area of life where the influence of the New Age has not reached. To a very small extent the Lucius Trust has tried to serve as a clearinghouse for many of the New Age groups, but it is far too large, too diverse for any organization to fully encompass.

"This has not been the result of some 'conspiracy.' It was not planned by some mastermind. It is rather an outgrowth, a natural convergence of thought, and an alignment of mind among many people of the earth. It is not that they fully know what is coming — their knowledge is still very limited — but they do understand that one age is ending and another is set to begin. They understand the general goals."

Christopher asked Decker, "Do you remember why Uncle Harry named me Christopher?"

It had been a long time since Professor Goodman had told him, but right now Decker remembered it clearly. "He said he named you after Christopher Columbus because he hoped that, like Columbus, you would lead mankind to a new world."

"That is exactly it," Christopher said. "And that is what I am here to do. But, as was the case in the days of Columbus, there are many who still think that the world is flat!

"We must enlighten them. As Bob said, many have already been reached by our friends in the New Age movement. But there are still some who have never even heard of the New Age, much less had personal involvement in the spiritual realms. These are the ones you must help me to reach. That is why you have been prevented from journeying into the spiritual realms yourself: so that you can better relate to and understand these people.

"There have been two times in the past when you might have entered into the spiritual domain — once after your family died, as you sat catatonic for three days. You heard voices calling to you, and then another voice which said, 'No! This one is mine.' And then the voices stopped. You thought you were going mad." Decker had never told that story to anyone, not even Christopher. "Then again when you visited the Lucius Trust with Jackie Hansen — though you did not hear the voices that time, they were there. Had your mind been allowed passage into the spiritual realm, there is no doubt that you would be well on your way to spiritual growth by now. But you have been selected for a purpose. Your words must reach the millions who have never experienced the spiritual realm."

Decker was understandably overwhelmed. "I'll do whatever you ask," he managed.

"The truth will not be easy," Christopher warned. "Many will despise you for the truth. Some will wish you dead, and some may even try to kill you." Decker didn't waver, so Christopher continued.

"Decker, I was wrong about John and Cohen. They have been acting at the behest of God all along, just as they claim. Everything they have done has been at his direction."

Decker was stunned. "But how can that be?!! Over a billion people have been killed!"

"Far more than that, Decker. One point four billion — one

third of the earth's population — just as a result of this most recent plague. Over 2¼ billion altogether — nearly half the world's population." Christopher shook his head. "I should have realized it before," he said. "It's so obvious now. I guess I didn't want to believe it, but now it's inescapable.

"Decker, everything that has happened to the earth over the past three and a half years was predicted in the Christian Bible! The nuclear devastation of the China-India-Pakistan War, the destruction of one-third of the earth's forests, the tsunami, the earthquakes, the eradication of sea life in the Pacific, the ash-filled skies, the locusts, and now the madness which is sweeping the earth, all of it has occurred exactly as it is described in the book of Revelation in the Bible. I had thought that John and Cohen were simply following the pattern of Revelation, but I was wrong. There's no way that they could have caused this much destruction on their own.

"Decker, all that has happened, all the killing, all the suffering, all the destruction, has been carried out by the will of God! Everything that has happened, all of it, was planned out to the very last detail, thousands of years ago."

The expression on Christopher's face was as somber as Decker had ever seen it. This was obviously very painful for him to say. "Decker," he said slowly, agonizing over every word, "God is not at all what we have perceived him to be!" Christopher paused and Decker waited, not wanting to interrupt. "Almost nothing about God is as we have understood it. The one who man thought to be his friend is instead his enemy! And the one who man thought to be his enemy is instead his friend."

"What do you mean?" Decker asked, wrinkling his brow and shaking his head instinctively at the strange riddle.

"In a way," Christopher said, with a sorrowful, awkward smile as he began his explanation, "Uncle Harry was right about me being from another planet. But at the same time," he added, "I **am** the son of God!

"Nearly four and a half billion years ago, as the first step toward colonization, the people of a planet called *Theata*, which is 17,000 light years from earth, **did** launch thousands of life-bearing probes throughout the galaxy, just as Professor Crick hypothesized in his book,[12] and just as Uncle Harry suspected after he found the cells on the Shroud.

"At the time the probes were launched, the inhabitants of Theata had progressed only slightly beyond the place where the people of earth are today. Their life form was remarkably similar to humans, but their history showed that there had not been a single evolutionary change in the physical structure or intellectual capabilities of their species in tens of thousands of years. Many of the Theatan scientists came to believe that evolution had progressed as far as it ever would. No one even remotely suspected that throughout those tens of thousands of years of stagnation, the next major evolutionary step had been fully within their grasp, waiting for them to simply reach out and take it.

"And then finally it was found, not by the scientists, but by the spiritual leaders. Just as it is here on earth, so it was on Theata: some truths are beyond the bounds of science. As a result, instead of advancing civilization, science itself shackled Theata to the past. The same can be seen here on earth. For example, many scientists look at a quartz crystal and see only a mineral consisting of silicon dioxide. But, as some spiritual leaders have been telling us for decades, it is actually far more. Properly purified and tuned, quartz crystals can be used to correct negative energies within the human body, promote healing, empower those who are willing to see the future, and a plethora of other things.

"Less than a thousand years after the launch of the first deep-space probes from Theata, and long before any of the planets they had seeded became habitable, the Theatans took the next great step in their evolution: they grew beyond the need for

---

[12]   Francis Crick, *Life Itself* (New York: Simon and Shuster, 1983). See also original reference, *In His Image, Book One of the Christ Clone Trilogy*, p. 31.

physical bodies, into pure 'spirit' beings. In their spirit form, the Theatans gained the ability to travel to other planets and solar systems and beyond the boundaries of this galaxy to the thousands of other galaxies throughout the universe. They learned to travel into other dimensions, as well as forward and backward in time, and they can do all of this instantaneously and effortlessly through just the power of thought. For eons since then, the Theatans have existed in this state as immortal spirit beings, traveling, exploring, observing, discovering the wonders of the endless universe. With these abilities, their plans to colonize other planets with space ships became obsolete.

"The planets they had previously seeded by the probes were allowed to progress at their own pace, with life evolving according to the particular dictates of the host planet's environment. Over time it became evident that there are endless variations that evolution may follow. Of those variations, only a very few possess the potential to emerge as a sentient life form. In fact, of over 500,000 planets in the universe with advanced forms of life, only a few hundred different types of self-cognizant creatures exist. And of those few hundred, only two paths have been found which can lead to eventual evolution into spirit beings.

"One of those paths first emerged on a planet in a stellar system just thirty-two light years from Theata. The evolutionary dictates of that planet brought about a life form which is instinctive and totally logical. They evolved much more swiftly into spirit beings than did the Theatans, but it turned out that the development of emotions was key in the Theatans' evolution. Because the beings of this other planet were incapable of emotion, they could never advance as far as the Theatans. In all, there are seven planets with this type of life form: three have achieved spirit form, the other four will do so over the next 3½ million years. In literature, these beings have been known as angels.

"The other evolutionary path which can lead to the emergence of spirit beings," Christopher continued, "is, as I said, the path taken by the Theatans. But in all the universe, on all of the billions of planets, throughout all history, only one other life form has evolved along a parallel course with Theata. Besides the Theatans, only that one life form is capable of achieving true godhood. And that life form exists only on the planet earth."

Decker felt his breath escape him as he was struck by the universal magnitude of the drama they were playing out.

"On the whole," Christopher continued, "Theatans are very reluctant to interfere in the affairs of other life forms. But when it was discovered how closely earth's evolution mirrored that of the Theatans, one of the Theatans took on the responsibility of preserving life on this planet."

Christopher paused both as a transition and to give Decker a chance to take it all in before he continued.

"What I'm going to tell you next," Christopher began again, "will be the hardest part of all for you to deal with. But you must try. I need you to try." Decker was overwhelmed already, and instinctively braced himself as though Christopher's words might physically impact him. Decker nodded for Christopher to continue.

"Fifteen thousand years ago, one of the Theatans claimed that, through a method he refused to reveal, he had advanced to an even higher state on the evolutionary scale and had become superior to the other Theatans." Christopher paused again, though no pause of any length could have prepared Decker for what Christopher was about to reveal. "The Theatan who made that claim was named . . . Yahweh!"

"Yahweh?!" Decker repeated in question. "The Hebrew name for God?!"

Christopher nodded. "Yes, Decker. The same. Yahweh claimed that his was the *final* step in evolution, and that it was an *exclusive* evolutionary state, one to which only a single being in the universe could advance. He said that in achieving this final step, he had become 'one' with the power that brought the universe into existence. And he expanded this claim by saying that because of this, he himself had *become* the 'Creator.' But it didn't stop there. Yahweh went on to demand that the other Theatans worship him.

"But the Theatans had abandoned the belief and worship of gods long before they reached spirit form — indeed, doing so was **the single most important step** in their evolution to spirit form — and they weren't about to revert to worshiping anyone again!

"Eventually, when it became clear that the other Theatans would not worship him, Yahweh went into a self-imposed exile. Only his son went with him. The other Theatans were only too glad to see Yahweh go. But even though he claimed he no longer wanted anything to do with the other Theatans, in fact, he needed contact of a sort, even if it was only in the form of conflict. He also had not given up his desire to be worshiped. He chose for his exile, therefore, the planet earth. If the Theatans would not worship him, he reasoned, then the next best thing was to be worshiped by the spirit-destined people of earth. But because humans *are* spirit-destined beings, it is against their true nature to worship a god.

"The Theatan who had taken the responsibility of caring for earth objected to Yahweh's interference, but he was not strong enough to resist Yahweh. He tried to reason with him but to no avail."

"But couldn't the other Theatans stop him?" Decker interrupted.

"Actually, yes; if enough of them had chosen to," Christopher answered, "but, as I said, the Theatans generally have taken a course of non-interference throughout the universe."

Christopher continued his explanation. "Decker, have you ever wondered why it is that people have an unquenchable desire for more, or why 'having' is never quite so pleasurable as 'wanting'? Why the rose that is picked is never so desirable as the rose just beyond the grasp?" Christopher asked. Decker nodded; he knew that Christopher was not the first person to raise this question. Poets and philosophers had been asking it for thousands of years.

"It's because man is ultimately seeking what has been denied him: his spiritual destiny. Man can never be truly happy because he is a dichotomy of flesh and spirit. What satisfies, satisfies only for a season. Man seeks happiness but he can never truly find it because he is prevented from reaching his ultimate potential!

"You know the story of the garden of Eden?" Christopher asked rhetorically. Decker nodded anyway. "Well, even though the details of the account as reported in the Bible are incomplete and somewhat misleading, it is essentially correct in several areas. Genesis, the first book of the Bible, reports that earth was like a beautiful peaceful garden inhabited by Adam and Eve. Into this peaceful world Yahweh entered, taking on a bright and magnificent appearance, such as the people of earth had never seen, telling them that he was the one true god, their creator, and that they were to worship him and obey the laws he would give them. In their innocence and ignorance, they submitted.

"As his first law, Yahweh gave the people a command that seemed absurdly simple, even to their primitive culture: he ordered the people not to eat the fruit of a certain tree. And to compel the people to obey, he threatened an insanely harsh and unjust punishment: Yahweh said that if they ate from that tree, they would die.[13] It was not that the tree bore some magical fruit as the Bible suggests. There was a much more insidious reason that Yahweh chose such a ridiculous law: for the very fact that it *was* ridiculous!

"You see, if he had given them a reasonable law, a law designed to protect them, one made for their own good, then they would have followed it for the very reason that it **was** for their own good. Such laws promote understanding, as when a parent tells a child not to touch the hot stove. But Yahweh sought *not* to promote understanding. He wanted ignorant and blind obedience! Yahweh's objective was to give the people a law so

---

[13]   Genesis 2:17.

senseless that by obeying it they would be doing so simply out of subservience to him. *That* was the truly insidious nature of his plan!

"Yahweh knew that the final step in Humankind's evolution would require putting away childish beliefs in gods and turning instead to trusting in oneself. He knew that if he could make the people of earth subservient to him, then they would never evolve into the spirit realm and they would be bound up for eternity, remaining in their fleshly bodies and worshiping him!

"The other Theatan, the one who had watched over the earth before Yahweh came, knew that he must do something to thwart Yahweh's plan. He agonized over his decision. Up until that time, he had never appeared to the inhabitants of earth because he knew that, with their primitive understanding, they might think he was a god — something he wanted to avoid at all costs. He knew that belief in a god, any god, would interfere with their intellectual growth and their self-reliance, both of which are vital for evolutionary growth. But because Yahweh had already appeared to them, there was little choice. He knew he had to try to set things right by exposing Yahweh's lies.

"To minimize the risk of being mistaken for a god himself, he appeared to the man and woman in the form of a simple animal that would be familiar to them. He spoke to the woman first and explained that Yahweh had lied to them and that if they ate the fruit of the tree they would *not* die.[14] He told her that if she ate the fruit she would realize that Yahweh had lied and that he was not what he claimed to be, but was instead a cruel tyrant who would stop at nothing to control them. She understood and instinctively trusted the Theatan's words, and in a truly remarkable show of courage and strength that has been recalled in song and legend a million times on a thousand different planets throughout the universe, she ate the fruit. She knew that if she was wrong she would die; but she also knew that if she did not eat, her people

---

[14]   Genesis 3:4-5.

might never know the truth that would set them free of Yahweh's repressive domination.

"And, of course, she did not die! Yahweh had lied! Quickly she shared the fruit with others and they did not die either. Even the Bible acknowledges this and says that instead of dying, as Yahweh had threatened, 'Their eyes were opened!'[15] That should have been enough to convince mankind for all generations that Yahweh was a liar, but within a few centuries that knowledge was lost."

"Wait a minute," Decker said with puzzlement written all over his face. "Let me see if I understand you on this. The other Theatan you're talking about . . . are you talking about . . . Satan? Are you saying that Satan had Adam and Eve's best interest at heart when he tempted them to eat the apple?!"

"Well," Christopher answered, "I suppose to begin with I should clarify that the other Theatan's name is actually Lucifer, which means 'bearer of light.' 'Satan' is simply a mispronunciation of 'Theatan' — there are many languages that do not have a *th* sound, and over the centuries 'Satan' has become the accepted pronunciation. Yahweh initially refused to use Lucifer's name and addressed him simply as 'Theatan,' the implication being that Yahweh considered himself superior to the Theatans, the race that had given him birth. Now, as to whether Lucifer 'tempted' them or simply informed them of the truth — much of that depends on your point of view."

Decker's face revealed that he was very troubled by these revelations. "Christopher, is there any possibility that you're mistaken about this?"

Christopher shook his head. "There's no mistake, Decker. Over the past three days, while my body lay dead, I was spiritually in the presence of Yahweh. I spoke with him 'face to face.' I discovered that the cold inhuman laughter and voice in my dream about the box was the laughter and voice of Yahweh.

---

[15]   Genesis 3:7.

"Yahweh's 'final evolutionary step' did indeed make him more powerful than other Theatans, but in many ways he is a throwback to the past, possessed of greed, pride, and jealousy. Yahweh himself acknowledged this in the commandment he gave to Moses in which he stated: 'You shall have no gods before me, for I am a jealous god.'[16]

"But even if I hadn't talked to him myself, Decker, the Bible itself convicts Yahweh. It is filled with examples of Yahweh's oppression and cruelty to the world. Besides threatening to kill the people for the simple act of eating the fruit, we need look only a few pages past the account of the garden of Eden, to the eleventh chapter of Genesis, where it tells the story of the Tower of Babel." Robert Milner opened his briefcase and pulled out a Bible he had brought along for this very purpose. He handed it to Decker who quickly found the reference. "Starting in verse five," Christopher said, and Decker found it, "it says,"

But the Lord came down to see the city and the tower that the men were building. The Lord said, 'If as one people, speaking the same language, they have begun to do this, then nothing they plan to do will be impossible for them. Come, let us go down and confuse their language so they will not understand each other.[17]

Christopher quoted it perfectly without looking over Decker's shoulder at the text.

"When Yahweh saw the people of the earth cooperating, working together to build the tower at Babel," Christopher explained, "he interfered in order to crush that unity. In the same way, he sees the unity that the world has reached through the United Nations; and just as he crushed the cooperative efforts at Babel, he seeks to crush them today.

---

[16] Exodus 20:3,5.
[17] Genesis 11:5-7.

"It was not the goal of building a tower that frightened Yahweh. It was that the people of earth were unified in the effort. In unity there is power — power that Yahweh fears because he knows that when people depend on themselves and each other, they no longer have any need for him. God thrives on division and suffering. Indeed, he promotes it at every turn. The self-righteous hatred Yahweh promotes and which has led to so much religious persecution and so many wars in the past, is the very fuel by which he corrupts the human spirit. God does not want peace on earth or good will among men. The Bible itself proves it!"

Christopher took a drink of water and continued. "Now, look over at the fourth chapter of Exodus. At this point, Yahweh has just told Moses to go to Egypt and tell Pharaoh to free the people of Israel. But now listen," Christopher said, to drive home his point, "here's what's really significant. Yahweh says,"

> *But, I will harden Pharaoh's heart so that he will not let the people go.*[18]

"Then to make it even worse, Yahweh tells Moses,"

> *Then say to Pharaoh, 'This is what the Lord says: Israel is my firstborn son, and I told you, 'Let my son go, so he may worship me.' But you refused to let him go, so I will kill your firstborn son.*[19]

"Decker, can you see the sheer unmitigated evil we're dealing with?" Christopher asked. "Yahweh sent Moses to warn Pharaoh, but he had already hardened Pharaoh's heart so he would ignore the warning. And then to top it all, Yahweh blames Pharaoh for everything and kills Pharaoh's son.

"The whole thing was just a big game to Yahweh! And, of

---

[18]   Exodus 4:21.
[19]   Exodus 4:22, 23.

course, it wasn't just Pharaoh who suffered. All of Egypt suffered as Yahweh dumped one plague after another on the unsuspecting people. And today the world is suffering from another volley of Yahweh's accursed plagues.

"If you read on through the next few verses," Christopher continued, "you'll see what can only be explained as unequivocal insanity! After Yahweh sent Moses on the mission to Egypt to talk to Pharaoh, he decided to kill Moses for doing the very thing he had told him to do![20] Fortunately, Moses' wife understood something about the cruel, bloodthirsty nature of Yahweh, and she cut her son with a knife and smeared his blood on Moses' feet so Yahweh wouldn't kill him.[21] I know it sounds crazy, but that's the whole point! And it's all right there in the Bible for all to see. And talk about bloodthirsty, have you ever read the gruesome details of how Yahweh instructed the Jewish priests to slaughter sacrificial animals?[22] As if it's not bad enough that he required animal sacrifices in the first place, he instructed them to slit the animals' throats and let the poor beasts slowly bleed to death.

"And it wasn't just animals! In the eleventh chapter of Judges, verses 29 through 39 is an account of where Yahweh required a man named Jephthah to sacrifice his only child, a young daughter, as a burnt offering in return for a military victory over the Ammonites.

"Now look over in the twenty-second chapter of the book of Numbers. There's the story of the king of Moab who sent messengers to get the prophet Balaam. Balaam refused to go with them unless Yahweh approved. Read starting right there," Christopher told him, pointing to a place on the page.

Decker found the reference and began,

That night God came to Balaam and said, 'Since these

---

[20]   Exodus 4:24.
[21]   Exodus 4:25.
[22]   See for example, Leviticus 1:5-17.

men have come to summon you, go with them, but do only what I tell you.' [23]

"Keep reading," Christopher said.

Balaam got up in the morning, saddled his donkey, and went with the princes of Moab. But God was very angry when he went, and the angel of the Lord stood in the road to oppose him. [24]

"Now look down at verse thirty-three and you'll see that Yahweh instructed the angel to kill Balaam. And for what?!! For doing exactly what Yahweh had told him to do! And then Yahweh has the **unmitigated audacity** in the very next chapter to declare,"

God is not a man, that he should lie, nor a son of man, that he should change his mind! [25]

"But, as the stories of both Moses and Balaam demonstrate, Yahweh changes his mind whenever he damned well pleases!

"When the Israelites finally reached the land Yahweh promised them, there was just one 'small' problem: there were already people living there. So what did Yahweh do? He told the Israelites to go into the land and kill or drive out every man, woman and child they found, showing no mercy." [26] Christopher was clearly in control of his emotions but his voice revealed growing anger with each example he raised. "Later on, in the fifteenth chapter of First Samuel . . ." Christopher paused. "Well, you read it, Decker. It's First Samuel, chapter fifteen, starting

---

[23] Numbers 22:20.
[24] Numbers 22:21-22.
[25] Numbers 23:19.
[26] Numbers 33:51-52 and Deuteronomy 7:1-2.

with verse three."

Decker flipped the pages and found the place and began to read.

> *Now go, attack the Amalekites and totally destroy*
> *everything that belongs to them. Do not spare them;*
> *put to death men and women, children and infants,*
> *cattle and sheep, camels and donkeys.*[27]

"What kind of a god would order the killing of innocent children, even ordering that the babies be slaughtered?" Christopher asked.

Decker had never been a very religious person. Still, at first it had been difficult to accept what Christopher was saying. Slowly, however, he was beginning to realize that Christopher must be right.

"Oh, and look back toward the front, to the book of Exodus in the twentieth chapter," Christopher said. "That's where the ten commandments are." Christopher waited while Decker found it. "Start in the fifth verse."

Decker read the words of the second commandment,

> *You shall not bow down to them or worship them; for*
> *I, the Lord your God, am a jealous God, punishing the*
> *children for the sin of the fathers to the third and fourth*
> *generation . . .*[28]

"I think you get the point," Christopher interrupted. "How much more cruel and unjust could someone be than to punish a child or a grandchild for something their father or grandfather did?

"But there's much more. The Old Testament book of Job is about a man named Job who had always served Yahweh faithfully.

---

[27]   I Samuel 15:3.
[28]   Exodus 20:5.

And yet Yahweh took everything from him, killing his children, taking away all that he owned, plaguing him with boils all over his body. And Yahweh did all of it in a cruel game just to prove that Job was so devoted to him that he wouldn't curse Yahweh no matter what.

"As amazing as it may seem, Decker, it's all right there in the Bible, recorded in black and white, for all to see. Because even when the writers of the Bible put the best face on his actions, ultimately they could not disguise the sadistic, twisted being that Yahweh truly is.

"We could go on for hours with other examples. It's all right there in the Bible," he said again. "'God's Word,' and yet sown throughout are the atrocities of an arrogant, self-serving, maniacal despot! Oh, he may claim to be a 'God of love' but by his own word we see him for the *beast* that he really is! Even if you were to totally disregard everything I've said about Theata and Yahweh's origin, all you have to do is just read the Bible and you cannot help but come to the same conclusion!

"As if all of these examples aren't bad enough, when you look below the surface at Yahweh's motives you'll find that he's guilty of a far worse crime against humanity. In the first chapter of Genesis, the Bible says that God made man in his own image.[29] This, of course, is a lie — though humans did evolve in the image of Theatans. But even if we accept the Bible's claim, we are faced with this question: after God created man in his image, did he allow man to become what his very nature dictated he *must* be? No!!" Christopher's anger now grew with every word.

"According to the Bible, Yahweh created man in the image of a god, and yet he demands that man be a servant!!" Christopher began to pound his clenched fist on the arm of his chair. "If he wanted servants and worshipers, he should have chosen beings who had the nature of servants and worshipers, not people who **by their very nature *must be free*** to exercise

---

[29]   Genesis 1:26.

independent decisions and judgment!

"What could be more **insidious**, more **depraved**, more **demented**, or more **sadistic** than to take men and women — **beings made in the image of a god** — and then to bind them up by pronouncing laws which go against their very nature — **laws that are, in fact, designed to prevent them from ever reaching their rightful place in the universe?!**"

Christopher took a deep breath to compose himself. "Now, I'm not saying all of Yahweh's commandments are wrong. Many of them, such as not murdering or stealing, and the like, serve a very good purpose — though Yahweh obviously doesn't mind breaking those laws for his own benefit. But as every good liar knows, the way to make people believe a lie is to mix in some truth. Besides, laws like not murdering and stealing are obvious to everyone and no 'god' was necessary to tell us that. But many more of Yahweh's laws, like giving him a tenth of your income, or his endless repressive laws against basic human sexual desires and relationships, are not only *not* for man's good, they are actually harmful.

"Since the dawn of time, man has asked the question: why, if God is a loving god, does he allow all the evil that's in the world? Or put another way, why do bad things happen to good people? The answer is as simple as it is frightening. As hard as it may be to accept, the answer is clear: Yahweh is *not* a god of love! He is a sick, demented, unstable being with a consistent history of sadistic behavior and oppression of the human species."

"Please," Decker said, shaking his head and trying to deal with all this completely unexpected information, "I don't understand. Didn't you say you are God's son?"

"Yes," Christopher confirmed. "I am his son, just as Jesus is. And that is the key to the whole mystery of my purpose on earth."

"Shortly after the incident you just read about in First Samuel — where Yahweh tells King Saul to murder every man, woman, child, baby and animal — the Theatan, Lucifer, went to Yahweh. He had tried on numerous occasions to reason with

Yahweh, but time after time he met with nothing but Yahweh's ridicule.   But when he saw what Yahweh had done to the Amalekites, he knew he had to try again.   He pleaded with Yahweh to reconsider the way he was dealing with the people of the earth.   He showed Yahweh the bodies of the children and babies that King Saul's men had murdered and mutilated.   He hoped that some small measure of decency might still exist in him. But Yahweh would not repent. He actually found it amusing, and he laughed at Lucifer for making the attempt.

"Then Lucifer made a bold proposition, a challenge to Yahweh's pride: he argued that the reason Yahweh placed so little value on human life was that he had forgotten what being mortal was like because it had been so long since he had been confined to a physical body on Theata.   Lucifer's challenge was that Yahweh become a man for one normal human life cycle and experience life as only a human could know it.

"Not surprisingly, Yahweh refused, but Lucifer was persistent, and finally Yahweh agreed to have his son — the only Theatan who had followed him into his exile — become a man for one human lifetime. Yahweh agreed that, after that period of time, if his son agreed that he had treated humans unfairly, then he would at least consider what Lucifer had to say.

"And so, his son, Jesus, took on the form of a human being, came into the world as an infant, and grew up among the people of Israel. But by the time Jesus had lived thirty years among the people of earth, he began to wonder if Lucifer might have been right. It was a terrible struggle for him because he remembered all too clearly why Yahweh had sent him and he knew the conclusion that Yahweh wanted him to reach.   Finally, Jesus began to question his father about some of these things. He also began to have the same dream about the wooden box that I have had. That's why in my dream it always seemed that I had had the dream before, long, long ago.   The dream about the box is symbolic. To look inside the Ark is to see it for what it is: an old wooden box with a gold facade, just as when you look past

Yahweh's vainglorious facade you find a common, egotistical, self-centered tyrant.

"Yahweh began to fear that if he didn't intervene, Jesus' questions and his boldness would grow and that ultimately Jesus might even ally himself with Lucifer to try to free the earth from Yahweh's stranglehold. It was at that point that Yahweh decided to end Jesus' stay on earth. But rather than simply having him return to his spirit form, Yahweh decided to arrange for his brutal crucifixion at the hands of men. He hoped that Jesus would respond by turning against the people of earth forever. Yahweh's intent was to cause Jesus to hate and distrust humans by having one of those he counted as his best friends betray him. That was when Yahweh struck a bargain with the Apostle John. Yahweh promised to give John eternal life if he would betray Jesus. But John, as it turned out, was too much of a coward to do it himself, so he tricked Judas into doing his dirty work for him.

"Unfortunately, Yahweh's plan worked. Of course, we'll never know what Jesus might have done if he had lived out the rest of his normal lifespan. Would he have ultimately sided with Lucifer and the people of earth?" Christopher shrugged. "I now possess Jesus' complete memory up until the time of his death and even I can't be sure. I suspect that he would have stayed loyal to Yahweh. His allegiance was too strong.

"Jesus was never fully able to see himself as a person of earth. The problem was that he was born into this world with the full knowledge and memory of his father and of his previous life. Because of this he could never really form an unbiased opinion about Yahweh. On the other hand, because of the trauma of the crucifixion, resurrection, and nearly 2,000 years of dormancy before the cloning, I had very little memory of either Jesus' life or his memory of Yahweh; that is, until through my own death, these things were revealed to me.

"Remember, Decker, when I said that Theatans can travel into the past or future? Well, I need to qualify that somewhat. You're probably familiar with the theoretical debate about time travel. Simply put, the issue is: Could a person go back in time and do something like kill his own father as a child? If he did, then the time traveler would have never been born. But if he had never been born, then how could he have ever traveled back in time to kill his father in the first place? The Theatans discovered the answer to that paradox. When a person travels in time, he is powerless to change anything, not even so much as breaking a twig or lifting the smallest object. He cannot be seen, heard, or felt. In fact, since he cannot change anything, he cannot even displace air or occupy space. The only reason time travel is possible at all is that it is done in the spirit form where the traveler occupies no space. In effect, he is only an observer. He is totally incapable of changing the past and he can change the future only by returning to his own present and attempting to set in motion the circumstances needed to change the future as desired.

"I tell you all this because you need to know that the cloning of the cells which were left on the Shroud had been planned from the very beginning, even from the time of Lucifer's proposition to Yahweh to take on a human form. Lucifer had seen the future and knew that Jesus would be crucified before he could make his own choice about mankind. After Jesus' death, Lucifer sent his angels to the tomb to ensure that the Shroud would be pressed firmly against Jesus' wounds so that when he was resurrected, his dermal skin cells would be left behind. He did this knowing that one day, nearly two thousand years later, men of science would come to examine the Shroud. When that day came, he would arrange for one of the scientists to find the cells and clone Jesus.

"But one other thing was necessary for any of this to work: he needed to conceal his plan and the cells themselves from Yahweh. I told you about the spirit beings which men call angels. What I did not tell you is that most of these spirit beings — or angels — have chosen to associate with the Theatans. Because of the uniqueness of earth, Yahweh and Lucifer each have many millions of angels who have chosen to align themselves with them and do their bidding. To protect the cells on the Shroud, Lucifer directed a group of his angels to conceal the existence of the cells from Yahweh. Since the time of the cloning, that same group of angels has also concealed my existence.

"I told you about the feeling I sometimes had that was as if a battle was going on between someone trying to get to me and someone else trying to prevent it. It happened whenever I did something which required the use of my abilities as a Theatan, such as healing people — including when my blood was used to cure Secretary Milner in the hospital. When I did that, Yahweh's angels could sense my presence. The battle that I felt was between the angels of Yahweh who wanted to get to me and the angels of Lucifer who were sworn to protect me."

"Wait a minute," Decker interrupted. "But then who was it you talked with during those forty days in the Israeli wilderness?"

"Lucifer," Christopher answered.

"But he identified himself as your father."

"Well, I think you can understand that at that time — before I knew the truth — I would not have been very receptive to the idea of conferring with Lucifer. Besides, he *is* my father in a much more important way than Yahweh is. Just as you have cared for me and protected me and helped me to reach my destiny, so also has Lucifer. Which is more important — who gave me life nearly four billion years ago, or who has loved and cared for me?" The question was rhetorical.

"Finally," Christopher continued, "after the series of healings at the U.N., Yahweh found me. That is when he sent Tom Donafin to kill me. Yahweh knew you'd blame yourself for my death — exactly as you had 2,000 years ago. Perhaps he even knew you'd plan to take your own life again as you did when you were Judas."

Despite all that Christopher had said thus far, there was still a little surprise left to be felt from this revelation. Instinctively Decker put his hand over his jacket pocket where he had placed the brochure from the life completion center.

"You know?" Decker asked.

"I know," answered Christopher.

Decker pulled the pamphlet from his pocket, looked at it briefly — seeing in it the tragic mistake he had almost made — and then tore it in two and threw it away. He was glad to be rid of it.

"There was one other thing Yahweh hoped to accomplish by having your friend, Tom Donafin, kill me," Christopher continued. "He hoped that I would blame you and as a result I would distrust all men, as Jesus did after he was betrayed.

"But I do not blame you, and I harbor no anger toward you **or** toward Tom. Tom Donafin was just a poor innocent pawn who was misled by those around him, just as John misled you 2,000 years ago." Christopher put his hand on Decker's shoulder. "Decker," he said consolingly, "it wasn't Tom's fault. And it certainly wasn't your fault." Decker didn't respond but it was obvious that he appreciated Christopher's solace.

"Over the last three days, while I was spiritually in his presence," Christopher continued, "Yahweh tried to sway me to his side with promises of power if I followed him and threats of punishment if I didn't. But, as my presence here indicates, he failed. Now I know that win or lose, I have to fight him, just as Lucifer has, in an effort to free the earth from his slavery. Yahweh knows my decision. I have dedicated myself to the victory of the human race over Yahweh's maniacal desires."

Christopher turned again to Robert Milner. "And you've known all along."

"Well, not all along," Milner confessed. "Actually, Alice Bernley knew long before I did. That's why, if you check the charter of the Lucius Trust, you'll find that the name was originally the *Lucifer* Trust. You have no idea how much we argued over that before she finally conceded that calling it the Lucifer Trust might scare away too many people. Actually, I didn't realize the truth until after Alice's death, when the Tibetan, Master Djwlij Kajm, came to me and prepared me to receive the spirit of the ancient Hebrew prophet Elijah. After fifteen months of his training in the Israeli wilderness I came to understand that Master Djwlij Kajm was in reality the Theatan Lucifer, the light bearer."

"But I thought Elijah was a prophet of God, that is, of Yahweh," Decker said. "Did he switch sides?"

"To put it concisely, yes," answered Milner. "You see, there was one thing about Elijah that made him stand out among the other prophets of the Old Testament. He had won such favor with Yahweh that Yahweh rewarded him by bringing him into his presence without Elijah ever having to die.[30] Elijah was taken physically into the heavens and into the presence of God. But what Yahweh had not counted on was that over a period of time in his presence, Elijah would come to realize what Lucifer already knew. Later, without Yahweh's knowledge, Elijah began to train under the tutelage of Lucifer. Soon he was able to advance nearly to the level of the Theatans. Now he has returned to earth and his spirit shares my body. He is here to assist Christopher in what must be done."

Decker took a deep breath and asked, "So what do we do now?"

"Decker," Christopher answered, "until now, I've been describing the New Age as being similar to a birth, and so it is, but perhaps a more appropriate analogy would be a 'coming of age.' In every person's life there comes a time when they must break away from the bonds of childhood and set out on their own course, reach for their own goals, live their own lives. I know it's not an easy thing to do. I remember when I left you to go to college in Costa Rica. I remember the pain of leaving as though it was just yesterday. But I knew that if I was ever going to grow, to mature into the kind of man that you'd be proud of and that I would be proud to be, then I would have to learn to rely upon myself.

"The time has come for the human race to take that same

---

[30] II Kings 2:9-12.

kind of step of independence. Of course, it will not be easy. I remember how supportive you were when my time came to leave the nest, and it still wasn't easy for me — for either of us, I guess. But breaking away is especially difficult if the parent refuses to allow the child to go, or puts obstacles in the way of the child's growth. In situations like that, the best thing for all concerned is for the child to steadfastly set his resolve and do what he knows must be done. He does no one any good by staying under his parents' rule. Certainly there will be some pain involved — for both the parent *and* the child — but refusing to accept and deal with that pain will only result in even greater, more prolonged suffering. And if the separation is put off too long, ultimately the child's spirit will be broken.

"Humankind now stands at that crossroads. Their spirit must be free. And whether we believe God to be a tyrant or simply a parent who is unwilling to release his child to become what destiny calls him to, the course of action is the same.

"The human race must be free, and the time for freedom is now! That is what I meant when I said that the task before us would require an act of will of every man and woman on the planet. Just as the child must be steadfast in his resolve to break free of his parents' control, so the people of the earth must, of one accord, in unity and faith in themselves, break free of the bonds placed on them by Yahweh.

"It is for this purpose that the prophets and teachers of the New Age have prepared us," Christopher said. "From the centuries-old beliefs of Freemasonry, the teachings of Madame Blavatsky's Theosophical Society and the Rosicrucians to the books of David Spangler and physicist Fritjof Capra; from the teachings of Mary Baker Eddy and Christian Science to the prophecies of Bahá'u'lláh, 'Abdu'l-Bahá, and Shoghi Effendi of the "Most Great Peace" to the enlightenment of Elizabeth Clare Prophet's Church Universal and Triumphant; from the theories of psychologists Carl Jung, Abraham Maslow and Carl Rogers to Dianetics and Scientology, est, Forum, and Lifespring; from the spiritual teachings of the martial arts to Transcendental Meditation taught by Maharishi Mahesh Yogi; from the revitalization of astrology and the awareness of the Aquarian Age imparted by the musical *Hair* to *The Aquarian Conspiracy* of Marilyn Ferguson; from the positive mental attitude books of Napoleon Hill to the *Megatrends* books of John Naisbitt; from José Silva's courses in Mind Control to Helen Schucman's book *A Course in Miracles*; from Richard Bach's story of a sea gull to *The Road Less Traveled* by M. Scott Peck; from the later spinoffs of *Star Trek* and the *Star Wars* movies of George Lucas which initiated millions to the concept of the power of the 'Force' that is within us to the books and lectures and movies of Shirley MacLaine, proclaiming that we must be our own gods; from the prophecies of Edgar Cayce to the pronouncements of Ramtha, Seth, Lazaris and other ancients through channelers like J.Z. Knight, Jane Roberts, Jacques Purcell, and Kevin Ryerson; from the later works of John Denver to the articles and lectures of Apollo 14 astronaut Edgar Mitchell; from the resurgence of nature religions such as Santeria and the Wiccans to the exponential growth in eastern religions such as Buddhism and Hinduism and the millions involved in yoga, shamanism, and holistic medicine; from the Club of Rome to 'World Goodwill,' the 'Planetary Citizens,' and the literally thousands of other New Age groups; and of course, to the United Nations itself . . . the list goes on and on: all of these have played their parts in bringing Humankind to this point of decision. The earth stands at the precipice. But we have not come to this place unprepared.

"We must decide now for ourselves and our children. The choice is not just between slavery and freedom but between life and death. There is only one weapon in this war and that is the strength of the informed, self-actualized, and self-empowered will. If all of Humankind will join together in steadfast defiance, we will prevail! Of that much, I am certain!

"It may not look like it when you survey the death and destruction that have befallen us, but our victory is close at hand.

Despite the calamities that have plagued the earth, the human spirit remains strong and unbroken, and that is where the real battle and our real hope lie.

If you look closely at Yahweh's tactics so far, you can see that they have been designed specifically to break the human spirit. With the China-India-Pakistan War, Yahweh disguised his actions as a man-made disaster. Of course, it was no accident that the target of that attack was the birthplace of both Hinduism and Buddhism — the predecessors of the New Age. Later, with the three asteroids, he used what appeared to be natural disasters. With both the war and the asteroids Yahweh's goal was to make mankind call upon the supernatural, that is, upon him, for relief.

"By doing that, mankind would have had to turn their backs on the only thing that can save them — their self-reliance. When Yahweh's tactics proved unsuccessful and the people of the world did not go crawling to him on their knees, he grew desperate. Turning to the plague of locusts, he began to use methods which are more obviously of a supernatural nature. He knows he is losing and his goal now has changed from wanting Humankind to call on him for relief to making people fear him. This same strategy can be seen in this current plague of homicidal madness.

"But by using forces which are so obviously supernatural, Yahweh has exposed himself and given us the opportunity to reveal to the world that he is the one to blame for what has happened! We must strike quickly at this weak point. That is why our first objective must be to make it clear to everyone that this is a spiritual war. We must make them understand that it is not nature or circumstance that has caused our suffering; it is the very hand of God carrying out the plagues he threatened in the Bible. Once the blame is placed squarely where it belongs, our next step will be to help the world see that instead of fearing Yahweh's power, we must stand firm against his attacks.

"Revealing the spiritual nature of the battle is another reason that I had to die. It would have been simple enough for Lucifer to protect me from Tom Donafin's bullet, but it was necessary that

I die and then be resurrected so that the world could clearly see the spiritual nature of the conflict. Suffering death was a small price for me to pay if it helps to buy the freedom of the people of earth.

"I must warn you, Decker, that what I'm asking you to do must not be taken lightly. If we lose this war, we risk an eternity worse than you can imagine. But if we win, we will end man's eternal hell of slavery to Yahweh."

Decker nodded his understanding but his expression seemed to reveal something else as well. A question had just occurred to him and he wanted to ask it, but he was reluctant to bring it up.

"What is it, Decker?" Christopher asked, "though I think I already know."

Decker bit his lower lip in thought. "Well," he said, finally, "admittedly, I'm not much of a Bible scholar, but I do remember a little, and it just occurred to me that if we're living through the plagues of the book of Revelation, that . . ."

Christopher began to nod in understanding.

" . . . well, are you mentioned in Revelation? I mean . . ."

Christopher nodded again in answer to Decker's question. It was obvious that the question hurt Christopher a little, but at the same time, he knew it had to be answered. No doubt it would have to be answered again and again in the future. "Yes, Decker. I'm in there. That is, my role is in there. By deciding to oppose Yahweh and side with the people of earth, I have fulfilled the prophecies concerning the Antichrist; the Beast, as John called me."

Decker's jaw dropped despite himself.

"But you must consider the source," Christopher added, shaking his head slowly and sadly. "Yahweh knew that this day might come and so has cast me in the role of the villain, second only to Lucifer in my alleged evil. But in reality, I am guilty only of trying to tell the world the truth about Yahweh — the same thing Lucifer tried to do in the Garden. If that makes me 'evil' then so be it," he continued with resolve. "I will not shy away from my responsibility or abandon the people of earth simply because Yahweh calls me names and attacks me with his lies. In truth, I am *not* 'anti'-Christ! Indeed, I am Christ, I am the Messiah, fulfilling what I began 2,000 years ago. And that mission is to tell the world that they must not worship at the feet of a tyrant! My mission is to tell them that they can depend upon and trust themselves. They must believe in themselves and in their own potential for divinity!"

Chapter 17

Clearing the Temple

March 12, 2023 — Jerusalem (4:30 a.m.)

The predawn April air was cool but exceedingly dry as Andrew Levinson walked with his father, brother, uncle, and two cousins across the dusty, parched ground toward the ancient city of Jerusalem. Before them the rebuilt Jewish Temple rose in unequaled splendor above the city's walls. Already they could hear the faint bleating and lowing of lambs and cattle brought to Jerusalem for sacrifice. The six Levinson men had come from their homes northeast of the Sea of Galilee in *Korazin* and had spent the night at the home of Andrew's grandparents near Bethany.

Despite the total devastation that surrounded their country, this was not the time to think on such things: this was the Levinsons' week of service in the Temple. As members of the ancient Hebrew tribe of Levi, their duty to their nation and their God was as clear as it was uncompromising and unyielding to the events around them — no matter how severe. Twice a year they came, just as in the ancient days, to serve for a week carrying out the myriad duties required for the efficient operation of the Temple.

To Andrew Levinson the fact that Israel survived while the countries around them had all perished was reason to believe and fear God, and therefore to serve him. Certainly Israel had its own problems, having been plagued by drought these past three and a half years, but at least they were still alive.

At first, when only the Arabs were dying of the madness and it became clear that Israel was being miraculously spared, Andrew, like most of the other religious people in Israel, had actually celebrated, believing that God was punishing Israel's enemies. But the madness continued to spread, reaching countries far beyond their region. Now Israel's friends and foes alike were dying in bloody acts of dementia and Andrew began to fear, as did many others, that the killing might consume the whole world.

It was a dreadful thought, a terrifying thought, and yet Andrew could not dwell on it. It was God's will and the will of Yahweh was not to be questioned, and so the six men walked in silence toward the Temple where they would go about their work as if all was normal, offering themselves in service to their God.

As it was with most of their extended family, Andrew Levinson's father, uncle, and cousins were members of the Temple Guard — not a position of any great honor, but still a relatively choice position compared to some. The men of each family from the tribe of Levi were assigned for life to one of the duties at the Temple. Some served as assistants to the priests, others as doorkeepers or groundskeepers. Some hauled away the entrails and manure of slaughtered animals or cleaned up where the sacrifices took place. Some skinned the animals for sale to tanneries. The types of jobs seemed endless. Which families were assigned to which jobs was based on some unexplained and unchallengeable judgment of the High Priest, and the Levinsons were just pleased that fate had not given them something far less desirable than serving among the Temple Guard. It was the responsibility of those in the Guard to ensure that order was maintained and that all Temple laws and customs were obeyed by the thousands of worshipers and visitors who passed through the Temple each day.

Andrew and his brother James would have been members of the Temple Guard as well had it not been for the training that both had received since early childhood from their mother. For a minimum of two hours a day she had tutored them in the singing of the psalms and playing of the Temple harp, an instrument believed to closely resemble that of Israel's great king David. Because of their musical abilities the two had been selected to be among the Temple musicians and singers — James played the Temple harp, and Andrew, because of his robust tenor voice, had been selected as a singer. Both positions were greatly coveted, but their mother also taught them humility and so they handled the honor well.

As they approached the gate to the city their numbers grew. There were dozens of other Levites, all headed for the Temple. The Levites who served with Andrew's family were all members of the Levinson, Levin, or Levine households, which made up this, the seventeenth course. In all, there were twenty-four courses or shifts of Levites, each of which served in the Temple for one week twice in each Jewish year. That is the way it had been in the ancient days of the Temple and so that is how it was today. The change from one course of Levites to the next always came on Saturday, the Sabbath, before the afternoon sacrifices. Today, being a Sunday, was the second day of the Levinsons' week of service.

It was still before dawn, but as they entered the city they saw them — thousands of them. There were whole families: some with doves or pigeons in cages; others with young goats or lambs on makeshift leashes; a few held small lambs in their arms. There had not been nearly so many the day before because it was the Sabbath, a day on which no private offerings were to be made.

People from all over Israel had come to the Temple to offer

their sacrifices to God. Some brought their 'sin and trespass offerings,' some their 'goodwill offerings,' still others their 'thank offerings.' All of them had one thing in common: fear. Those with sin offerings wished to ask God's forgiveness in hopes that he would continue to spare them from the madness. Those with goodwill offerings wished to show their loyalty to God and to ask his protection. And those with thank offerings came to thank God for protecting them thus far and to ask for continued preservation from the destruction that encircled their country.

Passing through the crowds, Andrew and his relatives reached a set of passageways beneath the Temple where they were granted entrance by the Levite guard. While priests guarded the inner precincts of the Temple at night, Levites were posted at the outer gates. Here Andrew would prepare for the day's service.

Andrew pulled the curtain behind him and placed his robe in a pile with others on a table. He had checked his sandals with another Levite before reaching this point. Naked, he stepped quickly into the cold spring water of the *mikvah*. The ritual bath was meant for cleansing the soul far more than the body and though the chill was unpleasant, it lasted only long enough for him to get fully wet. Altogether there were 500 to 600 members of his ancestral tribe of Levi and perhaps 400 priests who served with him this week. All of them would bathe in these same waters or in one of the other six mikvahs built beneath the southern entrance to the Temple, so it was extremely important that those bathing be quick about it. It was also expected that, in order to keep the slow-flowing spring water as clean as possible, each would bathe before he arrived. Like the others in his party, Andrew had bathed only a short time earlier at the home of his grandparents. Because of the drought, water was strictly rationed, but an exception was made for Levites serving in the Temple.

Emerging from the water, Andrew stepped into a small room to dry and dress himself in the traditional garments of the Levite.

As commanded by God through the prophet Ezekiel,[31] the Levites were to dress only in linen with no wool or any other fabric which would make them perspire. First were the white linen undergarments; over them a close-fitting, ankle-length, seamless robe bound at the waist by a long girdle, also of white linen; and finally, a white linen turban. Like the priests, all Levites went barefoot in the Temple, even in the coldest weather, for it was demanded by the laws of their God. Once properly attired, Andrew Levinson joined the others of his order to wait for the procession into the Temple.

The design of the Temple had been the result of numerous compromises between politicians, religious leaders, and the builders. The religious leaders, or at least the most vocal among them, had been split between those who insisted that the design be the one that was laid out in the vision of the prophet Ezekiel,[32] and those who wanted something closer to the design of Herod's Temple. The politicians were divided, as politicians usually are — concerned both with holding down costs and with pleasing their constituents. The builders, on the other hand, were unified in their contention that what everyone else wanted could not be built for what they were willing to pay. In the end no one was completely satisfied, but since its dedication no one had had anything negative to say about it. It was, after all, the Temple of God and no one thought it wise or useful to criticize it.

The main entrances to the Temple were similar to Ezekiel's model, with long wide stairs rising well above the surrounding landscape, leading to massive entrances on the north, south, and east. It was through these entrances that most visitors and worshipers came into the Temple. Those coming from the mikvahs entered through a long enclosed stairwell in the outer court known as the Court of the Gentiles — so called because even Gentiles were allowed into this portion of the Temple. In

---

[31]   Ezekiel 44:17-18.
[32]   Ezekiel 40-44.

this respect, the Temple bore a marked resemblance to Herod's model.

The procession of Levites, including Andrew and James Levinson, ascended the stairwell, crossed the Court of the Gentiles, passed through one of the gates in a low stone wall called the *soreg*, and then through another gate past massive stone walls into the first of three divisions of the inner court called the Court of the Women. Here the procession ended and the Levites who were assigned to duty within the inner court split up to go on to their respective posts. For Andrew and James Levinson, the Court of the Women was as far as they would go.

The Court of the Women, which occupied the eastern-most third of the inner court, was surrounded by massive stone walls 12 feet thick and 37 feet high. Within these walls, a colonnade encircled the court, and above the colonnade was a balcony. This court was open to all Jews but was as close to the Temple proper or 'Sanctuary' as women could come — hence its name. In the first century, this court had served as the natural meeting place for Jews seeking to vent their frustration out of earshot of the Roman legions who occupied their land. Here, in this refuge that even the Romans had respected (except for one brief incursion by the Roman general Pompey in 63 B.C.), they could speak freely. But conversation was not limited to politics. It was in the first century version of this court that the young Jesus had sat speaking with the Temple scholars on matters of religion shortly after his twelfth birthday.[33]

The Court of the Women also included the Temple Treasury and the thirteen chests shaped like rams' horns into which came a constant flow of monetary offerings. In the four corners of the court were large rooms in which other Temple activities were conducted.

In the center of the western wall of the Court of the Women, a semicircular flight of fifteen steps rose more than 13 feet (7½

---

[33]   Luke 2:42-50.

Temple cubits) from the floor to the magnificent Nicanor Gate which opened into the Court of Israel. At their widest point the steps spread to 90 feet. It was upon these steps, and before this huge, ornately carved and decorated gate that Andrew and James Levinson performed, along with the other Temple musicians and singers. Among the instruments were cymbals, skin-covered drums, reed pipes, ancient forms of flutes, harps like the one played by James, lyres, and various other types of stringed instruments.

When dawn broke, the gates to the Temple were opened and the worshipers poured in. In the Court of the Priests, beyond the Court of the Women and the Nicanor Gate, the Temple priests began the day as they began every day, by cutting the throat of a young lamb with a razor-sharp knife and then holding the lamb over a basin until its life had gone and it was drained of blood. The blood was then splashed out upon the stone altar, and the lamb's body was quickly skinned and placed upon the fire which burned atop the Altar of Sacrifice.

Six days a week — every day except the Sabbath when no private sacrifices were offered — the scene was repeated hundreds or even thousands of times for eight and a half hours. As worshipers led or carried their animals, teams of priests performed the rituals of the sacrifice. In mass production fashion, some slit the animals' throats and drained the blood; others removed the hides; one team splashed the blood upon the altar; and still others kept the fire atop the altar burning sufficiently so as to quickly consume the animals. The skins became the property of the priests and most were sold to tanneries to supplement their incomes.

Not all sacrifices involved blood, however. The very poor had the option of offering a small amount of fine flour. But while most worshipers who made animal sacrifices also made grain offerings and drink offerings of wine, few worshipers would ever admit to being so poor that they could offer *only* grain or wine. At the very least, most found a way to bring a dove or a pigeon.

□   □   □

Though the day was busier than most, it progressed normally and it was now nearly eight o'clock in the morning. Andrew Levinson had just finished singing one of David's psalms when a strange feeling came over him. He blinked several times, trying unsuccessfully to shake it off, then saw darkness closing in on him. Despite his rapid loss of vision he could see that the others were having the same problem. *Is this how the madness starts*, he wondered. Within seconds, his sight was completely gone and as he tried to call out for help he realized that his sight was not the only sense he had lost: he also could not hear. Realizing the precarious nature of his position standing upon the steps, he began to try to feel his way to the floor of the Court of the Women. But no sooner had he chosen this course than someone bumped into him and he tumbled down the stone steps. It was not much comfort for him as he lay there smarting to realize that he had not lost his ability to feel.

Despite his pain, Andrew Levinson got to his feet quickly before someone could step on him or trip over him. He turned in all directions, reaching out to find something to regain his orientation, when suddenly he realized that *all* was not black. Ahead of him, at a point seemingly about 20 yards away, was a single tiny point of light. With no other reasonable option before him, he walked slowly, carefully toward it, feeling his way along the floor with his feet and extending his hands in front of him to keep from running into something.

As he moved toward the light, Andrew soon realized that he was not getting any closer to it. He knew it seemed crazy, but it was almost as if the light was leading him somewhere. Sliding his feet along the stone floor to keep from falling down any more of the Temple's many sets of stairs, he felt the floor ahead of him drop away. He had reached the steps from the Court of the Women to the outer Court of the Gentiles, and he carefully made it down the steps without falling.

With his slow progress, it was nearly fifteen minutes before Andrew began descending the long flight of stairs which he knew from the number of steps must be taking him out of the Temple. He was still no closer to the light ahead of him. Following it thus far had seemed like the best idea considering the lack of alternatives, but with limited sight and no hearing he had no intention of leaving the Temple which he knew fairly well, to go into the open streets of Jerusalem. No sooner had he made this decision, however, than the light before him began to grow larger. A moment later he realized that he had regained some of his hearing. He had no choice: he had to follow the light out of the Temple. With each step he took he began to see and hear more. He could now tell that he was not alone. When he was about 200 feet away from the Temple, his sight and hearing were completely restored. Looking around, it became clear that what had happened to him had also happened to everyone else in the Temple, including the priests, chief priests, Levites, worshipers, and even the High Priest Chaim Levin, who Andrew saw feeling his way down the same steps from whence he had come.

Spotting the High Priest groping his way along, some of the priests near Andrew ran to help him. But as they neared the Temple, they again lost their sight and hearing and had to turn back. Surveying his situation, Andrew realized that those leaving the Temple were not the only ones on the steps. Standing there looking out over the people in the street were two men dressed in burlap and covered from head to toe with ashes. Andrew recognized them immediately as the men called John and Cohen.

Tel Aviv (8:30 a.m.)

Ben Gurian Airport in Tel Aviv, Israel, was all but shut down. Because of the spreading madness there were no planes coming in and, accordingly, there were no planes leaving. Had there been, they would have been packed with passengers hoping to flee the area of madness. Not everyone in Israel accepted the idea that the best way to ensure their safety was to trust the Jewish God to continue to protect them. Many just wanted to get as far away from the danger as possible. Some had attempted to leave by land but all had failed as they were overcome by the madness within seconds of crossing the border. But surely, most reasoned, it would be safer in North or South America or in Australia or some other place which might be isolated from the madness by the oceans.

It had been the middle of the night in Israel when Christopher was resurrected and most Israelis did not learn of it until the morning. As the news spread, the story left everyone dumbstruck. Repeated almost as frequently as the footage of the resurrection was Decker's parting statement as he boarded the plane with Christopher and Milner in New York. When asked where they were going, he had called back, "Jerusalem, to put an end to the killing!"

Some of the people of the world may still have been skeptical that spiritual forces were causing the madness, but that skepticism was not evident in the reports of the world press. Perhaps it was in part because of the media's constant need to simplify, but from the perspective of the news reports the matter was clear: The madness was somehow the result of the spiritual or at least psychic powers of the two Israelis, John and Cohen; and Christopher Goodman, following his resurrection from the dead, was headed to Jerusalem to somehow put an end to their atrocities.

So to many, the thought of Christopher's impending arrival in Israel was seen as a sign of hope. However, there were those who thought of a more concrete utility which Christopher's pilgrimage would serve. For them, Christopher's arrival meant only that a plane was coming in and therefore would be going back out. When it did, one way or another they intended to be on it, whether by begging and pleading or, if necessary, by taking the plane by force.

People began arriving at Ben Gurian Airport by 7:00 a.m. By 8:30 anxiety was high and tempers on edge, and airport security was limited — a dangerous mix — as Christopher's plane landed. Someone heard someone else say that they had heard that the plane would be pulling in at one end of the terminal. That was all it took for people in the airport to rush in that direction. At the other end of the terminal, someone else thought the plane would be pulling in at the other end. Neither was right but that didn't matter; the result was stampeding crowds and utter chaos. Then someone, employing neither common sense nor logic, decided to run out onto the runway toward the taxiing plane. Not only was it dangerous, but it put the person far beneath the plane with no possible way to get aboard. Nevertheless, when one person ran out, others followed. Airport security was no match for the mob.

As the plane rolled to a halt, Decker saw the problem out the window and called to Christopher, who looked out without comment, then phoned the pilot, who anticipated his question. "I'm afraid that until airport security can clear the tarmac, we can't move from this position, sir," the pilot said. "If we move now, we risk injuring people on the ground."

"It's all right," Christopher replied. "Just stay where we are."

"I'll make arrangements," Robert Milner volunteered without missing a beat as he picked up another phone and called out.

A few minutes later Decker spotted a helicopter approaching. "That's our ride," Milner said.

"But how do we get to it?" Decker asked.

"We'll have to rely on Christopher for that."

Decker and Milner followed Christopher to the front of the plane where a crew member stood by the door. The young crewman was obviously uneasy with the prospect of coming face to face with a man who, until very recently, had been dead. "I'm sorry, sir," he stammered, "but we can't move the plane any closer to the terminal because of the people on the ground. The ground crew has a mobile stairway ready but if they roll it out with all those people down there, we'll be mobbed."

"Open the door," Christopher said.

"But, sir," the crewman began to protest, but then thought better of it and followed Christopher's command.

In a moment the door was open and Christopher stood looking down upon the clamorous and growing crowd. Raising his right hand just a little, he said simply, "Peace," and immediately the crowd fell silent. And then an even more curious thing occurred: all at once the people in the crowd began to smile, and then they turned and walked away. "Now call for that mobile stairway," Christopher told the crewman, who wasted no time in doing so.

Once aboard the helicopter, they headed directly for Jerusalem and the Temple.

Chapter 18

███████████████

Behold the Hosts of Heaven

The scene at the Temple was not much different than it had been at the airport. Even from a distance immense crowds could be seen, but the size of the crowds was not all that was unusual. The Temple was usually a swarm of activity, but now, despite the number of people in the streets, the Temple itself was empty. The inner and outer courts, usually bustling with priests and worshipers, were abandoned, and the steps leading up to the front of the Temple were equally barren, with two exceptions. As the helicopter circled, Christopher, Milner, and Decker could see two men standing on the steps, both clothed in sackcloth and covered with gray ash.

Farther away, 200 to 300 priests and Levites huddled near the High Priest, Chaim Levin, who stood a safe distance away in a tableau of mock defiance toward the men on the steps. A few steps farther back, the crowds watched from behind a line of armed Israeli soldiers. Reporters from the international news media, unable to leave the country and aware that Jerusalem was

Christopher's destination, waited for his arrival, ready to cover every second of the event. The unexpected arrival of John and Cohen an hour earlier and the subsequent clearing of the Temple while Christopher was en route from New York only intensified the level of expectation. Into this, but more specifically between the line of military personnel and the steps of the Temple, Christopher directed the pilot to set the helicopter down.

With television cameras rolling Christopher was the first to disembark the aircraft. His hair and long robes tossed wildly about him in the swirling winds of the helicopter's rotating blades, painting a striking portrait for television viewers and magazine covers as he stood unflinching before the challenge that faced him. Looking out as he waited to exit the helicopter, Decker could see that John and Cohen had expected Christopher's arrival.

Once they were all on the ground, Milner turned and signaled for the pilot to withdraw. Standing there face to face with John and Cohen, Decker, who was still not sure of all the details of what Christopher had in mind, could not ignore the sudden twinge of anxiety that swept over him. Was any of this feeling the result of animosity borne between him (in his previous incarnation as Judas) and John 2,000 years earlier, as Christopher had told him? Decker wasn't sure. To Decker's surprise, despite all else that was going on, Christopher turned to him and put his hand on his shoulder. "It's all right," he said, and somehow Decker understood that it was.

John was the first to speak. "*Hiney ben-satan nirah chatat haolam!*" he shouted in Hebrew, meaning: 'Behold the son of Satan who manifests the sin of the world.'

"So we meet again at last," Christopher answered in an ironic turn of the phrase, ignoring John's comment.

"You are mistaken," John replied. "I never knew you."

"No, Yochanan bar Zebadee," Christopher responded, using the Hebrew form of John's full name. "It is I who never knew you!"

For a long moment neither spoke, but only stared at each

other. Then Christopher dropped his gaze to the ground. "It's not too late," he said finally, addressing both John and Cohen. His voice had a sense of pleading but at the same time the tone indicated that he knew the attempt was in vain.

Quite uncharacteristically, John smiled and then began to laugh. In a moment Cohen joined in. Christopher looked back at Decker with an expression that seemed to say 'this is for both of us.' Then taking a deep breath and with no sign of anger but every ounce of conviction, he looked back at the two men and then shouted above their laughter, "As you will!"

Then raising his right hand, he made a quick sweeping motion, and immediately John and Cohen's laughter stopped as they were thrown backward through the air at incredible, almost unbelievable speed, their bodies slamming against the front walls of the Temple on either side of the entrance. The crunch of breaking bones was loud enough to be heard throughout the vast crowd and left no doubt as to their fate. Their blood splattered liberally on the wall, and remained there as witness of where they had hit. As Christopher brought his hand back down, the two lifeless bodies fell and, with a sweep of his hand, they tumbled slowly down the steps toward the street below, leaving two long trails of blood to mark their paths.

The crowd watched in stunned silence as Christopher, Milner, and Decker climbed the steps to the Temple while the crumpled bodies rolled on either side of them. As soon as the crowd realized that John and Cohen were actually dead, a shout went up from civilians and military alike. A spontaneous celebration began and was soon joined by people all around the world cheering the news as they watched on television or listened on radio. Members of the media quickly pushed through the lines of Israeli soldiers to get a better look at the bodies.

□   □   □

In *Chieti*, Italy, a man whose nostrils were filled with the rank smell of burning sulfur and whose heart was filled with the madness by which he had thus far made bloodied carnage of all but one member of his family, held a gory meat cleaver above his head and was about to bring it down upon his only remaining son when, as quickly as it had come upon him . . . the madness was gone. Carefully the man lowered the cleaver and laid it aside, and there among the dismembered bodies of his family, he dropped to his knees to hold his terror-filled son and wept. In *Rudnyi, Turskaja*, an old woman choked and gasped for breath as she pulled her head from a barrel of rain water in which she had tried to drown herself. In *Baydhabo*, Somalia, a teenage boy stopped only seconds before striking a match to set fire to his four gasoline-soaked younger siblings. Throughout the affected areas, at the moment John and Cohen died, the madness ceased.

□   □   □

When they reached the top stair of the Temple, Christopher turned to the crowds. "No one must touch the bodies," he shouted, pointing at John and Cohen. "There is still great power within them. It will not be safe for anyone to touch or dispose of the bodies for at least four days." Nodding to Decker to imply that he should reinforce the warning, Christopher turned back and then, together with Robert Milner, he continued into the Temple.

As they had planned before their arrival, Decker remained outside. Pulling a folded piece of paper from his jacket pocket, he waited for the press who would, no doubt, descend on him as soon as they finished taking pictures of the two dead oracles. Decker was pleased to see that the press were heeding Christopher's advice and not venturing too close to the bodies. There was no need to fear that the priests or Levites would touch them: their laws forbade contact with dead bodies. The only real problem might come from onlookers who for now were still held back behind police lines.

❑   ❑   ❑

Inside the Temple, Robert Milner and Christopher walked side by side. Crossing the floor of the normally bustling Court of the Gentiles, the only sound came from the column-lined portico that surrounded the court. There animals meant for sacrifices had been brought to the Temple for sale to worshipers. They had been left there untended by the shepherds and merchants when everyone was driven out.

A hundred and fifty yards ahead of Christopher and Milner, the buildings of the Inner Court and the Sanctuary within it towered more than 200 feet above them.

❑   ❑   ❑

Outside the southern entrance and framed on either side by the blood of John and Cohen, Decker waited as the members of the press hurried up the steps to find what light he could shed on the scene they were witnessing.

❑   ❑   ❑

Christopher and Milner reached the *soreg*, the low stone wall which separated the Court of the Gentiles from the inner courts of the Temple and which formed a sacred *balustrade* or enclosure into which no Gentile was permitted to enter. Inscriptions on the soreg warned visitors in more than a dozen languages, "No foreigner may enter the enclosure around the Temple. Anyone doing so will bear the responsibility for his own ensuing death." It was convenient that the Temple had been cleared, for the priests and Levites would never have permitted Christopher and Milner passage beyond the balustrade without an altercation.

Intentionally going out of their way to enter from the east, the men walked to the middle opening of the eastern end of the soreg. Quickly spanning the distance between the soreg and the first of three short flights of steps, Christopher and Milner ascended to the *Chel* or rampart, a flat area 15½ feet wide from which the massive stone walls of the Inner Court rose 37½ feet above them.

❑   ❑   ❑

"Ladies and Gentlemen," Decker raised his hand and shouted above the reporters' questions. "I have a brief prepared statement which I will read and after that, I'll be available for a few minutes for questions."

Someone yelled out another question but Decker ignored it. "Forty-five years ago, in 1978, I was a part of a scientific team from the United States that went to Turin, Italy, to examine the Shroud of Turin, a piece of cloth bearing the image of a crucified man," Decker began, reading from the statement he had prepared on the plane. In the limited time available, he provided as much detail as he could about the events that had followed the Turin expedition and which had led to this moment. He told them how, eleven years after the expedition, he had been contacted by a member of that team, Professor Harold Goodman, who asked him to come to UCLA to witness a discovery he had made concerning the Shroud.

"Professor Goodman," Decker said, "had discovered that among the samples taken from the Shroud was a microscopic cluster of human dermal skin cells. To my amazement . . ." Decker paused, still awed as he recalled what he had seen those many years before, "the cells from the Shroud were still alive." For some in the assembly, that piece of the puzzle and Christopher's resurrection were all that was needed to make sense of the whole incredible picture, but though there was an audible gasp, no one spoke. "Tests of the cells showed them to be incredibly resilient and possessing a number of unique characteristics," Decker continued. "It was from cultures grown of these cells that Professor Goodman conducted his cancer research.

"Unknown to me on that occasion, Professor Goodman had already performed a number of experiments with the cells," Decker paused as if to give the reporters a chance to brace themselves, "including implanting the DNA from one of the cells into the embryo of an unfertilized human egg and then replacing that egg into the donor, thus . . . cloning the person whose cells were on the Shroud. From that cloning a male child was born." For those who had not yet figured it out, this revelation provided the missing link; for those who had guessed earlier, it was undeniable confirmation. Christopher Goodman was the clone of Jesus Christ.

It was an incredible story but nothing else could explain what had happened at the U.N. or what they had just witnessed on the Temple steps. "That child was named Christopher," Decker said, adding further confirmation. "He was raised by Professor Harry Goodman and his wife Martha until their untimely deaths in the Disaster. At that time," Decker went on, "Christopher Goodman was fourteen years old and, having been directed by Professor Goodman to turn to me in the case of emergency, Christopher came to live with me. The rest of the story, at least the important parts, you know."

The inflection in Decker's voice let it be known that his prepared statement had drawn to a close and as he folded the paper to return it to his pocket he was surprised that no one seemed to have any questions. He needn't have been, for the reporters had plenty; they were all still processing what they had been told.

Looking around at their blank stares Decker should have realized the problem, but instead started to excuse himself. His movement was just enough stirring of the waters for the dam to break. Someone in the back started to shout a question and then a flurry of questions were suddenly hurled at him. There were no particular arrangements made for handling the questions, so Decker simply answered first the question that had been yelled the loudest.

Yes, Christopher had really been dead.

Yes, he was indeed saying that Christopher was the clone of Jesus Christ.

Yes, he *was* saying that Christopher was God's son, just as Jesus was. (This did not set well with the Jewish reporters, but it was not a point that was currently open to argument.) No one had any reason to suspect or ask for the specific details of that relationship — which Christopher had revealed to Decker on the plane — and Decker had no intention of volunteering them. Christopher would explain all of that soon enough.

"What about his arm and eye?" a reporter called.

"Though Christopher has the power to restore his arm and sight," Decker answered, "he has pledged not to do so until his mission is complete."

"What is that mission? Why has Ambassador Goodman come to the Temple?" someone yelled. Most of the rest of the reporters fell silent, also wanting to know the answer to that question.

Decker thought for a moment. "There are a number of reasons, actually," he said. "The first and most important reason was to end the reign of terror of the two men, John and Saul Cohen. That, as you have all just witnessed, he has done. Also, he came to the Temple because, I suppose, it is the most appropriate place to make the announcement that he intends to make."

"What announcement is that?" someone yelled, while someone else called, "Can you tell us what Ambassador Goodman intends to say?"

"He will be addressing the people of the world on the subject of the destiny of Humankind," Decker answered.

□   □   □

Christopher and Milner climbed three more short flights of

stairs through the Beautiful Gate and entered the Court of the Women. Only hours before, this court had been the center of activity in the Temple. Now it was silent except for the hollow echo of footfalls on the stone floor as Christopher and Milner walked without speaking toward the broad semicircular steps at the western end of the court. At the top of these steps, the magnificent Nicanor Gate, 60 feet wide and 75 feet high, extended far above the walls themselves, forming an arch, and opened into the Court of Israel.

Only Jewish men and boys were allowed to enter this part of the Inner Court. Unlike the Court of the Women, which was square and open to the sky, the Court of Israel was narrow and roofed, encircling the innermost court, and crowded with numerous columns. A series of rooms used for storage and small meetings lined the walls of the Court of Israel, further reducing the open space.

The third and final court, the Court of the Priests, rose 3¾ feet above the Court of Israel. Though adjoining and fully open to the Court of Israel, admittance to this court was permitted only to laymen bringing a sacrifice. At all other times only the priests and Levites could enter. In the gateway to the Court of the Priests were four tables of hewn stone on which lay the blood-drained carcasses of a half-dozen lambs and goats, abandoned there when the priests and Levites were driven from the Temple. The smell of blood, incense, and charred animal fat still hung heavy in the air. To the north and south of the gateway sat eight more tables in a similar state.

In the center of the easternmost part of the Court of the Priests, the Altar of Sacrifice rose 20 feet in stair-stepped pyramid form in a series of four immense, unfinished stones which, by commandment, had never been touched by metal tools.[34] Steps on the eastern edge of the altar provided access to the upper stones. The capstone, which was called *Ariel* by the priests and Levites,

---

[34]   Exodus 20:25.

was 21 feet square and, like the stone immediately below it, was 7 feet thick.   On this stone was the fire of sacrifice which consumed the burnt offerings. Unattended by the priests, the fire had been reduced to embers.

From the four corners of the altar's capstone, horn-like projections, each 21 inches long, reached skyward. On these horns and upon the altar itself, the priests would pour out the blood of the recently slaughtered animals as a sacrificial offering. Around the base of the altar was a gutter, 21 inches wide and 21 inches deep, with a containing rim of 9 inches and a total capacity of over 3,000 gallons to accommodate the huge amounts of blood that were poured upon the altar during the busier days. The priests and Levites had been driven from the Temple only a little more than an hour into their day and so only a few inches of blood now settled in the altar's gutter, coagulating and drawing flies.

Directly behind the altar, in the westernmost portion of the Court of the Priests, stood the Sanctuary. This was Christopher's ultimate goal but there was a mission he and Milner needed to accomplish before continuing. Looking around until he found what he was looking for, Christopher nodded his intention to Milner. "We must see to it that no more animals are slaughtered here to satisfy Yahweh's blood thirst. We must desecrate the altar so that it cannot be used again."

Followed closely by Milner, Christopher went to where he had spotted a number of brass shovels used by the priests for removing ashes. They each picked up one of the shovels, and went to a spot near the slaughter tables where a hill of animal dung had been collected for later removal. As best he could with the use of only one arm, Christopher scooped up a shovelful and then walked over and slung it against the sides of the altar. Again and again Christopher and Milner repeated the act until there was no dung left and the altar had been liberally splattered. Next they beat the brass shovels against each of the altar's four stones.

"That should do it," Christopher said finally, knowing that Jewish law would forbid ever using these desecrated stones as an altar again.

After finishing their chore Christopher and Milner proceeded on to the Sanctuary. From above, the shape of the Temple proper formed a huge **T** — the result of the compromise between those who wanted to rebuild the Temple according to the plans of the prophet Ezekiel and those who wanted to recreate the design of Herod's Temple. It was 175 feet across at the widest point, 105 feet at the narrowest, and stood 175 feet above the Court of the Priests. To the right and left of the entrance stood two tremendous free-standing bronze pillars, called by the priests respectively *Jachin* and *Boaz*.

Here Milner stopped. The rest of the way, Christopher would go alone.

Looking back only to nod to Milner, Christopher ascended the final set of steps to the Vestibule or Porch. Directly in front of him were immense double doors 6 feet wide and 35 feet tall made of olive wood, decorated with carvings of cherubim (angels), palm trees, and flowers and covered entirely in pure gold. Suspended above the doors, a spectacular multi-colored tapestry displayed a panorama of the universe. And above that, the full width of the wall was covered with huge carvings of grape vines and leaves with clusters of grapes as tall as a man and nearly that distance across, entirely covered with gold.

Christopher took a deep breath and continued. Pushing open one of the huge doors and then the other, he let in the light of day and stepped through into the next chamber, called the *Hēkhāl* or Holy Place. The ceiling of the Holy Place dropped 40 feet from the ceiling of the Porch to a height of 105 feet. The floor was covered with cypress wood. The walls were wainscoted with cedar, above which they were covered with gold. A golden altar for incense still smoldered, releasing the fragrant smell of frankincense. Another altar for *shewbread* (holy bread) sat undisturbed with twelve sheets of unleavened bread laid out in rows. The candles of a golden menorah, though nearly consumed by the flame, provided the only interior light.

□   □   □

Still outside the Sanctuary, Robert Milner turned and walked back the way they had come in. There was a matter outside the Temple which awaited his attention.

□   □   □

In front of Christopher, suspended from the ceiling at the western end of the Holy Place was the Veil, a divider between the Holy Place and the final chamber, the $D^e bh\bar{\imath}r$, or Holy of Holies. Beyond the Veil, where only the High Priest was allowed to go — and he, only once a year on the Day of Atonement — sat the ancient Ark of the Covenant. The Veil was actually two richly decorated curtains which hung parallel to each other with about five feet of clearance between the two, forming an entry corridor which prevented any light from reaching the windowless Holy of Holies.

Walking to the northern edge of the curtain nearest the Holy Place, Christopher took hold and pulled sharply until, bit by bit, it broke loose from the ceiling. He continued this until only a few yards of the curtain remained hanging. He then did the same with the other curtain, pulling it loose from the southern edge, thus leaving a wide entrance through the middle of the Veil and exposing the Holy of Holies to the light of day, which poured in through the Sanctuary's huge doors.

Before him in the Holy of Holies two enormous winged cherubim, each 18 feet tall, carved from olive wood and covered with pure gold, stood watch over the Ark of the Covenant. Their outstretched wings each spanned half the width of the chamber and met in the center of the room directly over the Ark.

Christopher entered the Holy of Holies and approached the Ark.

□   □   □

Outside, as Decker took another question from the press, a low rumbling began which shook the steps where he and the others stood. It seemed to come from inside the Temple. Without explanation to the press, Decker calmly announced that he would take no more questions and that the press conference was concluded. "I suggest that you may want to move to the bottom of the steps and away from the Temple at this point," he added in obvious understatement. Decker was beginning to enjoy himself.

□   □   □

Inside the Holy of Holies Christopher stood before the Ark and after a moment's pause, gripped the Ark's cover and slid it back, revealing its contents.

□   □   □

"What's happening?" several of the reporters shouted at Decker as the Temple shook again. "Ladies and Gentlemen, if you'll be patient, I'm sure you'll have answers to all of your questions, but for your own safety, I must insist that you move away from the Temple immediately." The resolve in Decker's voice and the urgency of his steps convinced the others to follow.

□   □   □

Reaching into the Ark, Christopher found the items he was looking for.

□   □   □

A thunderous rumble many times louder than the first two

rolled through the Temple like a freight train, sending reporters and onlookers running. A moment later Robert Milner emerged. He was alone. Resolutely, he descended about a quarter of the way down the steps. Looking out over the thousands of people and the dozens of cameras that broadcast the event around the world, he began to speak. It was his own voice, but it was different; at least Decker could tell there was a difference.

"See, I will send you the prophet Elijah before that great and dreadful day of the Lord comes. He will turn the hearts of the fathers to their children, and the hearts of the children to their fathers; or else I will come and strike the land with a curse," Milner said, quoting the prophet Malachi.[35] The words were familiar to many but especially to the priests and Levites. "Hear, O Israel," Milner said, no longer quoting Malachi, "for this day, this very hour, your lamentation is ended. This is the day of which the prophet spoke. Elijah has come! I am he!"

There was a great stirring from the Jewish priests and Levites at this proclamation and all eyes turned to see how the High Priest would respond. It was bad enough that they had been run out of their own Temple, but now for this Gentile to claim that he was the prophet Elijah, while it wasn't exactly blasphemy, it was a tremendous offense. No one was quite sure how to respond and they looked to Chaim Levin, the High Priest, to follow his lead. Had they even an inkling that at that very moment Christopher stood within the Holy of Holies before the Ark of the Covenant, they would not have waited for the High Priest, but already would have been tearing their clothes and dumping dust on their heads in Jewish ceremonial outrage.

Surprisingly, Chaim Levin was very calm. Dressed in the traditional Temple raiment of his office, the High Priest wore a bulbous blue hat with a band of solid gold engraved with the Hebrew words קדש ליהוה, meaning 'Holy to Yahweh.' Over the standard white linen tunic of the ordinary priest which hung

---

[35]   Malachi 4:5-6.

down to his ankles, revealing only his bare feet, he wore a richly embroidered robe which reached below his knees and was decorated at the bottom by golden bells which jingled musically as he walked. Over this, he wore a vest-like garment which hung to his hips and was lavishly embroidered with thick threads of gold, purple, blue, and crimson. In the middle of his chest, supported by heavy chains of gold attached to broad epaulets upon his shoulders and around his waist by scarlet strips of cloth, was the *ephod*, a thick square linen breastplate decorated with gold brocade and inset with twelve large gemstones in four rows of three each, representing the twelve tribes of Israel.

Whether Chaim Levin's tolerance of Milner was borne of gratitude for Christopher's dispatch of John and Cohen or because he simply did not want to ruin a perfectly good set of robes, he remained unruffled by Milner's claim. Instead, he looked him in the eye and very politely but with skeptical amusement asked, "By what sign shall we know that you are who you claim?"

"By that same sign by which I, Elijah, proved myself to King Ahab and to the people of Israel on Mount Carmel,"[36] Milner answered, loud enough for everyone to hear him.

Chaim Levin raised an eyebrow and frowned a bit. The boldness of Milner's claim impressed him, though he did not for a minute think that Milner could carry it out. "And when shall we see this sign?" he asked after a moment.

"This very hour," answered Milner. Then turning away from Levin and toward the crowd, Milner continued. "For 1,260 days Israel has suffered drought. Today it ends!" With that, Milner's hands shot skyward and from somewhere beyond the Temple a low rumbling was heard which in just seconds grew in intensity to an earthshaking peal of thunder. Faster than anyone could imagine possible, the sky grew dark as out of nowhere heavy gray clouds began to fill the heavens. In fear, the crowds and all but a few of the priests nearest the High Priest drew back. No sooner

---

[36]   I Kings 18:19-40.

had an area of a few hundred square feet been cleared than a bolt of lightning struck the earth and a deafening crack of thunder sent people running, clasping their hands over their ears. In the larger clearing that resulted from the evacuation, the first bolt of lightning was quickly followed by three more, each more powerful than the previous one. And then it began to rain.

It came down in a torrent; pouring down upon Milner, the High Priest, and everyone else except a very few who had made it to cover. Most stood there looking up with their hands upraised, thankful for the rain. Some began to dance.

For the crowd, who knew the biblical story of Elijah, the verdict was clear: this truly must be the prophet. What other explanation could there be? Although the High Priest was unconvinced, he could offer no more believable explanation and so he remained silent, staring at Milner as the rain turned his impeccably elegant attire to dripping disarray. Soon many of the priests and Levites joined in with the crowds, proclaiming Milner as the promised Elijah who, according to the prophecy, would come before the Messiah.[37]

It came as no surprise, therefore, when after a few minutes of drenching rain, Milner announced, "Behold your Messiah!"

With rain still pouring down, Milner turned and seemed to be pointing with his outstretched hand toward the Temple, but no one could see exactly what he expected them to find. Then above the southeastern corner, a break appeared in the clouds, allowing a single brilliant shaft of sunlight to shine through. "There he is!" someone shouted.

At the top of the wall, on the very edge of the southeastern corner of the Temple, 180 feet above them at a point which by tradition is called the pinnacle, stood Christopher, robes blowing in the wind and completely dry as the shaft of light shone down like a spotlight. Quickly the beam broadened, as from that point the clouds retreated in all directions, bringing rain to the parched

---

[37]   Malachi 4:5-6; Matthew 17:10-13.

countryside around Jerusalem. In just moments the area around the Temple was in full daylight again with the sun shining brightly overhead.

By now nearly every network in the world was carrying the events in Jerusalem live. Every camera was on him, broadcasting his words and image to the most distant corners of the earth.

"People of Earth," Christopher began slowly with a serene, peaceful tone calculated to restore calm. "For millennia the prophets and soothsayers, the astrologers and oracles, the shaman and the revelators have all foretold the coming of one who would bring with him the olive branch of peace for all the world. By a hundred different names the world has known him. And by a hundred different names this promised peace bringer has been petitioned to come quickly to those in distress. For the Jews, he is Messiah; for the Christians, the returning Christ; for the Buddhists he is the Fifth Buddha; for the Muslims, the thirteenth heir to Mohammed or Immam Mahdi; the Hindus call him Krishna; the Eckankar call him Mahanta; the Bahá'í look to the coming 'Most Great Peace'; to the Zorastrians he is Shah-Bahram; to others he is Lord Maitreya, or Bodhisattva, or Krishnamurti, or Mithras, or Deva, or Hermes and Cush, or Janus, or Osiris.

"By whatever name he is known," Christopher declared, "in whatever tongue he is entreated: this day I say to you: the prophecies have been fulfilled! This day the promise has been kept! This day the vision has been realized for all Humankind!" Christopher paused as the anticipation rose.

"For on this day I have come!" he shouted triumphantly, surprising no one — for the conclusion was obvious — and yet astonishing all, for no one could have been truly prepared for such a declaration.

Christopher's voice quickly picked up speed and fervor. "I am the promised one!" he chanted. "I am the Messiah, the Christ, the Fifth Buddha, the thirteenth heir to Mohammed; I am the one who brings the Most Great Peace; I am Krishna, Shah-Bahram,

Mahanta, Lord Maitreya, Bodhisattva, Krishnamurti, and Immam Mahdi; I am Mithras, Deva, Hermes and Cush, Janus, and Osiris! There is no difference. They are all one. All religions are one. And I am he of whom all the prophets spoke! This is the day of the Earth's salvation!"

To the displeasure of the High Priest, many in the crowd in Jerusalem roared their approval and the response was echoed around the world. They had all seen Christopher die at the hands of an assassin, and they had seen his resurrection. They had witnessed him powerfully dispatching John and Cohen, who had called down terrible plagues upon the earth. They had watched in amazement as Robert Milner called down lightning and brought rain to the drought-stricken holy land. But more than anything else they cheered because they were *ready* for a savior.

"I have not come to make pious religious pronouncements," Christopher said. "Nor have I come to demand your worship or insist that you pay me homage. I do not seek your praise and adoration or demand your devotion. It is not my intent that you venerate or adulate me or that you pay me your tribute. Nor do I wish you to glorify, deify, idolize, extol, exalt, or revere me.

"I have come instead to tell you to look to yourselves. For within each of you is all the deity, all the divinity, that you will ever need. You may call me a god and I do not deny it: I am a god! But I call *you* gods. All of you! Each of you!"

High Priest Chaim Levin had heard all that he needed to. This was obvious blasphemy and, new robes or not, he was obligated to tear his garments and throw dust upon his head; and so he began with a vengeance, though he had to settle for mud. Some of the other priests and Levites near him immediately followed his lead. But others, many others, were far too interested in what this man who had risen from the dead had to say.

"It is not my own godhood that I have come here to proclaim," Christopher continued. "It is yours!"

"I have not come to threaten or punish," he said reassuringly, undistracted by the actions of the High Priest so far below him. "I have come to offer to Humankind life everlasting and joy unimagined. I bring you the opportunity to build a tomorrow of abundance and life from a yesterday of hunger and death. Come with me. Follow me. And I will lead you into a millennium of life and of light."

The High Priest's over-dramatic rending of cloth and hurling of mud distracted Decker from Christopher's speech just long enough for him to notice that despite the distance between Christopher and the crowd, he could hear him clearly. Christopher's voice seemed to be coming from right next to him or, perhaps . . . even from inside of him. It was as though he was hearing Christopher's voice from within himself. This discovery was quickly followed by another, even more startling: Decker suddenly realized that Christopher was not speaking English; nor had he since he began to speak. Decker was not sure what language Christopher was speaking, but he was certain he had never heard it before; yet he clearly understood every word. Apparently, so did those all around him, and as Decker correctly assumed, so did every other person on earth, no matter what their native tongue.

He wondered if others had noticed that the language Christopher spoke was not their own. Under his breath, Decker tried to recall and repeat a few of the words Christopher was speaking, but discovered that though he understood every word Christopher said, he could not for the life of him duplicate a single word or even a syllable. Later Christopher would explain that he had been speaking in the root language of all human languages, one which was as universal and instinctive to humans as animal sounds are to the given type of animal. It was, as Christopher would explain later, the language spoken by all humans prior to the confusion of language which Yahweh used to scatter the people of the earth when they built the Tower of Babel.[38] This

---

[38]   Genesis 11:1-9.

language did not need translation. It *was* the translation.

"Three and a half days ago," Christopher continued, "before the eyes of the whole world, a follower of John and Cohen and the Koum Damah Patar fired a bullet into my brain and killed me. Less than twelve hours ago, again with the entire planet as witness, I was resurrected from the dead!

"But my resurrection is not a symbol of *my* victory over death. It is, rather, a symbol of *Humankind's* victory of life. My resurrection, my release from the chains of death, occurred because the time has at last come for Humankind to break the chains that have bound it, and to claim the glorious future that awaits.

"Let there be no mistake: the afflictions that have befallen the earth over these past three and a half years have not been accidental or the result of natural disasters. They have been cold, calculated acts of supernatural oppression, enacted through the men John and Cohen, against all Humankind. But John and Cohen did not act alone. They were in fact, merely the conduit for an oppressive, evil force — a spiritual entity whose savage, barbaric, selfish goal has been and continues to be to prevent the human race from fulfilling its destiny and attaining its proper place in the universe.

"The power which directed my assassination and the entity which has brought the world to the brink of annihilation are one and the same. But my resurrection is proof that this entity *can* be defeated, that the earth can be restored, and that Humankind is ready to throw off the yoke of bondage and to take the ultimate evolutionary step toward spiritual completion.

"I have returned to lead the world out of this age of destruction and death, into a new and transcendent age where suffering and death are no longer a fact of life. An age borne out of the trials that the earth has suffered and into a time of individual harmony with the universe. You, the ones who have outlasted the disasters, the floods, the earthquakes, you are the survivors and you shall be the victors!

"The human race has tasted the worst of this evil entity's spiritual oppression and has stood defiant. It is the power of this defiance which has restored my life. It is the power of this defiance which has weakened the enemy. It is this defiance and Humankind's self-reliance that have ushered in the New Age.

"Let there be no doubt: The New Age is not about replacing one religion with another: quite the opposite. This is *not* about reliance upon or faith in some distant, isolated god. This is about man coming to rely upon himself; upon the power and the god that is within him. This is *not* about a limited few self-righteous, self-serving oppressors bent on self-aggrandizement. This is about individuals taking control of their own lives, their own environment, and their own destinies.

"For 2,000 years calendars have been based upon the birth of the Christian messiah. My resurrection from the dead has marked the commencement of the New Age. The estimated date of Jesus' birth is now irrelevant and the calendars of the Christian era have been relegated to history. A New Age has begun. Therefore, let the calendars of the world mark the day of my resurrection as the first day of the first year of the New Age." Christopher raised his right hand and shook his head as he offered an explanation for his directive. "It is not that I wish you to mark the date of my resurrection for *my* sake," he explained. "Rather, it is to mark the beginning of your own liberation from the hands of the one who has tried to crush your spirit and to destroy your soul.

"Let this date also mark the end of claims to exclusive truth that are held by backward religions such as that practiced by the KDP. To the members of the Koum Damah Patar, I extend my hand in peace. John and Cohen are dead. Their self-righteous claims lay barren and lifeless with their bodies. I appeal to you to abandon your offensive ways; abandon your sanctimonious claims to exclusive truth and join us. We must purge ourselves and our world of such intolerant philosophies and religions. From this day forward the religion of Humankind shall be **Humankind**.

"Let no one boast that their way to god is better, for it is not a god we should seek at all. It is the power that lies within us. Let us no longer excuse ourselves as being '*only* human.' **Human** is all we **need** to be.

"It is in our humanity that divinity resides. Humanity stands poised on the brink of the final great evolutionary stride. But it is not through physical evolution that divinity and immortality will be achieved. It is through spiritual evolution. For some, this evolution will take only a few decades. For others, it may take much longer. But even if it takes a thousand years it will have been time well spent." Christopher paused to allow that thought to sink in. He wanted his audience to fully understand what he was saying. "Do not wonder," he continued, "that I say that it may take a thousand years. It will not matter if it takes 10 years or 200 years or even 1,000 years! Immortality is yours to take! Through the same power by which the man John lived over 2,000 years, the same power by which I was raised from the dead, the same power by which we shall overcome the evil entity that opposes us, you shall live! To those who follow me, I will give the power to live for a thousand years! After that, you shall take your rightful place as evolved beings and shall live forever!

"Again I extend the hand of peace to the Koum Damah Patar. Turn from your error and follow me and you shall be the vanguard of the evolutionary process. You, who have already begun to experience the evolutionary metamorphosis, as evidenced by your advanced extrasensory abilities, do not use your powers for oppression. Use them instead to look inside yourself. Turn from serving the evil entity who claims to be God, and instead serve Humankind. Cease your worship of the one who seeks to destroy the world, and instead glorify Humankind, and together we shall restore the world.

"Worthy are they who work for the advancement of Humankind, for the universe shall be theirs. Worthy are they who have learned first to love themselves, for they shall be as gods. Worthy are they who have not denied themselves the desires of their hearts, for they have understood that to do so is to deny themselves. Worthy are they who draw their strength and hope from within themselves, for they shall be strengthened. Worthy are they whose spirit is strong and defiant, for they shall be first in the kingdom of the universe. Worthy are they who forbid intolerance and crush that which restricts growth, for they will be called beacons of truth and guideposts to fulfillment.

"Hear me and believe! Honor truth and growth with your allegiance!

"Yet a third time to the Koum Damah Patar I offer the open arms of brotherhood. Understand, however, that there is no place for you in the New Age if you continue your onerous ways. Unto whom much is given, much shall be expected. If you, who are the first to experience the power of the New Age, and who have tasted the sweet flavor and experienced the awesome power which already grows within you, if you do not turn from your ways of persecution and intolerance, then you shall be the first to fall and feel the wrath of a planet which has grown beyond its willingness to submit. Those who seek to empower themselves by making Humankind slaves to their god, have enslaved themselves already by their own choosing.

"Were they satisfied with enslaving only themselves it would be little threat to Humankind and might therefore be tolerated for a time. But that is not in their nature. Instead, their desire is to impose that slavery upon others. They are weak and primitive; they are totally alien to the present reality and do not belong to the present millennium, much less to the New Age. They have no understanding of the present planetary situation. Their weakness must not be allowed to sap and corrupt the strength of those who are ready to proceed to the future. Under the leadership of John and Cohen, they have tried to do so by calling down every kind of disaster they could imagine. They have brutally and without sympathy brought about the deaths of untold millions of innocent people and they have caused unspeakable misery and suffering for those of us who survive. Yet still they have failed to break the human spirit! The human will stands unshaken before the ill winds of theistic persecution. We are defiant! We shall not bend the knee to any tyrant!"

Turning his attention from the KDP and again to his broader audience, Christopher declared, "It is not in your nature to be a servant to anyone!"

Because of the distance between the crowds and Christopher at the top of the pinnacle, and because of the way the wind blew his robes, no one had noticed the objects at Christopher's feet. They were more evident to those who watched by television, but no one had really given them much thought during his electrifying address. Certainly, no one suspected that the items had been taken from the Ark of the Covenant.

"I have told you of an evil tyrant," Christopher continued, "a spiritual entity who has held the world in chains. For many who are listening and watching it will come as no surprise that the one of whom I speak — the one for whom John, Cohen, and the Koum Damah Patar have inflicted such ruin — is the same one who has demanded that his people offer him the blood of innocent animals as tribute.

Christopher paused to pick up the articles at his feet and raised them above his head. It was still not clear to the audience in Jerusalem but it was now obvious on television that he held two stone tablets. On the tablets a strange script could clearly be seen as the cameras zoomed in. Christopher was holding the Ten Commandments. A sudden gasp swept through the crowd in Jerusalem.

"No longer," Christopher shouted, his voice now showing his full fury, "shall the senseless dictates of spiritual tyrants — be they called Yahweh, Jehovah, Allah, or by any other name — have dominion over this planet!!" With that declaration, Christopher hurled the two ancient tablets to the street, 180 feet below, where they shattered into pieces so small they could not be distinguished from the tiny bits of gravel. The crowd, which to this point had been largely favorable to Christopher, now stood stunned and motionless in shock. Christopher had just taken a national religious treasure and transformed it to dust. His address had been stirring, but no one expected it to result in this.

Christopher continued, aware that he must quickly recapture the crowd's attention if he was going to win their support. "The things I have promised are real and they are within humanity's grasp. I say this from experience!

"Earth is not alone in the universe," Christopher explained. "Just as scientists have long suspected, there are thousands of other planets in the universe where life exists. One of those planets, an ancient and beautiful world circling a star beyond the Pleiades, is known as Theata. Life there evolved long before it did on earth. The people of Theata had already advanced to the beginnings of their space age 4½ billion years before the first one-celled animals appeared on the earth. It is a planet where hunger and fear no longer exist; where death is unknown; where people have taken the final step of evolution and become one in spirit and flesh; a planet whose inhabitants have fully become the god that is within them! It is from this distant, highly advanced planet that life on earth came! The people of Theata are the parent race of human life here! I have come that all that is theirs may be yours!"

Christopher's account of the origin of human life on earth was interesting, but hardly sufficient to cause the people in Jerusalem to ignore what he had just done with the stone tablets brought down by Moses from Mount Sinai. Christopher sensed their unease and realized it was time to give the world a demonstration of his real abilities.

"The future I offer you is a future of power," he proclaimed. "Including the power to control nature, as Robert Milner, who is Elijah, has shown you. But power, like the final steps of evolution, cannot be given. For it to be truly yours, it must be taken. Take and it will be given to you! I have ended the reign of terror brought on by John and Cohen; I have ended the plague of madness which threatened the whole earth; and now I shall begin the restoration of the earth!!" Christopher stretched out his right arm with his palm down toward the earth. For a long moment there was no sound, and the crowd began to murmur. Chaim Levin, the High Priest, robes torn and covered with mud, saw his opportunity and began to try to draw the crowd's attention. But before he could speak a stirring at the edges of the crowd distracted the attention of everyone.

From the recently rain-soaked ground along the road and around the buildings, anywhere there was soil, there was a visible motion as, before the eyes of the crowd, grass and flowers began to grow where there had been none before. As if watching time-lapse photography, the people witnessed in awe the earth release plant life of beautiful greens, reds, yellows, and purples. Flowering bushes sprouted from the barren ground and suddenly the air filled with the fragrance of spring.

But the miracle was not only in Jerusalem. Christopher remained silent and motionless for nearly five minutes as throughout the world plant life began to spring up and grow. Many of the smaller plants grew to full maturity in just moments and in the fire-blackened areas, young trees grew to heights of six, eight, and ten feet. Finally Christopher dropped his arm and the amazing growth slowed again to normal speeds.

"I have come that power such as this may be yours," he shouted. There was evidence of exhaustion in his voice, suggesting that the proof of his powers had not come without a good deal of effort.

"As I have said," Christopher noted, making his point again, "I do not ask for or seek your worship. I ask instead for your allegiance." There was no hesitation now as the vast majority of the crowd, along with those around the world watching on television, clapped or cheered or shouted out his name.

Again Christopher raised his right hand, but this time it was to quiet the crowd.

"Some may ask," Christopher continued, "what of the billions who have died in Yahweh's disasters?" He paused to allow the thought to register with his listeners. He knew that while only a few might have that question in mind in the context of his speech, for many it undoubtedly would come to mind soon after. It was better to deal with it now instead of waiting for it to be asked.

Shaking his head sympathetically, he said, "It is not possible to restore their lives. But those of you who mourn the deaths of friends and family need not grieve. Instead, rejoice in the knowledge that they are not truly dead. They will feel the earth beneath their feet again, for gods cannot truly die. As Jesus told Nicodemus 2,000 years ago, 'You must be born again.'[39] So it is for those who have died. Whether it is called reincarnation or being 'born again' or by some other name, the truth is that some who died over the past three and a half years have already been born again; though thankfully, few will remember their former lives. Nonetheless, as the Hindus and Buddhists teach, the suffering they underwent in their previous lives serves as a stepping stone to higher, brighter futures. So do not weep or mourn. Dry your tears and rejoice that when they return, they will be born into the age to which Humankind has always aspired: the New Age, the Age of Ascension for all Humankind.

"People of the Earth, people of Jerusalem, the time has come to put aside those things which separate us. The *destiny* of all Humankind awaits the *unity* of all Humankind. No longer let us consider such differences as skin color, gender, language, or the place of our birth. No longer let there be division between races or nationalities. And no longer let there be Gentile or Jew. All of these distinctions are now null and void," Christopher said. "All people are the chosen people!

"As such, let this building no longer be a temple to Yahweh, but a monument to the godhood of man. No more shall innocent animals be led here for brutal slaughter to a bloodthirsty god. From this day forward the killing must cease and the Temple shall be open to all!"

Toward the front of the crowd, Decker Hawthorne braced himself for what he knew was about to come.

---

[39] John 3:7.

"If any still doubt," Christopher said, preparing to conclude his oration, "I offer a final proof that I am who I say. Four billion years ago, it took 23,000 years, traveling at nearly the speed of light, for the crude space vessels sent out by the people of Theata to reach the earth. Now that they have evolved to spirit form, that distance can be traveled in less than a second!

"All that is Theata's is yours for the taking. At this very moment there are millions of our brothers all around us. They have come to lead, to guide each of the people of earth in the way they must go to enter into oneness with the universe.

"Can you see them?!" Christopher cried. "Can you see them?!"

Christopher raised his right hand in the air, held his head back majestically and shouted, "Behold the hosts of heaven!" Suddenly the sky was filled with thousands or hundreds of thousands of beautiful lights, some hundreds of meters across, some as small as the head of a pin; some moving slowly, some darting about at incredible speed.

"Behold the hosts of heaven!" Christopher shouted again.

Now that you've read *Birth of an Age,*
Book Two of The Christ Clone Trilogy:

Visit our web page at
www.selectivehouse.com

- ෨ let us know what you think
- ෨ see what others are saying
- ෨ e-mail the author

Write to:
James BeauSeigneur
SelectiveHouse Publishers, Inc.
P.O. Box 10095
Gaithersburg, MD 20855

Order Form

🖥 On-line orders: www.selectivehouse.com

☎ Telephone orders: Call 1-888-CLONE-99

✍ Postal orders: SelectiveHouse Publishers, Inc.
                            P.O. Box 10095
                            Gaithersburg, MD 20898

Complete 3 book set, _Save $9.90_ off price of 3 books bought separately.   __ x $34.95 = $_____

In His Image, *Book One of The Christ Clone Trilogy*   __ x $14.95 = $_____

Birth of an Age, *Book Two of The Christ Clone Trilogy*   __ x $14.95 = $_____

Acts of God, *Book Three of The Christ Clone Trilogy*   __ x $14.95 = $_____

For books shipped to **Maryland addresses only**, add 5% sales tax ($.75 per book; $1.75 per 3 book set): $_____

SHIPPING AND HANDLING: $_____
U.S. Orders: Include $2.00 per book (for 1 - 3 week delivery)
                Or $3.00 per book (for 3 - 5 day delivery)
International Orders: Please include $8.00 for first book and $1.00 for each additional book ($10.00 for 3 book set).

☐ **Check**   TOTAL $_____

Credit card: ☐ **Visa**   ☐ **MasterCard**   ☐ **Discover**   ☐ **Am. Express**

Please Print:
Card number: _____ Exp. date: ___ / ___
Name on card: _____
Signature: _____
SEND BOOK(s) TO:

Name: _____
Address: _____
City: _____ State_____ ZIP _____
Phone: (_____)_____
AUTOGRAPH book(s) to: _____